Beyond the Cemetery Gate

The Secret Keeper's Daughter
(Chloe & Maggie Mystery #1)

Valerie Biel

Lost Lake Press

First edition 2024

ISBN Paperback: 978-0-9981736-4-1

ISBN ePub: 978-0-9981736-6-5

Library of Congress Control Number: 2024915562

"... **a must-read** and recommended for fans of mysteries looking for **a gripping and compelling story.**" 5-Stars - Reader Views Kids

"Not all secrets are buried in the grave. *Beyond the Cemetery Gate* is a nonstop read through a dark, twisting plot and the dangerous world of shadows and sinister people that 16-year-old Chloe must outrun and outsmart ... **A canny and gripping introduction to an exciting new series.**" - Patricia Skalka, Author of the Dave Cubiak Door County Mysteries

"Valerie Biel's writing is **fast-paced and sharp!**"- Christy Wopat, author of *Almost a Mother* and *Always Ours*

"**A haunting YA mystery**. Touching on everything from police ineptitude and community solidarity to the endless frustration of being patronized as a young person, **this paranormal thriller confidently combines timely and relatable themes within a page-turning storyline.**" - Self-Publishing Review

"Vulnerable but also **whip smart, brave, and daring**, Chloe investigates her dad's murder, ultimately putting her own life at risk. This heart-in-your-throat novel pulsates with suspense as Chloe roots out secrets and exposes lies, ultimately discovering who she really is." - Jeannée Sacken, author of the award-winning Annie Hawkins series

"With its many layers of secrets, tightly woven plot, and great characters, *Beyond the Cemetery Gate* **tops my list of books worth reading this year**." - Terri Karsten, author of *A Mistake of Consequence*

".. . **imaginative storytelling, emotional depth, and action-packed narrative** are artfully crafted . . . I devoured every page of this impactful and hope-filled book and eagerly await the next adventure in the Chloe and Maggie Mystery series." —Laurie Buchanan, author of the Sean McPherson crime thriller novels

"Biel's writing is **intense, suspenseful, and passionate**." – K.M. Waldvogel, award-winning author

"Blending **an amazing portrayal of a sometimes-stark reality with human willpower** and the hope that comes in friendships, Valerie Biel gives us a novel that is both **tender-hearted and thrilling**." – author Laurie Stevens

"Biel will take you on **a wild ride in this mystery**. She crafts a fantastic thriller that has **a splash of romance, and a wonderful cast of friends**." – Barbara M. Britton, award-winning novelist

"*Beyond the Cemetery Gates* is about family, friendship, and trust versus greediness, violence, and crime – **I was moved to tears by Chloe's tenacity and strength**." – G.P. Gottlieb, Author of the Whipped & Sipped Cozy Mystery series

Playlist

First Light ~ Hozier
Not Strong Enough ~ boygenius
Your Side of Town ~ The Killers
Baggage ~ Bishop Briggs
Ghost ~ Arly Scott
broken ~ lovelytheband
Routines in the Night ~ Twenty One Pilots
Falling ~ HAIM
Over ~ CHVRCHES
Nobody Knows ~ The Lumineers

DEDICATION

To RJ,
for everything.

1

Chloe

IN THE SPACE BETWEEN sleep and wakefulness, a sound seeped into my consciousness. The sense that something wasn't quite right pulled me fully awake. I listened beyond my own breathing for it to come again.

A wail pierced the silence. An animal in pain? Only it wasn't. I knew it was human. I slipped from bed to stare out into the cemetery. The tombstones always made for fascinating or eerie shadows, depending on how you felt about graveyards. I never minded, which was a good thing, considering my house was smack dab in the middle of one.

The sound came again, more of a moan this time, followed by a murmur of voices. I couldn't tell what they were saying, but people were definitely in the cemetery. One of them was scared or maybe hurt. Dad wasn't going to like this. He locked the gate tight every night. The only way in was to scale the tall, spiked iron fence or pick the lock. Either one was going to piss him off.

In the distance, a pinpoint of light moved away from where I perched. It was too small to be a flashlight . . . maybe a cell phone?

I padded down the hall to Dad's bedroom, calling for him. His door was ajar, and the hall light was enough to show his empty bed, the covers rumpled and thrown back as though he'd gotten up quickly. He must have heard the same thing.

His boots weren't in their usual spot by the back door, so I knew for sure he'd gone to investigate. I had to help because Dad and I were a team, *small and mighty,* he said. We always made it through everything together.

In my hurry I forgot to stop the screen door from slamming behind me when I stepped out onto the porch, cringing when the sound echoed through the night.

I waited a moment and then whispered, "Dad," as loudly as I dared.

No answer.

I angled toward the part of the cemetery where the small light had been, thinking I'd find him corralling some kids from high school pulling a prank. It happened once in a while but usually in a few weeks—closer to Halloween. I knew more than a handful of idiots my age who would think this was funny.

I hadn't heard the wailing or voices since I left the house. Maybe whoever it was had left? That hopeful thought disappeared as a weird combination of worry and fear crawled up the base of my spine. Just in case it was something more menacing than kids, I hid my approach behind the cemetery's largest and oldest tombstones. Maxwell, Bell, Ludington . . . I touched their cold granite and the mossy green lichen growing up their sides as I slid between them. I expected to find Dad by now. *Where was he?*

A terrible thought pushed me into full fear mode. What if the person making that horrible scream *was* Dad? It hadn't sounded like him, but . . . what if he was out here somewhere and hurt? I had to find him!

My breath quickened and a damp sheen of sweat prickled my skin.

I sped up, more concerned with finding him than being seen. The cemetery was big, but I had to be close to where I'd spotted the light. I calmed myself long enough to pivot in a slow circle, my bare feet sliding on the dewy grass. The main gate was open, obviously where the trespassers came in—and hopefully where they'd gone out.

It was quiet and dark.

The cemetery had no lights of its own, and the glow of streetlights reached only to the second row of graves. Here and there, solar decorations shimmered for dead loved ones as cheerfully as possible but didn't shine far enough to be helpful. The darkness didn't hinder me. The cemetery had been my playground since preschool, so even in the dark I was able to avoid every tree root, odd stone, or divot that might trip me up.

I decided to be systematic and jogged a grid pattern, snaking through the rows. I stopped short and gasped at the next turn. A body was slumped against the base of my favorite statue, a white marble angel holding a sword and shield.

"Dad!"

He didn't move. In two quick strides, I was at his side. "Dad!"

I gave his shoulder a gentle shake, and his head tipped sideways.

"Oh my god! Wake up!"

I needed a better look and found the light on my phone. What I saw scared me even more. Dad's face was pale, his eyes unfocused. I needed help—fast!

Dialing 911 seemed impossibly slow for three simple numbers.

"911. What's your emergency?"

"It's – it's my dad. He won't wake up."

"What's your location?"

"I'm in the city cemetery. My dad is the caretaker here."

"What's your name?"

"C-Chloe Cowyn."

"Okay, Chloe, can you check whether your dad's breathing?"

I bent low and placed my face close to Dad's mouth. "I don't think so. Please hurry!"

This didn't make sense. Had someone hit him? I didn't see any blood. I swept my eyes over his legs and arms—stopping abruptly at what I saw.

"Nooooo."

At first, I thought the wailing had returned, until I realized that I was the one making the sound eerily like what woke me.

"Chloe, are you okay? I have help on the way. Stay on the line with me until they arrive."

"No. No. No." My cell phone dropped from my hand as I backed away.

Tears blurred my view until I could no longer see the needle stuck in my dad's arm.

2

Chloe

THE SQUAD CAR ARRIVED in minutes, turning into the cemetery faster than anything I'd ever seen. I fumbled on the ground for my phone, waving its lit screen as a beacon. "Over here! Over here!"

The officer ran over and kneeled by my dad. "What's happened?"

"I don't know. I heard noises and came looking for my dad. I found him like this."

As I spoke, he eased Dad out of his position against the base of the angel statue to lay him flat on the ground. "Is he a habitual drug user?"

"No, never. He's not like that. This doesn't make any sense."

In the beam of the headlights, my dad looked even worse. His color was ashen, and his mouth now drooped open with foam at the edges of his lips. The officer checked for a pulse and began CPR.

I was unable to look away but I wanted to more than anything—to close my eyes and put everything back to normal.

The ambulance siren I'd heard in the distance became impossibly loud as the EMTs parked right behind the squad car and the paramedics jumped out.

"Looks like we have an overdose. I couldn't find a pulse." The cop backed away as the EMTs took over.

"Do we know what we're dealing with here?" barked one of the paramedics. "Heroin, oxy, meth?" He looked at me for an answer.

I shook my head. "My dad doesn't do drugs."

The paramedic snorted and shook his head. "Well, apparently he does."

The other paramedic opened a small case and jabbed my dad in the arm with a needle. "We'll see if some Narcan will bring him around."

I knew what that was. The town council had a big debate about how it was too expensive to put the anti-overdose medication in each of our town's squad cars. It hadn't seemed important to me. Until now. I searched my dad's face for some sign of consciousness—but he looked the same—pale and unresponsive.

Just like on television, they hefted him onto a stretcher. One paramedic continued CPR as they rolled over the uneven ground toward the ambulance. I was ready to get in too when the officer pulled me back. Surprised at his touch, I lurched away.

The cop put his hands on his hips, but then relaxed, saying, "You can ride with me. We'll follow right behind."

3

The Watcher

I SHOULD LEAVE BEFORE I'm spotted but I can't move, watching the paramedics work.

The emergency lights bathe everyone in flickers of red and white—the harsh flashes make Chloe's face, full of fear, nearly unbearable to watch, but I can't take my eyes off her.

Even in her panic, she's beautiful. With every fiber of my being, I want to swoop in to give her comfort.

But I'm not supposed to be here.

I back away into the darkness.

4

Dean ~ 15 Years Earlier

"HEY, DEAN-O, WAKE UP!"

Dean jumped and grabbed for his weapon as he pivoted off his cot.

"We're good, man. No attack. You've got a call on the SAT phone from home."

"What's going on?" Dean stared at his fellow Marine, before lowering his weapon and quickly lacing his boots.

"Don't know. They jus' told me to get you. Didn' like the look on Sarge's face."

"Shit." Dean hustled out of the tent, with a sick gut. Calls like this didn't get routed through on a mission unless it was something bad. Really bad.

In the command tent, his sergeant handed him the phone, barking, "Sit down."

The order made his head swim as he croaked out, "Hello?"

"Dean, it's Maggie. I've got terrible news."

"Maggie?" He hadn't expected his sister's voice.

"There's been a fire at your house. Dean, I'm so sorry, but – but not everyone made it."

His hand grew numb as he clutched the phone, dreading Maggie's next words, which shattered his heart.

5

Chloe

THE OFFICER PUT ME in the back of his squad like a criminal, but at least he drove fast enough to keep up with the ambulance.

"So do you know your dad's dealer?"

"What?! No, my dad doesn't do drugs!"

"Hey, I know this is hard to talk about, but if you know who his dealer is, then maybe we can go after him and keep some of these drugs off the street."

For a moment and only a moment, I wondered if it could be possible that my dad *would* do something like this, but quickly shook off the thought. *No. He wouldn't.* I knew I was right. As long as I could remember it was only me and him. Even now in high school, I considered him my best friend, even though that'd never be cool to admit, out loud anyway. *I mean what junior in high school considers her dad her best friend?*

"Look, my dad doesn't do drugs. I would know. I heard someone crying out in the cemetery tonight. It woke me up.

When I went to get my dad, he wasn't in his bed. Then I found him, just like you saw."

"But you didn't see anyone else?"

"I heard voices, but I never saw anyone. I only saw a little light. I don't know. There was someone else there. The gate was open."

"Did your dad always close the gate for the night?"

"Yes. Every night. It has a lock."

"Okay." The cop nodded thoughtfully. "I'll go back and have a look around."

When we pulled into the emergency room driveway, I had to wait for the officer to open the squad car door. I dashed inside right behind the paramedics, listening as they gave my dad's information to the emergency room staff. I heard words like overdose, Narcan, and no pulse as they wheeled the gurney down the hall and into one of the curtained areas.

"Damn," the nurse shook his head, "this is the fourth OD this month. There must be a bad batch out there. Was he with anyone who can tell us what he took?"

"His daughter, but she doesn't know." The paramedic nodded my way as I hovered near the edge of the curtain. I barely noticed the nurse's grim expression as his eyes flicked over to me. In the fluorescent lights Dad looked even worse than he had in the cemetery. His eyes weren't fully closed, but his gaze was flat and – dead.

Dead.

The edges of my vision darkened, I couldn't catch my breath, and that wailing sound escaped my throat again. The commotion around my dad grew—more people, gear, and rolling carts flew into the room.

Someone gripped my shoulders and pulled me backward, a soft voice whispering, "You don't need to see this. Come sit."

My butt hit the seat of a hard plastic chair with a thump.

I was so cold. My breath came in desperate gasps.

Just when I thought I might throw up, pass out, or both, a blanket of warmth enveloped my shoulders. I strained to hear everything the medical crew said while they tried to save my dad. As I concentrated on their words, the warmth seeped into my chest and unhitched my breathing.

A curtain blocked my view. I couldn't bear to look anyway.

I hunched forward with my hands on the edge of the plastic chair for what felt like ages. My legs were bare, my terrible burn scars clearly visible. I was rarely bare-legged in public, because of the scars. I'd forgotten I'd run out of the house in my pajamas. Barefoot, too. My bright pink toenail polish looked too cheerful and just plain wrong on my dirty feet. I tucked them back out of view and stared at the navy blue flecks in the bright white linoleum floor while I continued to listen.

"Are we gonna call it? We've been at it over an hour."

I watched enough medical shows to know what that meant and jumped to my feet.

"Dammit! Yes. Time of death 1:42 a.m.."

I ripped open the curtain and shouted, "No! Keep going! You have to keep going!" I shoved the closest person back toward my dad, but someone grabbed hold of me. I began to flail, trying to get loose. I needed to find someone to help my dad if they weren't going to do it. My fist made contact with someone's face, and I was tackled to the floor. The last thing I saw were the wheels of my dad's gurney before everything went black.

I woke on my own gurney, covered in an itchy wool blanket, staring at ceiling tiles.

"There you are." A woman in a white coat spoke while holding an ice pack to her jaw. "I'm Doctor Brady. You've had a shock tonight. I'm so sorry. Do you remember what happened?"

I simply nodded. My throat was tight and tears ran down my temples and into my hair.

"Oh, sweetie. I'm so sorry, but your dad didn't make it. We tried. We really did."

I nodded again. Curling into a ball, I wrapped my arms around my head as if to drown out her words. But I couldn't unhear her. I knew what it meant. The only person I had ever counted on was gone.

The doctor touched my shoulder. "We're so sorry. Can we call someone for you? Your mom or your grandparents?"

"No. It was just me and Dad. I – I have an aunt." I hiccupped. "She's our only family." I pushed myself up onto one elbow, looking around for my phone.

"Here, let me help you sit up. You went down pretty hard." The doctor held out her free hand, which I thought was brave given the fact that I'd recently slugged her. "I don't think you hit your head. Are you dizzy?"

"No, I'm okay. I'm sorry I hit you," I managed to croak out.

"I've had worse. You're quite strong though." She checked my eyes with a light before handing me my phone. I dialed my aunt, but it went straight to voice mail. I didn't know what to say. I saw her maybe twice a year. I couldn't tell her that her brother was dead in a message. "Hey, it's me, Chloe. Um. Give me a call back." My voice sounded shaky and weird.

Through the gap in the curtain, motion caught my eye as a stretcher wheeled past. It wasn't empty. The person was covered in a sheet. But the sheet kept going and going over the person's head. Then I knew it was my dad. His body.

"Where are they taking him?" I whispered.

"He'll go to the morgue until you and your aunt can make arrangements. Did you want to see him?"

My 'no' trailed off into fresh tears. I couldn't stand to look at him—not like that. I pulled the horrible wool blanket tighter around my cold shoulders, but it didn't help.

"I know this is terrible. I'm so sorry. Can I get you anything? Do you want some water or something to eat while we wait for your aunt to call back?"

I shivered again, thinking of the warmth of the earlier blanket. "Someone, a nurse I think, gave me a really soft blanket before. Out by the chairs. Can I have that one back?"

"Hmm." The doctor peered around the curtain toward where I'd been sitting. "I don't know who that would have been, but these are the only kind of blankets we have."

"Okay." The realization that *it* had happened again swept through me, but not in a bad way. I had a vivid imagination—or so my dad said.

Said.

He'd never *say* anything again. It would always be *said* from now on. I pulled my knees up to my chin and wrapped my arms around my legs, almost relieved that I'd dislodged the scratchy blanket.

Whenever I was scared or panicked, my imaginary friend—my guardian angel—comforted me. His name was Leb. Weird at my age, I know. But if ever I needed a friend—imaginary or not—it was now.

I caught the doctor staring at my legs.

She stepped over. "May I?" she asked.

I shrugged. I'd grown used to doctors being intrigued by my burn scars.

With care she examined the puckered skin that stretched from mid-thigh down to my ankles. "What happened?"

"It was a house fire. I was too little to remember any of it. My mom died, and I almost did. My dad said I was in the hospital for six months before I could come home."

"I'm glad you made it." She grabbed my hands and looked at me. "You're obviously a survivor."

6

Chloe

WAS I A SURVIVOR? I didn't feel like one. I was alone now, except for an aunt I rarely saw.

An aunt who hadn't yet called me back. But there was likely a good reason for that. Maggie Gill was a famous journalist, often away on assignment in dangerous, war-torn places. How would she react to needing to care for her sixteen-year-old niece? I was bound to get in the way of her work.

The emergency room doors down the hall whooshed open for a police officer, not the same one who'd come to the cemetery and driven me here. A different man, taller, broader, older. He strode toward my cubicle, but Dr. Brady stopped him.

I couldn't hear what they were saying. The officer gestured toward me and then trailed after Dr. Brady as they approached.

"Chloe, the police chief wants to talk to you, but you don't have to do this right now if you'd rather not."

"No, it's okay." I really wanted to know if the other cop found anything at the cemetery.

The police chief filled up the space when he stepped around the curtain, but not in an intimidating way.

"Hi, Chloe. I'm Chief Barnett. I'm sorry about your dad."

"Thanks, but you have to know that he wasn't a drug user. He really wasn't. Did the other officer find anything at the cemetery?"

"He didn't see anything out of the ordinary. He tells me you heard voices?"

"I did. There was at least one other person, maybe more, out there with my dad before I found him – like – like that."

"Do you know who that might have been?"

"No. I know how this looks. But you have to believe me—my dad didn't do drugs."

Chief Barnett's face flickered through a bunch of emotions, settling into a painful look of pity.

Pity for the poor girl who didn't realize her dad was a drug addict.

"Something else happened out there." My words were tight as my jaw clenched and I tried to tamp down my anger. "I don't know what it was or who was there, but that's your job, isn't it? To figure this out?"

The chief shifted on his feet and cleared his throat. "There's nothing to indicate a struggle or that other people were there. This really looks like a straightforward overdose. I know you don't want to hear that."

"Except *I did* hear other people."

"Right, except for that."

"And the gate."

"The gate?"

"Yes. My dad locked it every night, but it was open when I went out to look for him. There's also a small back gate, but no one ever uses it."

The chief drew his eyebrows together for a moment. "My officer didn't mention the gate. I promise I'll check on that personally. Look, maybe if we talk to a few of your dad's friends, we can figure out if someone had a problem with him. Do you know who we might ask?"

"My dad didn't really have any friends. He kept to himself. He did his job and he usually stayed home and read books at night."

"What about the people he worked with regularly?"

"He mostly worked with, well, *near* dead people, except for the funeral directors. He talked to them all the time." I thought through my dad's schedule. "A couple of mornings each week, he ate breakfast out at the coffee shop near the main highway with some old guys." On my days off school, if we ate breakfast out, they greeted my dad by name. "Maybe one of them saw or heard something." I truly couldn't think of anyone else. It hadn't occurred to me until then what a solitary life my dad led. But he didn't seem to mind it. Or did he?

"Okay. Chloe, I *am* sorry about your dad. We'll ask around." He shifted on his feet again. "So you're sixteen? Right?"

He already knew the answer to that, but I nodded.

"I hear you're waiting for your aunt to call back?"

"Yeah, she doesn't live around here."

"Okay, so I am going to send in one of the county social workers, to get you squared away so you have a place to stay."

I didn't think much about what that meant, until about an hour later when a tired looking woman slid into my space. She wore no make-up to cover up the circles under her eyes and her dark shiny hair fluffed out from the messy bun at the nape of her neck. Not that I was one to judge. I was exhausted and was sure I looked it, too. She wore jean capris, a Bucky Badger sweatshirt, and Birkenstocks.

I tucked the blanket more tightly under my thighs, again deeply aware of my bare legs.

"Chloe, I'm Ameena Alavi." She held out her hand to me, and I shook it automatically. "I've been called in as your social worker. I'm sorry to hear about your dad's passing. I'm here to make sure we can find you a safe place to stay until your aunt gets here." She pulled out a clipboard, snapping a thick stack of forms into place under the metal clamp.

"Okay."

"There are no other relatives nearby?"

"No other relatives at all," I corrected her.

"Hmmm. Okay." She began to write things down. "Can you give me your aunt's full name?"

"Maggie – er – Margaret Gill."

"Maggie Gill? The one from the news?"

"Yes." I shouldn't have been surprised that her name was recognizable.

"Her phone number?"

I read it from my phone contacts. "I left her a message already. I didn't tell her about my dad, I just told her to call me. I need to be the one to tell her!"

"Do you want to try calling again?"

I shrugged and dialed, but the call went to voice mail again. "Hi, Aunt Maggie. It's me again – Chloe. Um, I – well –

something bad has happened, and I really need to talk to you as soon as you get this message."

"Where does your aunt live?"

"Sometimes she doesn't live anywhere. Y'know, she's on assignment a lot. She had an apartment in New York City, but I don't know if she still does."

Ameena jotted down some more notes. "So, we have a couple of options here while you wait for your aunt. Maybe you can stay with a friend's family or a neighbor. Or, if that doesn't work, I can find a temporary foster placement for you."

My heart lurched at the idea of having to live with strangers. I didn't want that—at all. The only person I could possibly call was my friend, Emma. We ran on both the cross country and track teams together, and I hung out at her house a lot. I'd even gone on vacation with her a couple of times. I had a lot of friends, but Emma was the only *real* one. "Emma Phillips. Her parents are lawyers here in town. I have Emma's number, but not her parent's."

The social worker checked her watch. "It's early. Do you think Emma would answer?"

"She might." I waited while the phone rang. It went to voice mail. I dialed again out of frustration, and this time she picked up.

"Chloe? What the heck? It's like five o'clock." Emma was croaky and cranky.

Just hearing her voice—even her cranky voice—made me want to cry. "Emma," I choked out. "Emma, something terrible has happened. I am at the hospital—"

"Oh my god, Chloe. Are you hurt?"

"No, it's not me. It's my dad. Emma, he – he's dead." With that I started sobbing uncontrollably. This was the first time I had to say those words to anyone. It made it so much more horrible to say it out loud.

Ameena took the phone from my hand and spoke to Emma, now that I couldn't. It became clear when the conversation shifted to either Mr. or Mrs. Phillips.

She hung up and handed the phone back. "They'll be right here. I told them to bring you some clothes, too. I didn't figure you wanted to leave here in your pajamas."

"Thanks." I sniffled and gratefully took the wad of tissues she passed my way.

"I'll need to talk to your aunt to make sure you're in her care once she gets here. I'll check in with you at the Phillips' home until then. It's good that you have people in your life who will take care of you. Some kids aren't so lucky." Ameena sighed and returned to her clipboard.

"I don't feel very lucky," I whispered.

Ameena's head shot up. "Oh, oh. That was really thought-less of me. I'm sorry. I wasn't thinking about how that sound-ed. I deal with such sad cases all of the time. Abuse and neglect. Clearly people love you, so that's all I meant. Please forgive me."

I was on the verge of tears again. The only person who really, really loved me was Dad.

Ameena stepped closer. "Would you like a hug?"

Even though I'd just met her, I sank into her arms. She smelled like a mix of spices and oranges. Except for the mys-terious soft blanket, the hug gave me the first real comfort of the night.

It wasn't long until Emma rushed in, followed by her parents.

"Chloe!" she shouted and smothered me with a hug that nearly toppled me back on the gurney, but somehow it felt like I was comforting her rather than the other way around.

Mr. and Mrs. Phillips and the social worker talked in the hallway, but their voices carried to me and Emma. "Drug overdose . . . in the cemetery . . . yes, that's what the police believe."

Emma's eyes grew round as she overheard the discussion.

"I don't know what happened, but my dad was not an addict! Someone murdered him!" I looked down at my hands, now curled into fists. I needed someone to believe me.

7

Chloe

I REPEATED THIS SAME thing, more than once, to Emma's parents on the ride home, but I knew they didn't believe me. Just like the police department and the doctors and nurses in the emergency room, everyone believed my dad died of a self-inflicted drug overdose.

I didn't have the energy to challenge them. I collapsed onto Emma's bed the minute I got into her room. I snuggled into her blankets. The hug of my imaginary friend cozied around my body, protecting me from the world so I could rest.

I didn't wake up until Emma came back from school hours later.

"Chloe, you awake?"

"Yup," I mumbled into the pillow and rolled over to look at her. "I slept a long time. Are you back from practice?" Cross country practice usually ended by 5 o'clock. I was surprised I slept that long, but not entirely ungrateful. Sleeping was better than being awake and having to deal with reality.

"No, it's only 3:30. I skipped practice, but I told Coach why you were absent first. I think he already knew though."

"In this town everyone knows everything."

Emma laughed and abruptly stopped as though she realized that maybe she shouldn't laugh about anything with me right now. She bit her lip.

"No, it's true. Everyone probably already knew before you even got to school this morning."

"You're not far off," Emma said, cringing slightly.

"Ugh. I don't want to go back."

"I can guarantee that's not an option. My parents aren't going to let you stay home for long. You might get an extra day or two out of them but that's it. They're sticklers for law and order and attendance."

"Law and order." Repeating this made me realize it wasn't going to be easy to make people believe what I knew to be true about my dad. Even though it wouldn't bring him back, it mattered to me. A lot. Dad's death didn't deserve to be dismissed as "just another overdose."

Emma knew what I was thinking. "Chloe, I believe you. I liked your dad. I don't think he'd do anything like this either." She shivered. "It's really scary to think there's someone out there who did this to him."

"Well, you're the only one." It didn't even pay to ask if her parents were on my side.

—◇—

Mr. and Mrs. Phillips were perfectly kind to me but visibly stiffened when I again explained my dad's lack of drug use and my belief that he'd been murdered.

Later, when the chief's squad car pulled up to the curb at the edge of their pristine, gardener-maintained lawn, the neighbors came out of their equally perfect homes to gawk. This was not a neighborhood that generated police calls.

Mrs. Phillips noticed the attention immediately, scowling before ushering the chief quickly inside. Her tight voice was most polite, but definitely not warm. "Thank you for coming over."

I, however, was grateful Chief Barnett stopped by with an update. "Have you found anything that proves my dad didn't do this to himself?"

"No. We looked through your house and searched the cemetery again, and except for some stray garbage, we didn't find anything."

"What about the lock?"

"We know the gate was open when police arrived, but the lock didn't appear to be tampered with. Is it possible your dad forgot to lock it last night?"

"No. I remember watching him do it." In fact, as I replayed this memory, I realized it was the last time I spoke to him. He came back into the house and put his keys on the counter. I'd said goodnight and went to bed.

The chief nodded, his lips pressed into a thin line. "Who else has keys?"

"Well, I do—and I'm sure there are other people who have them, like my dad's boss. His office is at City Hall." I stared at the chief's expression. He looked uncomfortable, like he wanted to tell me something but couldn't find the words. I stopped him before he could say it. "I know you're thinking I just didn't know what my dad was doing, but it was only the two of us and – and – I would have known if he was doing drugs. I would have!" I hated that I sounded like a crabby grade-schooler trying to make herself understood.

"Look, we haven't closed the case. The official cause of death is overdose, but that's not saying he inflicted it himself. It's just what killed him." The chief cringed as if he realized how insensitive that might sound.

He cleared his throat and handed a manila envelope to me. "Here are the things he had on him. We're done with them. You can have them back now."

It weighed more than I expected and made me think of all the things my dad carried in his pockets. I resisted the impulse to look inside so I could feel close to my dad for a second. My dad didn't deserve this—any of it.

"Here's my card. If you think of anything that might help us, you give me a call. And if we learn anything new, I'll let you know." He reached out and patted my shoulder.

I shrugged him away. They weren't taking this seriously. They were probably only looking for evidence that proved my dad *did* drugs. I knew that without saying it, he *was* saying "case closed."

Maybe it was for him, but it sure as hell wasn't for me.

———◇———

I spent the weekend mostly in Emma's room, waiting for my aunt to call.

She didn't.

I got a pass on going to school on Monday. Mr. and Mrs. Phillips agreed that was reasonable. But by Tuesday morning, it was clear they wanted me to go.

Mrs. Phillips was the one tasked with providing the *encouraging* conversation. "Chloe, I know this is a rough time, but you don't want to fall behind in your classes. It'll be that much harder to catch up later. And I'm sure you want to keep your spot on the cross country team."

I knew she was right, but at that moment I had more pressing things to do than go to high school. My aunt was still gone, and the police hadn't been by with more news on the investigation—that is, if they were actually still looking into my dad's death. I had my doubts.

"I'll go tomorrow. I promise." My words were muffled by the pillow I pulled over my head when Mrs. Phillips came in the bedroom. *Childish I know, but I just wanted her to leave me alone.*

"C'mon Mom, let her have another day," Emma shouted from the hall. "Let's go, we're gonna be late."

Thank you, Emma!

I could hear Mrs. Phillips sigh before she quietly shut the door behind her.

Once everyone left the house, I got to work. I needed to track down my aunt. I didn't try her cell phone again. Instead, I called her employer, International News Day, and after a lot of fast talking, I was transferred to the right desk where I finally got some answers.

I explained who I was and that we had a family emergency. I finally convinced her producer I was legitimately Maggie's niece by telling him the secret that my aunt never traveled without her ratty stuffed monkey named MoMo. He told me she wasn't answering calls because she didn't even have her cell phone with her. He wouldn't say why exactly but that it was a matter of safety, which didn't make much sense to me. *Didn't a cell phone provide a safety net?* I'd have to ask her about that once I finally talked to her. The bad news was that she was completely unavailable for at least three weeks. He did promise that if she happened to check in, he would tell her to call me asap.

Great.

I was so over the stiff, awkward looks from my temporary host parents. Three more weeks before Aunt Maggie showed up. Nearly a month. There was no way I was staying here. I could be on my own for three weeks. It wasn't that long. No one needed to know I was alone. Plus, it would give me the freedom to find out what really happened with my dad. It was clear the police were not likely to do much more.

I grabbed the thick, monogrammed notepad by the anti-quated landline phone on the kitchen counter and penned a note.

Dear Mr. and Mrs. Phillips,
My aunt flew in without calling ahead today.
Headed back to my house with her.
Thanks for all your help.
Love, Chloe

I choked a little on the love part, but it seemed appropriate to be sweet, even if the idea of a "drug addict's" daughter in their home was uncomfortable for them.

To make my plan complete, I texted Emma with the fake good news of my aunt's return, too. I felt worse lying to her.

Going home, I walked from one side of town to the other, actually crossing railroad tracks into my neighborhood of smaller, slightly shabby houses to make my journey as cliché as possible.

The cemetery gate was open. I didn't know if it was *still* open or if someone else was opening and closing it each day.

For now, I detoured away from the angel statue where I found Dad. It was the tallest monument in the cemetery, standing at least two feet higher than other statues and headstones. I liked it so much because it was a warrior angel, an avenging angel, with a sword raised to the heavens in one muscular arm and a shield held protectively in the other. You wouldn't want to mess with this angel.

The moment I stepped onto the porch of my house, a wave of wrongness washed over me. It didn't feel right returning here knowing dad never would. The door was shut, unlike how I'd left it. I was grateful for that, knowing there *had* been others in this cemetery.

I attempted to turn the handle, but it wouldn't budge. Someone had locked it, too.

Fear ran through my body. *Would the city have locked me out already?* We didn't own the house. We only got to live here because my dad was the cemetery caretaker.

My keys were still in the house. I hadn't grabbed them when I ran into the cemetery the night I found my dad. The only thing I carried with me from Emma's was the now-crumpled manila envelope the police chief had given me.

I hadn't looked inside. But now I really, really hoped his keys were there.

I bent the tiny metal prongs open and tipped the contents out onto the small wicker porch table.

His cell phone, wallet, and, thankfully, his keys tumbled out. I grabbed the key ring, shaking as I lined up the key with the lock, nearly crying with relief when the deadbolt slid open.

I was glad they hadn't been heartless enough to change the locks so quickly, but I knew my days here had to be numbered.

I put everything back in the envelope and stepped inside, locking the door behind me.

The house was strange and empty and, if possible, it even smelled funny. Here and there, I saw evidence of the police search—kitchen drawers partly open, couch cushions out of place, and closet doors ajar.

I'd only been gone for a few days, but everything was oh so different. I'd been wearing Emma's clothes, so slipping into my own running shorts and T-shirt made me feel a little more normal. Even though I had no idea what normal would even mean from now on.

A knock on the door made me jump.

I froze for a moment, knowing it was time to begin my charade for real.

I ran to the bathroom and turned the shower on full blast. On the way to answer the door, I shouted, "It's okay, Aunt Maggie. I'll get it."

At the door, I was greeted by my dad's boss, Frank.

"Hey Chloe. Gosh darn, we're sure sorry to hear about your dad. A drug overdose they're sayin' down at the police station. I really can't believe it."

"It isn't true."

His sad eyes and pinched expression told me he was uncomfortable that I believed this. I changed my mind about inviting him into the kitchen and left him standing on the porch.

"So I hear you've got an aunt coming in to take care of – er – things."

"Yeah, she got in this morning. She's in the shower. Long flight." *Lying had never been so easy.*

"Ah, okay. So, here's the thing. Um, I hate to do this to you, but you know we're gonna have to post your dad's job as caretaker now. It usually takes some time to fill these positions, and you can stay here for a couple more weeks, you know, until you can get things in order."

"That's fine." I expected this. But two weeks wasn't much time. Plus, it left one week before Aunt Maggie might be here.

"Are you going to have a service for your dad?"

"We haven't figured all that out yet." But now I wondered, just how long would they keep a body in the morgue? I wasn't prepared for the emotions that swamped me. My throat tightened, but I managed to squeak out, "Thanks for letting me - us," I quickly corrected, "stay for a couple of weeks."

Frank nodded. He'd done his job delivering the news of my pending eviction and turned to go.

I gently closed the door and sank to the floor, thinking about my dad in a cold drawer on the other side of town. I curled up with my face on the wavy, old vinyl floor, crying and staring at the spot where my dad's boots always sat.

8

Dean ~ 15 Years Earlier

THOSE HOURS IN THE air from his Middle East deployment were the worst, not knowing what he'd hear when he landed. He rushed to the hospital to be with Chloe and hadn't left her side.

Except for today.

He put on his dress blues, his formal U.S. Marine Corps uniform, for the funeral—even though it was going to be small, with only his sister by his side.

He gave Chloe a kiss on the forehead, whispering, "I'll be back soon, sweetheart," and joined Maggie in the hallway.

The staff glanced up and then quickly down as they passed by the nurses' station. No one knew what to say, and he couldn't blame them.

At the gravesite, the sweat trickled down Dean's back—a typical muggy day for central Florida—with the heat shimmering above the flat headstones that stretched in every direction.

He didn't break down until the minister's final words, ". . . and to dust you shall return," letting out a muffled cry as he sank to his knees, staying that way until Maggie tugged gently on his arm and equally gently said, "C'mon, Dean, let's go now."

He swiped at his face as grief mixed with guilt and anger—so much anger.

"That bitch," he hissed. "I'm glad I never have to see her again."

Maggie sucked in a breath by his side.

"I should never have left on my deployment. She was supposed to be clean."

"Dean, you couldn't have known she was using again."

"And those scum dealers she got involved with—" his voice broke.

"I know, I know. But you can't blame yourself. I could have checked in, too, but she sounded good on the phone. She put on a good show for us." Maggie hugged him tight.

"I'll never forgive myself. I should have been here."

With that they turned, leaving the funeral director and the cemetery workers to their jobs. The grave would be filled in. The sod would be placed over the top.

Stepping through the cemetery gate, Dean knew he would never visit here again.

9

Chloe

THE SOUND OF CARS driving nearby woke me. Stiff and grog-gy, I pushed myself off the kitchen floor to peek out the low window, hoping I was not getting more visitors. A funeral procession snaked through the main gate toward the newer section of the cemetery. Thankfully, these people didn't care about me.

My absent aunt's fake shower was still running. *How could I have forgotten to turn that off?* The bathroom was a steamy mess.

Two weeks.

I had to get moving.

I pulled out my suitcase and an old backpack and plopped them near the door to offer visible proof that Aunt Maggie had arrived if anyone came poking around.

At the kitchen table, I slid dad's things from the envelope once more. This time a piece of paper I hadn't seen earlier fluttered out as well. Dad's scrawl jumped out at me. He'd written a phone number on the slip—out of state it looked like because I didn't recognize the area code.

This might be the first clue to what happened to my dad.

I started to dial the number from my phone but stopped. Would it be better to use my dad's phone? I hoped the person on the other end might think it was him calling and answer at least so I could ask questions. His phone was off, but luckily it still held a charge, and I knew his security code. My dad used the same passcode for everything because he always forgot.

The call was answered on the third ring. "Cypress Grove Correctional Facility, how may I direct your call?"

I nearly hung up but managed to gather my wits. "I'm sorry. What did you say?"

"Cypress Grove Correctional Facility."

"Wait, like a prison?"

"Yes, exactly like a prison because we're a prison. Is this a crank call? You need to know that all the calls coming in and out of here are monitored and you could get into trouble."

"No, I'm sorry. I think I dialed you by mistake."

"You think? Do you need to speak to anyone here or not?"

"I guess not."

"Alrighty then, you have yourself—"

"Wait. Where are you located?"

"Pinellas County, Florida. Bye bye now."

That made no sense. We lived in Wisconsin. We'd never been to Florida. Well, at least, I'd never been, and Dad had never mentioned going there.

What was he doing with the phone number for a prison in Florida? I switched screens to his phone log to see if he'd actually called this number and was stunned by what I saw.

My technologically-challenged Dad had deleted his entire call log.

I flicked to another screen. He'd also deleted his text messages.

There was no way that was accidental.

Nothing made any sense. I didn't even think he knew how to do that.

I pawed through Dad's wallet next. He didn't carry a ton of stuff—his drivers' license, a debit card, and his library card. He never had a credit card, always saying he didn't believe in them. "If you don't have the money for something, you shouldn't be buying it anyway."

There was nothing surprising in his wallet. That is, until I checked to see how much cash he had. There was no cash at all, and Dad *always* had some money in his wallet.

Panicked, I stepped to a kitchen cupboard and snagged an old popcorn tin from the top shelf. It hadn't held popcorn in a long time, but it was where we kept emergency money. Not much—only a couple of hundred dollars. Enough for me, *probably*, until Aunt Maggie got here.

The lid clattered to the counter when I popped it off.

Empty.

There was no cash in the house and none in his wallet, and he might have been calling a prison in Florida. *God, was it possible my dad was doing drugs?*

I forced myself to take a deep breath. There could be logical explanations for all of this, right?

Back at the table I eyed his debit card.

Now, really worried about my financial situation, I tied up my running shoes and sprinted out the door, gripping the card in one fist and my dad's keys in the other.

The first ATM was a few blocks away on the town square. Yes, we were that cute little town with a perfect park at the center of everything. Only now it didn't feel so cute and charming, knowing there were people out there willing to kill someone and make it look like an overdose.

I slid into the bank alcove that held the cash machine and poked the keys with my dad's pin as my anxiety grew. I pressed the balance inquiry button and gasped.

The amount read $0.00.

That couldn't be. Where would all of Dad's money have gone?

Someone cleared their throat behind me. "Excuse me. Are you finished?"

Without answering, I stepped back onto the sidewalk and leaned against the wall of the bank.

There had to be an explanation for this, but I couldn't think what that would be. Wondering when he'd cleaned out his account, I pushed open the door to the bank lobby and rushed over to the teller that was free.

"Hi," I said, trying to sound normal and not like the panicked, frantic person I felt welling up inside. "Could you help me get a printout of my account transactions?"

The woman smiled at me. "No problem. Do you have the account number?"

"It's the one for this debit card." I slid the card over to her.

"Oh, it's easier if I look it up by account number, but I can just type in your name." As she began to type, she slowly stopped and looked over to me. "You're not Dean Cowyn."

"No. I'm Chloe Cowyn. It's my dad's account."

"I can't give you access to that information unless it's a joint account. Is it?"

"I don't think so."

"Well, let me check." She typed in something and then looked back at me. "It's not a joint account."

I leaned in closer. "Can you please help me. My dad—the person whose account this is—has passed away. I need to know where the money went that was in this account."

"Oh, I'm so sorry, honey. Okay, in that case, I can give you access, but first you have to bring in a death certificate along with your identification and then we can get you what you need."

I stood there for a moment, feeling completely defeated. A death certificate? How did I get one of those?

"Can you at least tell me when the money was taken out of the account?"

"Look, I'm not supposed to do anything like this without the proper paperwork. I could lose my job. I'm sorry. Bring in the death certificate and we can get you all squared away. Okay?"

I crossed the street in a daze and plunked down on one of the benches that flanked the square. I was flat broke, except for maybe the five bucks in my backpack at home. Staying independent was the key to finding out who murdered my dad. And I needed money for that. My entire plan was going down the drain.

Heaving myself off the bench, I cut across the square toward home, passing by Molly Bell's Diner with its neon sign flashing more cheerfully than I cared to see right now. I was daydreaming about how nice it would be to sink into a piece of cherry pie and nearly missed the small sign in the corner of the window. **Now Hiring.**

10

Chloe

I WASN'T DRESSED RIGHT to apply for a job, but I was desperate.

Oldies music blared from a jukebox as I opened the door. I loved this diner. The retro vibe was fun. Everything was authentic to the 1950s: the red vinyl booths, metal-legged tables, and a long counter with stools. The owner was truly named Molly Bell, and she was as retro as her restaurant, although she probably wasn't even forty years old. Her poodle skirt swished as she came around the corner to deliver a plate of fries.

"Hey doll, sit anywhere you like." Her quick smile was highlighted by bright lipstick in—you guessed it—red.

I slid onto the stool at the end of the counter.

Molly came back and picked up an order pad. "What can I get you?"

"Well, actually. I saw the sign in the window."

"You want to apply for the job?" Molly smiled again and her dark short curls bobbed.

"I do."

"But you don't know what kind of job it is yet."

"I don't care. I really need a job."

Molly tilted her head to the side. "Okay. Ever done any restaurant work?"

"No, but I'm a hard worker and a fast learner."

"Are you good with numbers?"

"Yes. I'm in honors math at the high school."

"Are you sixteen or older?"

"I'm sixteen."

"If you think you can waitress, I'm happy to train you. I need a server for the dinner shift 4:30 to 8 Monday through Friday and breakfast on Saturday from 6 to noon. Will those hours work for you?"

"Yes, definitely," I said, although my heart sank. I'd have to quit the cross country team to earn money. But learning what really happened to my dad was worth giving that up—even though we had a good chance at going to state this year as a team. For a moment I seriously considered calling the social worker and asking about foster care, but I highly doubted any home they put me in would think it was cool if I was investigating Dad's death. And everyone knew foster care was a crapshoot.

I could go back to the Phillips's, but I truly couldn't stand living with people who would never believe anything good about my dad. Now that I'd lied to them, I wasn't sure they'd want me back. I imagined their discussion: "A druggie for a dad and now she's a little liar." I could already hear the town gossip. No. This was the only way.

Molly was staring at me quizzically but then smiled. "Alright, we'll give it a try with a one-week probationary period."

She grabbed a form from under the counter and handed it to me. "Fill this out, and we'll go from there."

I penned my answers into the blank spaces. Molly slid a cherry coke toward me when I was part way through. When the sweetness hit my taste buds, I realized that this was a real cherry cola made the old-fashioned way with cherry syrup. Nice.

When I was done, I waved her over. She scanned the document and nodded. "Okay. Here's your uniform shirt. Wear it with jean capris or rolled up jeans if you don't have any capris and some tennis shoes. We're not fancy here. I prefer that you pull back your hair in a ponytail for sanitary reasons. Can you start tomorrow?"

"Yes, definitely. I'll be here!" I kept up my cheerful façade until I walked out.

My life was in shambles. I was on my own with a murderer on the loose, and no one believed me, but at least now I had a way to survive while I worked it all out.

11

The Watcher

CHLOE IS FAST. NEARLY too fast for me to follow. I catch up with her when she stops at the bank. The trees in the square are a fabulous cover. Here I pretend to enjoy the day like the others do while watching the bank door. When she comes out, even at a distance, I see she is upset.

I feel it too—we already have an emotional connection—the way we should.

Again, I want to go to her. Offer comfort.

But not yet.

I am startled when she darts into the diner. This is unexpected.

I wait.

When she comes out, she is holding a shirt, and the Help Wanted sign is taken out of the window.

This is going to work out better than I could have planned.

12

Dean ~ 15 Years Earlier

CHLOE LOOKED SO TINY in the hospital bed; the lower half of her body swathed in a mass of white bandages. Dean couldn't bear the days when they cleaned her burns and changed the dressings. She was so tough, but it was hard to hear her cries—even with the pain medication they gave her. The funny thing was that just when the process was at its worst, she would calm down and stare at him with her big eyes. It was eerie really, the way her pain magically disappeared.

While he couldn't fix her current pain, he sure as hell was going to do his best to protect her from future pain, and that meant putting the darkest chapter of their lives behind them. Chloe didn't need to know any of it. So, there was no way they were staying in this small town where everyone knew what happened and where anyone might dredge up their personal tragedy over and over again as Chloe grew.

No way in hell was that happening to his baby girl. She'd been through enough.

He'd already scoped out where they might go. He was initially tempted to go as far away as they could get but still stay in the United States—like to Alaska. But, instead, he settled on a nice small town not far from Wisconsin's capital.

While it would be easiest to blend anonymously into city life, Dean had a motive. It was easier to pick out the people who didn't belong in a small town and that was part of his plan to protect Chloe.

He'd already bought cold-weather clothes. He'd filed the paperwork to change their last name to Cowyn, in honor of his maternal grandmother. And as soon as Chloe was released from the hospital, they'd hit the road.

13

Chloe

SLEEPING ALONE IN THE house, mere feet from where I found my dad, was not easy. The gate to the cemetery remained open until late. I waited to see if someone from the city might come, but apparently no one remembered this job was no longer being done by my dad. I finally summoned the courage to do it myself. I ran out as fast as I could, banging the gate shut with a clang and turning that key. The whole thing probably took three minutes. I was breathing heavier than I ought to have been from the short sprint, and my nerves felt jangly when I got back to the house. I slammed the kitchen door shut and flipped the lock. I couldn't settle down until I rechecked all the other locks in the house.

In the dark, I stared out my bedroom window, hoping to see something and also hoping I wouldn't. Tomorrow before school, I was going to search the cemetery for the clues I was sure the police had missed.

I couldn't fall asleep until I felt the warmth of my guardian angel in my room, sheltering me. Now safe, I was able to drift off.

When my alarm dinged at 6 a.m., I initially resisted, thinking it was a normal kind of day in my normal kind of life. My groggy brain struggled with why I would have set my alarm so early. Then it all crashed down on me.

Dad was dead. Murdered.

Sadness and a low level of panic slid through me.

It was up to me to solve this.

I jumped out of bed.

The autumn air hit me when I stepped out—that nice kind of crisp that has just a bite of cold to it. The trees rustled in the breeze as more and more leaves let loose and floated downward. I stood on the porch surveying the cemetery. I liked the peacefulness and order of the rows of headstones. The dead never bothered me. I'd always felt at home here, even when the location of my house had briefly earned me the nickname, Creepy Chloe, in elementary school. And normally, I loved this time of year, but now realized that the new fallen leaves were going to make my job harder as I looked for clues.

I zipped my hoodie and walked slowly in the direction I assumed Dad took to where I eventually found him. I moved leaves aside with my feet as I walked—swoosh left, swoosh right—like an uncoordinated ballet dancer. I was a runner not a dancer.

The still-green grass underneath held no clues.

I walked all the way around the avenging angel statue. I circled the neighboring grave markers too. Nothing seemed out of place except the faint marks in the grass from the gurney the paramedics had used to transport my dad.

I sat down in the spot where I'd found him. I tried to copy his exact position, letting my arms go limp with my hands resting atop the grass. *What was the last thing he saw?*

From here, lower to the ground, most of the view was blocked by the staggered rows of headstones. I couldn't see clearly to my house or to the street. However, the chapel that was sometimes used for smaller funeral services was visible. I'd look there next.

When I pushed myself up, my fingertips on my right hand felt a bump in the grass.

I looked more closely and dug in a little bit, assuming I'd find a small piece of gravel or maybe even an acorn.

Instead, I pulled out a dark blue stone.

Rubbing off the dirt, I saw that it had holes drilled through it like it had been used for a piece of jewelry. This definitely didn't belong here. Anyone could have dropped it at any time. But it was right where Dad's hand had been resting. I put it in the baggie I'd brought along and zipped it shut. It probably was nothing, but then again, maybe it wasn't.

The chapel was built of reddish-brown brick with dark brown wood trim and heavy double doors. The windows were low enough to look into from the ground, but I didn't need to do that. I had a key. Finding the right one took a while though. Dad had so many keys. Finally, one fit and the door opened easily on well-oiled hinges.

I'd been in here before with Dad. He was in charge of keeping it clean. Nothing was out of place. I looked out the windows facing the angel statue. There was a clear view but no indication that anyone had been in here since the last time it was used. I quickly walked to the other side and looked out the windows that faced our—*my*—house. I nearly left before remembering the small crypt underneath the chapel. I didn't really want to go down there, but I knew I should check it. The short staircase was tucked behind the altar area. I turned the knob at the bottom and shoved the door open with my foot—not willing to go any farther. Luckily, daylight from above showed me the room was empty.

I knew the space hadn't been used for a long time, but way back before they had digging equipment, coffins were stored here during the winter months when it was impossible to dig a grave in the frozen soil with a shovel.

Happy to be outdoors to continue my search, I opened the gate for the day, feeling better about doing something to earn my keep since no one else seemed concerned about cemetery security. I walked along the wrought iron fence, looking for anything that looked out of place but finding nothing except stray garbage . . . cigarette butts, a cheeseburger wrapper, and a dirty plastic army man. As gross as it was, I tucked everything in the baggie I'd brought with me. I could always throw it away later.

School was going to be a chore today. Not only would I be seeing classmates for the first time since Dad died, I had to tell Coach Brooks I was quitting the team. That was going to be hard.

I didn't need to pack my cross country clothes, but I grabbed my new uniform shirt for work. I took a good look at it for the first time, a red short-sleeved blouse with white cuffs and a white collar. I threw in some jeans and my red converse. Then

I remembered what Molly said. She wanted me to roll up my pants 50's style. Ugh. My scars would show. Probably not a great idea to gross out the customers on my first day.

I had a solution, but it was an ugly one. Although it was less ugly than my scars. I rummaged in my sock drawer and came up with some flesh-colored knee high socks. Yup, ugly, but serviceable. I threw them in on top and zipped the bag shut.

The closer I got to school, the more nervous I became. I pulled up the hood on my sweatshirt and kept my eyes down in an attempt to remain anonymous. I nearly snorted at the thought—I knew that was impossible. The most that would do was buy me a few more peaceful minutes.

Once inside, a few of the girls from the cross country team came over to my locker to say they'd heard what happened and were sorry. I appreciated that more than I expected I would. But mostly kids looked away if we accidentally made eye contact—now *that* I hadn't expected.

Was this how people acted when someone lost a loved one or was this how people acted when it was a drug overdose? Supposed overdose, I mentally corrected. I had no experience with this. My mom died when I was too little to remember. I hoped they were simply avoiding me because they didn't know what to say.

Then Emma was there giving me the hug I needed.

"Hey, Chloe. I wished you waited until I got home to leave, but I'm glad your aunt is here."

I nodded, not wanting to lie again (*at least out loud*).

"Maybe I can come over and meet her after cross country practice." Emma was already moving away to her first class. I didn't have time to tell her I was quitting the team or more importantly, come up with a plausible excuse why meeting my aunt was impossible because she was really on some special assignment, likely in a foreign country, for three more weeks.

About to enter my first class, I heard my name called in the hall. Mrs. Hartman, the school guidance counselor strode toward me, her black wedge heels squeaking on the hard tile.

"Chloe, we should talk. Will you pop into my office for a few minutes?"

I didn't think I really had a choice, even though I would have rather gone to my first class after missing three days of school.

"I cleared it with your first hour already."

Well, that was that. Silently, I followed behind to her office.

I think Mrs. Hartman's office had once been a janitor's closet. There were no windows, but she made up for it with bright and cheery floral prints on the walls mixed with posters with positive sayings like "You've got this" and "Hard work pays off." There were also a ton of family photos, showing five kids, a husband, and two large golden labs. The photos annoyed me. A stabby feeling hit me right in the chest, and then I realized what it was. Jealousy—plain old happy family jealousy. That was new to me. I'd truly never felt bad about our family being only me and Dad. Until now when it was just me.

I sat in the chair she motioned to.

"Oh, Chloe," she started.

Here it comes. I was getting used to that look of pity. A tight look that said, we had no idea your life was such a nightmare with your drug addict dad.

Before she could continue, I blurted out, "My dad was murdered."

She looked startled initially—her mouth moving as though she was going to say something but thought better of it. She covered it up well by grabbing her can of cola and taking a sip.

"I was told that he died of a drug overdose."

"That's what everybody thinks, but my dad didn't do drugs. Seriously, I would know. No one believes me."

"Okay. What do the police say?"

"Chief Barnett asked around, but I know they think it is a closed case—just another overdose—just another casualty of the drug epidemic. Good riddance." My sarcasm surprised even me.

"I'm sure they're doing everything they can." Mrs. Hartman cleared her throat before continuing. "So, I want you to know that I'm here for you if you want to talk. Losing a parent is really hard. My mom died when I was about your age. It was awful."

"My mom died when I was a baby. My dad was my only real family. And you can't possibly know how this feels. I knew my dad, and he didn't do drugs!"

Mrs. Hartman sighed, but not like she was frustrated. "Do you want me to talk to Chief Barnett?"

"I don't know what good it would do, but, yeah, if you feel like it. See what he tells you. Maybe there's stuff he doesn't want to say to me. I don't know." I rapidly became less irritated with her now.

"I have a notice here that you're staying with Emma Phillips, right?"

"Um, no." Here I go—*liar, liar, pants on fire*. "My aunt actually got here yesterday."

"Oh, that's good. I'd really like to meet her or at least talk to her."

Trying to avoid all of that lying business, I stood to go. "Um, sure. I'll let her know. Can I go to class now?"

"Yes, of course. But you can stop in anytime you need to, Chloe. I mean it. You're not alone in this."

Then why did it feel like I was utterly, completely alone?

14

Chloe

COACH BROOKS SAT AT the desk in his office with the door wide open. Somehow I made it through the whole day, dreading what I had to do next.

He looked up as I approached and called out, "Hey, Cowyn, you doing okay?"

I nodded. "Listen, Coach, I've got to talk to you."

"Sure, sure. C'mon in." He moved a giant stack of jerseys off a chair to make room for me. "I'm so sorry about your dad."

I nodded and took a deep breath. There was no way to do this slowly. "I've got to quit the team."

"What? You've got the best times." His mouth pressed together in a thin line, like there was more he'd like to say but was holding back.

"I'd stay if I could, but things are more – more complicated now. I had to get a job."

"Really? Maybe you should give it a while before you make a final decision. This has been a rough couple of days for you.

I'll bet if I ask around, we can pull together some donations to get you through the rest of the season if money's that tight."

For a moment I considered the idea, but I wasn't sure if Coach could deliver. I didn't know if other parents might feel the same way Mr. and Mrs. Phillips did about my dad. People don't have a lot of sympathy for drug users and by extension, me. I almost wanted to take the chance on the hope that others would be more kind, going so far as to rationalize that I could eat my way through the canned goods left in the pantry in the meantime. I loved running cross country.

I could hear some of my teammates approaching on their way to the locker room, and I wished I'd done this faster so I was gone by now.

I heard Hailey's snorting laugh, and then Alyssa said, "Maybe the coach will have to drug test *her*."

"Not likely. She's the star of the team." Hailey laughed again.

My stomach sank.

Coach's booming voice made me jump. "Girls. Get in here."

I let my head drop into my hands and hid my face. I thought Alyssa and Hailey were friends. Not like good friends but like teammate friends. I wished he had ignored them.

I didn't look up when they came in.

"What's wrong with you?" Coach asked. "You owe Chloe an apology."

Hailey was first. "Oh my god, Chloe. We were just goofing around. I'm so sorry."

Alyssa wasn't nearly as contrite. "I'm sorry, too." But she didn't sound it.

Coach sighed. "Get your butts changed for practice, now. You'd better be running hills in five or you won't run at the invitational this weekend."

They nearly tripped over each other in their hurry to get out of Coach's office. It almost made me smile. Almost.

"Ignore them, Chloe. They're jealous of you. That's all. I know you're not the kind of kid to do drugs."

"Thanks, but I don't want to be late for work."

"Look. You can change your mind anytime and come back, okay?" he called after me.

I passed Emma and a couple of my other teammates in the gym hallway.

"Hey, where are you going?" Emma asked.

"I quit."

"Nooo! Don't do this, Chloe. We were going to make state together this year." Emma reached out like she wanted to hug me, but I pushed past her, my anger sparking.

"Is that all you care about? Really, Emma, is that all that's important to you? Because my whole world has changed, and no one believes me when I say my dad didn't do this to himself!" I was screaming at this point, and Coach was now in the hall too, watching the whole thing.

"I believe you!" Emma shouted back.

"I meant anyone important!" I felt bad when Emma flinched, but I couldn't take back the words.

"That's a shitty thing to say, Chloe!" Emma turned and was halfway into the locker room before I realized she was right—it *was* a shitty thing to say. By the time I formulated my apology, the locker room door swung shut.

And now I really did have to hurry to my first night of work.

Which was a nightmare of mistakes.

When I got there, Molly glanced at the clock and then back at me with her eyebrows raised. I was on time—barely. But I still had to change.

When I presented myself at the counter for my first task, Molly gave me another look, reached into her pocket, and handed me a hair tie.

Dang. I usually had one of those with me. "Sorry," I said and quickly pulled my long blonde hair into a ponytail. We went through drinks first. Soda was no problem, everyone knew how to do that. Even adding the syrup to make a real cherry cola wasn't hard, two pumps and a quick stir. The shake mixer also seemed straightforward.

As the early dinner crowd trickled in, I shadowed Molly for the first few orders before she turned a bunch of tables over to me.

I did my best. I really did.

But I mixed up one order, forgetting to hold the onions on the patty melt. Then, I turned around too fast with a tray of drinks. They all went flying, and when I stepped on the edge of the puddle, I went down, too. My embarrassment was complete when I looked up and saw that my chemistry lab partner, Jarvis Keen, was sitting at the counter with a front-row view of my colossal wipe out. He didn't laugh, but he didn't offer to help either—although that wasn't his job. Surprisingly, I thought I caught a glimpse of compassion cross his face. It took forever to clean up. Eventually, Molly sighed and grabbed a mop from the back and helped me out.

I felt like I *was* running cross country as I flew from table to table and back to the counter and the kitchen window to grab orders that were ready. I hadn't figured out the trick for balancing more than two plates on a tray, and scared that I'd drop them all, I very inefficiently delivered them two at a time.

When I placed a burger and fries in front of a woman sitting alone, asking her if I could bring her anything else, she glared at me in a way that made me step back. She seemed confused at first, but that morphed into something else—I wasn't sure what exactly. She narrowed her eyes at me but didn't speak.

"Did I get your order wrong? It's my first night." I was afraid she was going to make a scene. "I can fix it," I offered as my hands turned clammy.

"I doubt it." She snorted.

"Wha – what?" I stammered.

"You got my job!" She jabbed her finger at me, her beaded bracelets punctuating each word with a jangle.

"I don't—"

"Molly wouldn't hire me," she interrupted even louder, earning glances from people at nearby tables.

"Um – I'm sorry. Do you want me to get her?"

"Don't bother." She was nearly shouting. "Like I'd want to work in this dump anyway."

I wanted to point out that she *was* eating food here after all, but I fled back to the kitchen. "Molly, there's a lady out there who says I took her job. She seems mad."

"Oh, lordy. She's back. I'll take care of it."

Molly swished out to the table and along the way grabbed a to-go box. I watched while she spoke to the woman, sliding her entire dinner efficiently into the to-go container, handing it to her, and pointing to the door. The woman sat there with her arms crossed over her chest for a moment, finally getting up and taking the food from Molly. Before she stomped to the door, she pivoted back to the table and maliciously tipped over her nearly full soda glass. Molly followed her out, and I rushed to stop the soda from flowing onto the floor.

Molly came back to me while I cleaned up.

"Who was that?" I asked.

"She came in last week and applied for the waitressing job, but she couldn't provide any references. You didn't take her job, I never offered it to her."

"Okay." Thinking of all my mistakes, I added, "Maybe you should have, given the kind of night I've had."

"Don't worry about that and don't worry about her. I told her not to come back."

Despite that crazy scene, I finally felt like I was getting into the groove by the end of the shift.

When there was only one lady left in the corner booth, sipping her coffee and nibbling on her pie, Molly told me to have a seat at the counter and brought me a burger and fries.

I was hungrier than I realized and dug in immediately. Yum!

Molly flipped the sign to closed and sat down next to me. "Rough night."

Ugh. Maybe she was going to fire me. Maybe I could convince her to give me another try. "I know I messed up, but I'll get better. Please give me another chance. I need this job so bad."

"Hey, calm down. I'm not going to fire you. Everyone thinks this looks so easy, but anyone who has ever been a waitress knows it's not. I'm not worried about that. I can tell you're a hard worker. We're good here."

Tears welled up in my eyes.

Molly handed me a napkin from one of the black and silver holders on the counter. "Do you want to talk about it. Why do you need this job so bad? Saving for college?"

I had so many more immediate concerns than college that the suggestion almost made me laugh. "No. I need the money for regular things."

"Well, I can understand that." Molly laughed. "Don't we all?"

"My dad died this week." I wished I could take it back the minute I said it.

Molly's face froze. "Whoa. That's awful. What happened?"

Now I froze. Did I tell her the truth or make up some kind of illness (the kind that instilled sympathy rather than disdain) like cancer or a heart attack?

My hesitation had Molly reaching for my hand. She gave it a squeeze. "If it's too hard to talk about, you don't have to, honey."

I looked around as if someone might overhear, but I already knew there was only one customer left. "I think he was murdered," I whispered.

"Murdered?!" Molly nearly shouted.

The woman in the corner did look up then for just a second.

"I didn't hear about any murder," Molly continued. "And we hear pretty much every bit of news around here. Was this somewhere else?"

"No. Here in town. The police think it was an overdose, but I know that my dad didn't do drugs." But a teeny-tiny smidge of doubt coursed through my mind as I thought back to the missing money—the reason I was even in the diner having this conversation in the first place—and that strange prison phone number. There had to be another explanation for those things.

A light popped on in Molly's eyes. "Oh, you're the daughter of the cemetery guy. I'm so sorry. I know a bit about that. Jim, I mean, Chief Barnett, was in here and mentioned the case."

"What'd he say?"

"Not much. The other morning he stopped in for a late breakfast, and I asked him why he looked so tired. He said that the cemetery caretaker overdosed and they were looking into who might have been with him at the time."

I nodded. That's what I thought. They were actually trying to catch my dad's supposed dealer or something, never really believing me at all. "He didn't do it." I whispered, even more defeated, grabbing more stiff napkins to dab at the corners of my eyes.

Molly leaned closer. "You stick to your guns. If you know your dad wouldn't do drugs, then don't let anyone tell you otherwise. I know what it's like not to be believed about something. I'll stand by you."

I simply stared at her. How could she be willing to back up my belief in my dad when she'd just met me?

Molly's face flashed briefly with a mix of concern and fear as her eyes narrowed and her perfectly manicured eyebrows pulled together. "But that means there's a murderer in town."

"I think there is. I heard other voices in the cemetery that night."

"Well, that's scary. It's not only big cities that have problems like this. I believe you. You're on my team now, Chloe."

I found a smile for her and impulsively gave her a hug.

When I pulled back, she gestured toward the corner booth. "Now, see if Candi needs anything else, so we can close up."

"Is she a regular?" I figured she must be if Molly was calling her by name.

"Nah. She's new to town. I like to get to know people if I see them more than a few times. It's builds customer loyalty."

I went over to the booth. Candi was taking a sip of coffee but her pie was gone. "Candi, do you need anything else?"

The woman looked up at me and stared for a minute. In a weird way, like she was thinking of something else and hadn't heard me. Or had Molly gotten her name wrong? That had to be it.

"I'm sorry. That's not your name? Molly thought—"

"No, I'm Candi." Her gravely smoker's voice surprised me, but it shouldn't have as I noticed the tell-tale wrinkles around her mouth that smokers usually have. She probably looked older than she was because of it, although her medium brown hair had streaks of gray.

"What's your name?"

I hadn't expected her to ask *me* any questions. "Chloe."

"That's a lovely name." She set her coffee cup down and smiled at me. "I'm done, Chloe. You can bring the bill."

Once she left, Molly showed me the closing routine, which was fairly simple: wipe everything down—tabletops, booths, chairs, salt and pepper shakers, ketchup bottles, basically everything that was out on the table; wrap everything in the dessert display cooler with plastic wrap; send all the dishes to the kitchen for one final load in the washer and that was it. I didn't mess up once.

"See you tomorrow, Chloe." Molly let me out the front door and relocked it behind me.

Stepping into the cool air felt good. I survived my first waitressing shift. I hadn't gotten fired, and I had an adult ally who trusted my instincts about my dad.

15

The Watcher

TONIGHT SHE REALLY NOTICES me. I trail after her as she walks back to the cemetery. Back where I first began watching her.

She locks the gate, but then she stops. I swear she looks directly at where I stand, and my heart skips a beat. But I'm in the dark. She can't possibly see me. I move farther back into the shadows to be sure.

After a moment, she turns and makes her way to the house. I wait for the lights to turn on, so I know she's safe inside before I leave.

But my elation turns to dread when I realize that I'm not the only one watching her. He's here, too. We stare at each other for a moment, his sly grin making me feel sick, before he speeds away.

16

Dean ~ 13 Years Earlier

THAT FIRST WINTER DEAN questioned his decision to pick Wisconsin, particularly with the job he landed as a cemetery caretaker. Even with equipment, digging graves was no joke in the winter. He didn't mind the job, appreciating the solitude. The pay was decent, and it came with free housing.

They were gradually making a home here. He found Chloe a spot at the local daycare center where she first happily joined in the melee of the two-year-olds in the Bumblebee Room, graduating now to the three-year-old Ladybug Room. People were kind but curious. A single dad wasn't typical, and a few of the single moms he'd met expressed interest in being more than friends. But Dean didn't return the sentiment, and they eventually gave up.

It's not that he wasn't tempted by the sweet, kind Midwestern women he met. He would have liked to have found a companion, someone he could trust, but he didn't figure he'd ever trust a woman again. Sweet and kind didn't always stay that way, and his heart ached every day for what they had lost.

Sure, Chloe was doing fine, but she'd carry physical scars with her for the rest of her life. That was another good reason to have picked a cooler climate. It wasn't strange to keep Chloe in leggings, tights, or long pants most of the time.

He hoped she'd never remember the fire and the long months of painful recovery. But he suspected on a deep level it was burned into her soul the same way the fire had scarred her chubby toddler legs. She woke up crying sometimes, like she'd had a nightmare. He'd watch on the video baby monitor to see if she'd settle down on her own. The first time he saw her reach out to someone who wasn't there, as if to embrace them, was freaky. She laid down in her toddler bed, scooching over as if to share the space. He heard her having whole conversations when no one was there, but later when he asked her who she was talking to, she'd just say, "my Leb." Dean would have asked her more about her imaginary friend, if his heart hadn't been lodged in his throat. By the time he could speak, he'd decided to leave it be. If this was how Chloe coped with all that had happened, who was he to judge?

17

Chloe

BEFORE SCHOOL, I TOOK stock of my food situation. There was enough to get by for a few more days. I was grateful for the dinner Molly gave me last night and reminded myself to ask her what day I got paid.

I was still shocked that she believed me when I told her there was no way Dad died the way everyone thought. I was no closer to solving his murder, but Molly's support made me feel better.

But better didn't last long as I entered school and Emma deliberately turned away from me when we walked past each other. I tried to tell her I was sorry, but she held up her hand to ward me off and kept walking. Then, before I could even get to my first class, Mrs. Hartman found me.

"Chloe, are you doing okay?" she asked very kindly and quietly, but no matter how quiet she was, this kind of attention in the hall from the guidance counselor always made kids take notice. I felt their glances.

"I'm as fine as can be, Mrs. Hartman."

"Stop in if you need to—if you need a break from the day, I mean."

That was a nice offer. I actually needed a break from my entire life, but I didn't think she could provide that.

"Don't forget I need your aunt's contact information for the school file. I'd really like to meet her, too."

That was so not happening, but I would have to come up with something.

"Okay. I'll get that for you later." The class warning bell rang. It was the perfect excuse to disentangle myself from this conversation.

"Sure, sure." She waved me toward my class as I melted into the groups of students maneuvering their way through the hall.

I was wondering how to make my absent aunt appear more – er – present when a warm hand gripped my shoulder.

It was Jordan, one of the other top runners on the cross country team. I braced for her to be mad at me, too. "Chloe, I'm so sorry about your dad. I hope you come back on the team. We miss you."

Jordan actually seemed sincere about wanting me back, maybe really for me and not for my top time that could help bring the team to state. The three of us, Emma, Jordan, and me, were the best runners. Our times combined were some of the fastest for a team in our sectional. Individually, we might not make it to state, but running together we had a good chance.

"I'm sorry, Jordan. I really am." It was all I could manage.

Guilt on top of my grief on top of my anxiety about my absent aunt—well on top of everything—had me slogging the last few steps into chemistry.

I slid onto my stool at my lab station next to – ugh – Jarvis Keen, star witness to my blazing act of clumsiness the night before.

Jarvis was an interesting guy—weird interesting. He was new to school. Obviously smart. Noticeably good looking and rocking all that with a grunge vibe that radiated "I don't care what you think" from his hoodie down to his disintegrating Chuck Taylors. He kept his head down and didn't talk unless it was necessary. Plenty of girls had tried to talk to him but gave up when the most they got in reply was an uh-huh.

I remembered my dismay at being paired with him for an entire year as lab partners. I'd been late to class on the first day. A crucial error. We were odd numbered, so our teacher allowed me to make a lab team of three with two other students who were already paired up. But then Jarvis came in even later than me, and I was shifted over to be his partner. He'd nodded when I said hello, and I'd been hopeful for a few minutes, but he never said anything else that day. Since then, he only spoke when necessary for the experiment that we were performing. I'd given up trying.

But today I really, really hoped that Jarvis would be as quiet as he always was. I didn't need him mentioning last night or my dad or anything.

No. Such. Luck.

"Hi, Chloe."

I whipped my head around to look at him. He had never once greeted me in the four weeks since school started. I stared at his dark eyes as he pushed his over-long black hair off his forehead.

"Hello, Jarvis."

"I heard about your dad. That sucks."

Whoa. Were we actually having a conversation?

"It does, Jarvis." Was I supposed to also say thanks? He hadn't really said sorry or given me any condolences. It was more a statement of fact. *Having a dead dad sucks. Yes, it does.*

"I saw you last night . . ." His voice trailed off like he was going to say more.

I waited, eventually answering. "I know. I saw you, too. It was my first night."

Jarvis nodded.

Class began, and we went back to all business, measuring this, heating that, trying not to blow up the room.

When class was over, he surprised me again. He leaned over and whispered in my ear, "Be careful, Chloe."

18

Chloe

Jarvis' warning bothered me all morning. For weeks, we don't have a conversation, except about chemistry, and then he says something cryptic like that? *Be careful of what or who?* Could Jarvis possibly know something? I was too stunned (and weirded out) by what he said to ask him more questions during class. My guess was that he probably wouldn't answer me anyway.

At lunch, I tried once more to apologize to Emma, but she ducked me *again*—this time by turning away and sitting at a table that had no more open seats. I went outside to eat the meager peanut butter and jelly I'd packed on the last of the bread I found in my kitchen. As I ate, I scrolled through my phone. There were no new messages. I hadn't really expected any, but I still hoped Aunt Maggie might check in.

Mrs. Hartman wasn't going to give up on needing my aunt's contact information. If I gave her Maggie's cell phone number, there was no way she'd get an answer if she dialed it. I decided to try something sneaky. I was becoming a pro at sneaky.

I could give her my cell phone number. The school didn't have that on file anywhere to notice my dishonesty. Then if I changed my voice mail to something generic, she'd never know it wasn't Maggie's number. That way I'd know if she dialed it and what information she was looking for. I could stay one step ahead of her. Maybe.

Killing off my old cheerful voice mail message felt therapeutic. My previously chirpy voice didn't feel like me anymore. I chose the automated voice mail greeting and played it back. "Your call has been forwarded to an automated voice message system. Please leave your message at the tone."

Perfect.

I scrawled the phone number and my aunt's name on a sheet of notebook paper and tore it out, planning to leave it in Mrs. Hartman's mailbox in the school office. Best to avoid talking with her too much. The halls were chaotic as lunch period was almost over. I bumped along with everyone else and was nearly to the office when I saw a familiar face. The social worker from the hospital, Ameena Alavi, was talking with the school secretary. Thankfully, she didn't notice me. I ducked into the alcove for the bathroom doors and peered around the corner. Mrs. Hartman appeared, and they walked together toward her office. *Phew*. I avoided a major problem there.

A voice behind me made me jump. "Who are you hiding from?"

I turned and nearly bumped into Jarvis Keen, who was standing a bit too close, sidestepping just in time to brush by him and not stumble out into the main hallway.

"Um, no one." *Anymore*. Strange. Two conversations in one day.

"Looks like you were hiding from someone. Do you need any help?"

I stared at him, incredulous that he'd now spoken more non-Chem-Lab words to me in one day than he had all year.

He stared back.

Maybe he could help me. "Well, yeah. I need to get this phone number for my aunt to Mrs. Hartman, but I just saw the social worker who talked to me at the hospital the night my dad died. I'm not really – um – up to talking to them both. Y'know. So if you could maybe deliver this to either Mrs. Hartman or put it in her mailbox in the office, that'd help a lot."

"Do you think they're meeting about you?"

Whoa, more conversation. "I don't know. Maybe? Probably."

Jarvis grinned. "Don't you want to know what they're saying if they're talking about you?"

"Um. Yeah. But it's better if I don't get too close."

"I can find out." Jarvis seemed almost excited about the idea.

He nearly set off on his mission before I remembered that I'd already given Aunt Maggie's real cell number to the social worker. I snatched the paper back from him and balanced it on top of the books I was holding, quickly writing "new number" across the top of the paper. *It was plausible my aunt might have a new number, right?*

Jarvis strode toward Mrs. Hartman's office door and knocked rather loudly. I stayed back far enough to avoid notice if either of the women looked out into the hall. Jarvis went in. Less than thirty seconds later he returned.

"Mission accomplished." He smiled again, and this time it lit up his face.

I didn't think I'd ever seen him smile before today, and I smiled back, suddenly unsure of all the assumptions I'd made about him. "Thanks, that avoided a big . . . complication."

"Meet me after school at the picnic tables, and I'll fill you in."

How strange. I had no clue why Jarvis was suddenly talking to me. I was grateful for his help, but this interaction combined with his odd warning had me on edge.

Later, when I approached the picnic tables under the big pine trees that surrounded our school, Jarvis was already there, but he wasn't alone. Jarvis sat stone still, hunched over with his head down, while two of the more popular guys hovered around him.

My stomach sank.

"Hey, Jerkis, what are you doing here?" one of them said, shoving Jarvis' shoulder.

Jarvis tipped backward and nearly fell off the bench.

"Get lost, Freak," another taunted, shoving again. This time Jarvis did fall, landing in the wood chips, where he stayed down.

Why didn't he fight back? He had a slight height advantage and enough muscle on him that he would have had a fair shot in taking them down.

"Stop it!" I shouted. As an athlete, I ranked somewhere in the middle of the general school power structure. I hoped it was enough to get these idiots to back off. "What's your problem. Get out of here."

I stepped between them and Jarvis, who was now standing and brushing himself off.

"Aw, did we interrupt something?" one of them asked.

"Probably a drug deal," said the other guy, earning himself a pat on the back as they laughed at their wit.

"You're such assholes. Just leave." My fists were ready at my sides in case I had to get physical. My dad had taught me the basics of self-defense. I didn't think they'd shove me around, too, but who knew? They *were* idiots.

Proving bullies only select easy targets, they backed away with one parting shot. "Looks like Jerkis has a girlfriend." They laughed all the way to the parking lot, probably congratulating themselves on their masculinity.

"You okay?"

"Yeah." Jarvis didn't look at me.

"Does that happen a lot?"

"Some." He sat back down. "I could have handled it."

I wasn't sure that was exactly true with his do-nothing tactic, but I said, "I know. It just made me mad to see you treated that way."

He continued to look down. I didn't blame him for not wanting to talk about it. I had other things to ask him anyway. "Jarvis, before you tell me about the social worker and Mrs. Hartman, I have a question. Why did you tell me to be careful this morning? Do you know something?"

"I know a lot of things."

"You know what I mean. Do you know something about me, something about my dad?"

"I know everyone thinks your dad died of an overdose but you don't. I know a lot of kids are talking about you. Some of them are mad."

"I know. Most of the cross country team is not happy that I quit."

Jarvis nodded. "I hear things. People don't notice me much, and they keep talking."

"Jarvis, what do you hear?"

"Only what I told you."

"Okay." It didn't seem like I was going to get more out of him. "What did you hear when you went to Mrs. Hartman's office?"

"They quit talking when I went in, but I saw a file on Mrs. Hartman's desk with your name on it."

That wasn't much. I could have figured out that my file might have been in plain sight during this meeting. "Is there more?"

"There were notes on a page. It said 'drug overdose' with a big question mark next to it. The name Maggie Gill was written there, too."

The first part surprised me. Maybe what I said to Mrs. Hartman had her wondering about my dad's death. It's weird how something as simple as a question mark could make you feel like you weren't losing your mind. The second part didn't surprise me at all—my aunt's name was bound to be written down somewhere.

"Anything else?"

"The social worker had a file on her lap with a card paper-clipped to the outside that said:"

Custodian Confirmation Needed

Minor: Chloe Cowyn
Custodial Adult: Maggie Gill
Deadline: October 6

That was just a few days away. I let out a long breath. I wondered if they required my aunt to show up in person or if a phone call would work.

"Thanks, Jarvis."

"I can do more. If – if you need it?"

"Jarvis, why are you helping me? I mean you hardly talked to me before today. Why do you even care?"

He was quiet for a minute. "It bugs me the way some kids are talking about you—about your dad. I figured you could use help."

"Jarvis, what kind of help do you think you can give me?"

"I'm good at mysteries. Solving them. You have a mystery."

I nodded, weighing whether I should accept his help. He was a little odd, but he was smart, and I'd clearly underestimated him. I loved watching crime dramas, but now, being at the center of one, I couldn't make the pieces fit together. I had a huge—horrible—mystery to solve and nothing was making any sense. I wouldn't mind some help. Who was I kidding? I *needed* his help.

"I'm trying to find out who would do something like this to my dad. I need to find the truth."

He nodded.

"Can you keep secrets too, Jarvis?"

He looked at me for a few seconds before answering. "I'm the best at that."

19

------◆◆◆------

Dean ~ 10 Years Earlier

"CHLOE, BE CAREFUL!" DEAN called as he watched his daughter nearly slam into another kid in her race across the playground.

"She's fast."

Dean pivoted toward the voice, which came from a woman wearing a black track suit trimmed in bright pink.

"Hi, I'm Bonnie Phillips. Chloe and my Emma are in the same class."

"Nice to meet you." Dean nodded to her politely. "Maybe a little too fast for her own good."

"What are you going to do?" The woman laughed. "I'm just grateful Emma's burning off some energy before we head home for dinner."

"There's that!" Dean agreed.

"You're the caretaker at the cemetery, right?"

"Yup."

"That's an interesting job. Do you like it?"

"Well enough."

"Ha—a man of few words."

"In my experience, there's no point in using more words than are needed to get the job done."

"I think you and my husband would get along rather well." She chuckled. "So, I'm sorry about your wife."

"What about my wife?" Dean choked out.

"Oh, the fire and all . . . I'm sorry that happened."

"How do you know about that?"

"I guess Emma asked Chloe about her burn scars the other day, and she said that she'd gotten them in the fire that killed her mama."

Dean was quiet. He didn't talk about that much with Chloe, but of course, over the years it had come up when he explained to her how she'd gotten the scars, and that they'd lost her mom at the same time.

Last week was the anniversary of the fire, and Dean had been looking at some old photos that brought back such sad memories. Chloe had seen him weeping over them, and he'd quickly shoved them back into the filing cabinet, hiding them away. But she'd been so sweetly relentless about why he was so sad that he had explained about it being the anniversary of the fire. With the subject coming up recently, Dean wasn't altogether surprised that Chloe had mentioned it to a friend—but he was taken aback by having to discuss it with someone he'd just met.

The silence grew to an uncomfortable length, and Bonnie finally said, "Look, I'm sorry for bringing it up."

Dean wanted nothing more than to leave it at that, but it was important to play nice in the parent sandbox, particularly in a small town where they'd likely be running into each other for years and years until their daughters graduated from high school. "It's fine. You surprised me, that's all. Last week was the anniversary of the fire, so I always feel – um – sad this time of year. I don't like to talk about it."

"I completely understand. Again, apologies for that."

They watched their daughters play tag, giggling and chasing each other through, under, and around the jungle gym.

A wave of gratefulness at their happy play washed over Dean, loosening his tongue. "It's a miracle that Chloe survived. The doctors weren't sure she would. She's lucky. And I'm lucky. I don't know if I would have survived if I had lost Chloe, too."

"I can't imagine. How horrible," Bonnie said quietly, her previously chirpy voice now more subdued. "That didn't happen around here? Did it? I think I would have remembered a fatal house fire in the news."

"Nope, different state." Dean had enough of her tactless chatter and shouted to Chloe, "Hey, kiddo time to go."

"See you later," Bonnie called after them.

Dean gave her a curt nod before boosting Chloe into the pickup truck.

20

Chloe

"Jarvis, I have to get to work, but we close at eight. Could you meet me at the diner then?"

"I can do that."

It felt good to have someone help me unravel this mystery, although I was still a little unsure about Jarvis.

My shift went without mishap—almost. I was on time, my hair was in the required ponytail, I remembered everyone's orders, and I didn't spill anything—until my last customer.

I was delivering chocolate cream pie to Candi, the lady who was the last customer the evening before. Somehow, I must have tilted the plate right as I was about to set it down, and the pie landed cream-side down right on her wrist.

We both stared at it for a split second before I began apologizing, and Candi started laughing.

"I'm so sorry. I'll get you another slice right away." I was grateful she wasn't mad.

I hurried back with a clean towel and carefully put the replacement slice of dessert on the table. "I really am sorry."

"No worries. Gave me the best laugh of the day." I watched as she stripped her wrist of a number of bracelets and wiped them clean with the towel before putting them back on. They were a mix of multi-colored stones. I liked them. They completely covered a faded tattoo of a watch that encircled her wrist. I thought maybe she did that on purpose to cover up the tattoo.

"You're new here." She handed the towel back and took a bite of pie.

"Yes. Obviously, you can tell when I dump food all over my customers."

"A simple mistake. It happens to every waitress. I know what it feels like to be new somewhere, too. I just moved here."

"Do you like it so far?"

"It's definitely living up to my expectations."

"Where'd you move from?"

"Oh, down south."

I didn't know if she meant farther south in Wisconsin or farther south in the States or, heck, for all I knew she meant South America. I didn't think it was my business.

"I'm glad you're liking it so far."

The bell over the door jangled, and Jarvis came in. I felt lighter for a moment, realizing how glad I was to see him. I wasn't completely positive that he'd show up, but here he was.

I turned back to Candi and impulsively placed my hand over hers. "Thanks for not being mad at me."

Candi laughed again. "At least it wasn't coffee."

She was being so kind, unlike that lady from the night before who was mad because Molly hadn't hired her.

Candi eventually left, and Molly let Jarvis stay while I did my closing chores.

"You're doing good, kid," Molly said as she let us out the front door.

"Thanks. Tonight was better—well—until I dumped pie on Candi."

"None of us are perfect." Molly's bright red (of course) dangly earrings swung back and forth along with her dark curls as she laughed.

Since she wasn't mad about my latest mistake, I finally had the nerve to ask a question that was growing more serious for me. "Molly, when's payday?"

"Not until next Friday."

My heart sank. It was only Thursday. My disappointment must have shown on my face. I was earning some tip money in cash from each shift. I could probably make it work if I was very careful. "Oh, okay."

"Listen, if you need a little money to get you through, I could advance you some."

"That might be good."

"Is tomorrow soon enough? I already closed out the till for tonight."

"Definitely. Thanks, Molly."

"See you tomorrow."

Jarvis and I stood awkwardly on the sidewalk. I hadn't really thought about where we would go to talk. The early autumn wind had picked up a chilling zing. It made the most sense to invite him back to my house, but I questioned whether that was really smart. I mean, I was alone there now, except for my fictitious aunt. Could I trust Jarvis? I mentally shrugged, deciding that if I trusted him enough to help me unravel this mystery, letting him into my house was no big deal.

"Let's go to my house."

We walked in silence until we got to the cemetery gate. Taking my security duties seriously, I locked it behind us.

Once inside the house, I gestured toward the kitchen table and chairs, and Jarvis took a seat. He looked around, stared at the decoy suitcase and backpack, and smirked. "You made up your aunt being here. Didn't you?"

How could he know? I didn't answer, wondering what I did to tip him off.

"The baggage tag on the suitcase is from a year ago."

I looked over and saw that he was right. The last time I used the suitcase was when I went to Colorado with Emma and her parents for spring break. I hadn't ripped off the tag from the airline. I tugged on it now and threw it in the garbage, impressed with Jarvis' powers of observation.

"So you obviously notice things other people don't. Is that why you're good at solving mysteries?"

"That and other things."

"I need to prove that someone gave my dad the drugs the night he overdosed. The police don't believe me."

"Did they investigate at all?"

"Chief Barnett says they did. He took down the names of everyone dad knew and was going to talk to them. He said they looked around the cemetery for evidence, too. But they didn't find anything that makes them think there was anyone else here that night. Jarvis, they think he's just another druggie."

"There'd be a police report. You could ask for a copy."

"They'd show me that?"

"They have to, if you ask. It's a public record."

"I didn't know that. How do you know things like that, Jarvis?"

"It's stuff that I picked up. I don't forget things once I learn them."

"Okay, I'll go down there tomorrow and see if I can get it."

"Do you have any real evidence that your dad didn't overdose on his own?"

Jarvis' question jolted me, but his expression was so honestly curious that I knew he wasn't trying to hurt my feelings.

"No, not really. But there are a few strange things. All of my dad's money is gone. There was nothing in his wallet, nothing in our emergency tin here in the house, and nothing in his bank account. That's why I got the job at the diner."

Jarvis' eyes widened. "That's weird. If someone robbed him, I could see the money being gone from his wallet or even from inside the house, but his bank account, too?"

"The bank won't tell me when the money was taken out of the account without a death certificate because my name's not on the account. I don't even know how to get a death certificate."

"Can't you get into his online account and view the transactions?"

"Maybe, if my dad believed in online banking—which he didn't. The only thing I have is his account number and the pin for his debit card."

"I might be able to help with that."

"There's more. All of the phone call records and text messages were deleted from his phone. I wanted to see who he'd been talking to."

"You have his phone—the police didn't keep it?"

"No. The chief gave it back to me with all of the other things my dad had in his pockets. But now that you mention it, that is weird, isn't it? Even if they believed he overdosed on his own, they would have wanted his phone to try to track down his dealer. The cop who drove me to the emergency room kept asking me if I knew who that was."

"Maybe they grabbed what they needed from his phone before they gave it back to you. They might be getting records straight from the cell phone company. They can do that, too."

I grew silent, wondering if the police department was doing their job at all.

"Is there more?" he asked.

"One more thing . . . in his wallet there was a slip of paper with a phone number on it. I dialed it and someone answered at a prison in Florida." I pulled out the paper where I scrawled the name of the prison next to the number. My heart lurched at seeing my handwriting next to Dad's. I used to complain that I couldn't read his handwriting. Now, I wished I hadn't. "Cypress Grove Correctional Facility in Pinellas County, Florida. As far as I know, my dad has never been to Florida. I don't know why he'd have that number, and now I can't see if he even called there because he wiped his phone logs."

"Or someone wiped his phone logs."

"*What?*"

"You don't know if it was your dad or someone else."

"I guess so." Jarvis was right. If someone killed my dad and staged it to look like an overdose, they'd want to cover their tracks and delete any evidence that might point to them.

"I definitely can help with that."

"Wait—with what? My dad's phone?"

Jarvis nodded.

"Really? Are you a hacker?"

"Something like that." Jarvis grinned and cracked his knuckles. "But I don't think I'll need those skills for this."

So, quiet Jarvis had another side indeed. Wow.

"Grab your computer."

I retrieved it quickly from the bedroom.

"Let's start with the bank. Which one did your dad use?"

"The Farmers & Merchants Bank downtown. But we can't hack into a bank. That's got to be a federal offense or something."

"Hacking into a bank is definitely a federal offense, probably a state one too, but there might be another way. Go to their website and let's see if we can set up an online bank account for your dad. Pretend you're him."

Typing in the name of the bank, I clicked on the link to their website. In the corner it said, log in or enroll now. I clicked enroll now, and the box prompted me to enter the type of account, my dad's name, and the account number. The next screen asked for his social security number. That I didn't know, but I knew where to find it. I dashed for the filing cabinet where dad kept important papers, like taxes. He was organized that way. After entering that, I was prompted to put in an email and recovery phone number along with the username I wanted. My fingers flew over the keys. This was going to work!

The next message deflated me. Thanks for registering. Your online banking access will be confirmed by email in twenty-four hours.

"So now what?"

"They'll either confirm your access or they won't."

I hated the idea of waiting, but I didn't have a choice. "What about the phone? Can we retrieve his call log?"

Jarvis checked the time on his phone and jumped up, suddenly eager to leave. "I've got to go, but I can work on it."

I handed him the phone and the pin on a post-it note. He looked down at the note, then crumpled it up and threw it in the kitchen trash.

"Hey, don't you need that?"

"I'll remember it. I should have some answers before chemistry class."

"Okay. I'll see if I can get the police report before then, too."

I walked Jarvis out to the gate and unlocked it for him. It felt so good to have someone to confide in—someone who would help me—even if it was the most unlikely person of all. Impulsively, I gave him a hug. I realized I probably shouldn't have done that when he stiffened up. I released him immediately. "I'm sorry, Jarvis."

"G'night." He didn't look at me as he slipped through the open gate.

With his head down he shuffled through the leaves covering the sidewalk, and I wondered if I was making a huge mistake by trusting him.

21

The Watcher

I'm GETTING CLOSER TO Chloe just as I planned. But others are, too. I have to make sure they don't get in the way.

I haven't decided how I will do that . . . yet.

I know I'm smarter than the cops in this town—at least the police chief. He's walked right by me and not even noticed that I'm watching her. My goal is to be invisible.

It's the other cop I need to be careful of. He's looked at me like he knows who I am and what I'm doing.

But he couldn't possibly.

Even so, I'm up for any challenge if it means I get to be with Chloe.

22

Dean ~ 2 Weeks Before Death

DEAN FELT THE PHONE buzz in his pocket but ignored it. He needed to finish prepping the grave for tomorrow's funeral so he could get to Chloe's cross country meet in time to see her run. Luckily, it was the one home meet they had each year. Even so, an hour later he knew he had cut it close and jogged the last hundred yards to the starting line on the golf course.

Chloe was just finishing her warm-up, jogging back and forth with her teammates. She flashed him a quick grin when she noticed him with the other fans. "Let's Go Tigers!" Dean whooped.

Chloe laughed and shook her head, taking her place at the line.

The announcer's voice echoed through his megaphone. "Runners get ready, runners set"—and with the bang of the gun the runners surged forward. Dean knew the drill, once the runners were all past, the spectators ran to the next point in the 5-kilometer race where they'd have a good view.

"We get nearly as much exercise at these things as the kids," one mom shouted as she sprinted along with the crowd. Dean hurried, knowing Chloe and her teammates would likely be near the front.

And there she was, in the lead pack of runners.

"Go Cowyn!" He shouted and she gave him a thumbs up.

Then the fans all flocked to the next point and the next—by then Chloe was first and maintained that lead until she ran across the finish line. Dean took photos as the top runners came in—Chloe, Emma, and Jordan—all in the top five. Chloe had said they had a good shot at state this year, and Dean didn't doubt it as he scrolled through the pictures.

The red voice mail notification caught his eye. He'd forgotten about the call he ignored earlier. He froze in place and nearly dropped the phone as he listened to the message.

"This is Warden Sanchez at the Cypress Grove Correctional Facility. I've got you on a victim notification list for the release of an inmate, Diana Johnson, regarding a Florida State Court Case. State law requires that I confirm you've received this message, please call me back at 850-488-7042."

"Shit," Dean said, sliding his phone back in his pocket.

"Dad!" Chloe bounded up to him like a puppy. "Did you see that? Fastest time so far this year!"

"I did – great job. You three looked awesome coming across the line so close together." Dean did his best to put enthusiasm back in his voice, but it didn't quite work.

"You okay?"

Chloe was always perceptive of mood shifts, even as a little girl. Now she looked at him with her eyes clouded with worry.

"I'm good, I'm good. I just got a work call that I need to take care of."

"Okay. Don't forget that a bunch of us are going to get pizza. I won't be late."

"That's right." Dean had indeed forgotten but was grateful for the time alone to return the phone call to the warden.

He waited until he was back in the house, sitting at his desk in the living room before calling the number back.

The phone only rang once before a recording clicked on. "You've reached the office of Warden Sanchez at Cypress Grove Correctional Facility. Our administration office is closed for the day but will reopen at 8:30 a.m.. Please try back then."

Dean scrubbed his hand across his face and leaned forward with his elbows on his knees. As much as he could, he'd put Florida and everything that happened there behind them. Once a year he pulled out the envelope and took a moment to look at the photos of who they had lost on that awful day. That's all he allowed himself—that one day to grieve and then move on. Nothing good could come from wallowing in his sadness.

He shoved out of the chair, going to the kitchen to grab a beer. He stared into the fridge, wondering what he could make for dinner, but all he could think about was that the person responsible for so much grief was getting out. He wished he could have gotten the call over with.

He went back to his desk with that once-a-year file calling to him, and he yanked the drawer open—breaking his vow. He'd concealed everything in a manila envelope that said tax receipts. He knew it was risky keeping these in the house, but

Chloe wasn't likely to open an envelope that held tax information.

Flipping up the tiny metal clasp that held it shut, he slid the contents out onto the desktop. A small plastic photo album was on top of a bunch of documents and newspaper clippings. He set the album aside, once a year was enough for that.

Instead, he re-read the papers from the court case and the news articles he had clipped. He didn't remember cutting them out originally—long before the internet made that sort of thing unnecessary. But he did remember how, in a fit of anger one year, he had torn away the grainy mugshot photos that were included with each article. He couldn't stand seeing that face.

He sifted absentmindedly through other documents in the envelope. His marriage certificate, birth certificates with their original names, an old life insurance policy. His fingers shook as he touched the name listed as beneficiary—his wife's name. It was an old policy, but he kept it—he didn't know why. It wasn't valid anymore anyway—he'd long ago changed the policy over to Chloe's benefit. He should throw that away. He wasn't sure why he hadn't.

He shoved everything back in the envelope, mashed the clasp closed, and threw it into the drawer.

Leaning back, he chugged what was left of his beer.

———◦———

Once Chloe was out the door to school the next morning, Dean dialed the correctional facility's number. With Florida in the eastern time zone, it was already approaching 9 a.m.. He was put through to the warden immediately.

"I received a call about a prisoner release—Diana Johnson."

"Right, right. Yes, she's set to be released this week, and you have a right to know that, as she was convicted of—"

"I know what she was convicted of. I was there."

"Of course. I see you're not living in Florida any longer?"

"No, we're not."

"You should know that she isn't allowed to travel out of state as a condition of her parole. She's been reminded of the restraining order you filed here in Florida. Do you have any questions?"

"No, I guess not. I knew her time would be up soon, but I didn't expect it for another year or so."

"Well, we're overcrowded, and she's been a well-behaved inmate."

Dean had no response to that, and when he didn't say anything else, the warden said, "Okay, then, I just needed to make sure you knew she was getting out."

"Thanks." Dean ended the call and let his phone clatter to the desktop.

Dean didn't trust for a second that Diana would obey the rules of her parole. He only hoped that their trail to Wisconsin was too cold for her to follow after so many years.

23

Chloe

THE POLICE STATION WAS a small building not far from the diner. Nothing was actually very far from anything else in this town, but most businesses were on the streets surrounding the town square or out near the main highway where people traveling from Madison to Fond du Lac and beyond might stop for a break.

The lobby was sparse with only a few chairs and assorted posters for community events. Not very welcoming. But I didn't imagine people wanted to hang out at the police station much. I stepped to the information window. The desk behind it was empty, but a sign said to press the button on the wall for assistance. The buzzer was loud—as jarring as a car horn blaring, unexpected and rude.

The same officer who arrived first at the cemetery appeared, giving me that dang pity smile that made me want to slap his face. *Probably best not to follow through on that desire.* Just looking at him brought back all his questions about my dad's supposed drug dealers. I really didn't like this guy.

"Hey, there. What can I do for you?"

You can quit being a smug, idiot jerk. I ignored my impulsive thoughts and pasted a sweet smile on my face, thinking of the old saying about using honey to catch some kind of bug. I noted his nametag. "Hi, Officer Mank. I was wondering if you could help me get a copy of the police report about my dad?"

He stared me down. It was probably only a second or two, but it felt like a minute. "There's a form you need to fill out." He rolled his chair back to grab a sheet of paper from a cubby and slid it across the counter.

It was a simple enough form. My name and address, my dad's name and address, the location and date of incident . . . all these locations were the same. My stomach sank when I read the notation at the bottom. "Requests may take up to 10 days."

Ten days! I didn't think there'd be much in the report, given what I suspected about the depth of the police investigation—if you could call it that.

I handed the sheet back to the officer and cleared my throat. "It says that it can take ten days to get this report. I was hoping to get it today."

"We put that on there in case we need more time. Check back later today. It might be ready."

On my way out the door, I passed Chief Barnett coming in. "Hello, Chloe. You doing okay?"

I liked him better than the other cop, at least for now. But who knows what I would think after I read the report. I muttered, "I'm fine," and stepped out onto the sidewalk.

Why did people say they were fine when they weren't fine? What a dumb thing. I was NOT fine! I was anything but fine.

I was horrible and sad and scared and mad. I wondered what the chief would have done if I said how I actually felt?

—◦◦—

Jarvis wasn't in chemistry class when I got there—unusual for him.

Relief flooded my tense shoulders when he ducked in right as Mr. Hughes was shutting the door.

I didn't even let Jarvis sit down before I asked, "How did it go?"

"I got everything."

"Wait—what? Everything?"

"You didn't think I could do it." Jarvis gave me a hard stare. "The email from the bank confirming online access came through and I logged in. I restored your dad's deleted calls and text messages, too. But I can't get the voice mails back."

"Jarvis, you must have stayed up late."

"I don't need much sleep." He rummaged in his backpack. "Here's the phone and a printout of the bank account information. Did you get the police report?"

"No. They might have a copy for me after school." Unable to wait until after class, I scanned the bank printout. The money was transferred out the day before Dad died. It went into an account at another bank.

Jarvis leaned over, pointing to the line I read. "This is an online bank. You can view the account number and the name of the bank, but I can't get in to find the name on the account. They have really great security. I'm sorry, Chloe."

My head shot up. "Jarvis, you've been great. You don't have to be sorry about anything. Don't do anything illegal on my account."

Jarvis' response was to laugh.

It rippled through me, but in a good way. He had a nice laugh. It was the first time I'd heard it.

We'd been so intent on our conversation that we jumped when Mr. Hughes' voice boomed, almost in our ears. "Mr. Keen, Ms. Cowyn, do we have a problem with attention to-day?"

Um. Apparently, we did. "Sorry," I said.

I tried to stick with chemistry for the rest of the hour, but I was distracted, screwing up my measurements more than once.

Finally, Jarvis held up his hands in exasperation. "Chloe, I've got this. Can you just – just not?"

I was fine with him taking over. I stood next to him, attempting to look involved, but I was dying to take a peek at Dad's messages and call log. It was difficult to resist pulling out his phone to begin my research, but Mr. Hughes had a no cell phone rule. One of the phones pinged from inside my bag. I wasn't sure if Jarvis had left Dad's phone on or if it was mine making the noise. I reached in and put both on silent.

The wait was nearly unbearable, but I survived until the bell before checking the phones.

My phone screen showed a voice mail notification. It had to be the social worker because my friends usually texted me. Except for Emma. But I didn't think Emma was going to be calling me anytime soon. I would apologize to her if she'd let me.

"Hello, Ms. Gill. This is Ameena Alavi with the Columbia County Human Services office. I'm the social worker assigned to Chloe's case. I need to confirm she's in your custody following your brother's death. Please accept my condolences for your loss. If you would let me know when we could meet, then I can close Chloe's file. Call me back at your convenience either at this number or on my office line."

Shit! This was exactly why I had given my number as my aunt's pretend contact information, but now I wasn't sure what to do. Could I get her to close the file over the phone by pretending to be my aunt?

I mulled this over on the way to the next class and nearly bumped into Emma. Here was my chance. I took a deep breath and quickly blurted out, "Emma, I'm so sorry."

She turned and went the other way, avoiding eye contact. It was worse than if she'd yelled at me and told me how mad she was. I vowed not to cry. Not here. Not in front of everyone. We'd been friends for years. Yes, I said something awful, but I was in the middle of a huge crisis. A real friend might see that and give me a break.

The only person acting like a true friend was the most unlikely one—Jarvis.

Later, I avoided everyone and ate my lunch outside again. It was nearly too cold for that today, but it was better than dealing with pity stares and angry glares. Lunch was kind of meager—two thin slices of turkey, a cheese stick, and an apple. We were out of bread. No, *I* was out of bread. I tried not to cry and set to work scanning through my dad's phone records. Jarvis really had managed to repopulate everything.

I looked back two weeks before he died and started writing down his outgoing calls.

Most of them were local. I dialed a few from my phone and crossed them out as people answered at locations that I knew my dad called regularly: funeral homes, the guy who delivered the burial vaults, Frank his boss at the city, someone about a lawn mower part, and a local law firm. I was struck by how grim and lonely Dad's life now seemed. One number rang at the motel at the edge of town, the one attached to the coffee shop my dad sometimes went to.

That one seemed a bit strange. I didn't know who he'd be calling there, but maybe there was a relative in town for a funeral that had a question or something.

Then I saw it. A number I already dialed a few days ago—the one for the prison in Florida. Dad *had* called the number on the slip of paper he was carrying around, twice, nearly two weeks ago.

I quickly scanned the incoming calls to see if he ever received a call from that number and saw it listed an hour or so before his first outgoing call, making me realize Dad was actually returning a call when he dialed the prison number. It still didn't make any sense to me. I went back as far as I could in his call log and didn't see the number listed again.

The rest of the incoming calls were easily eliminated as the same numbers dad called regularly, except for one. There were a bunch of missed calls from the same number, and then one short call that my dad had answered, followed nearly immediately by a longer one from the same number. Weird. I redialed the number from my dad's phone, but it just rang and rang.

I stared at the doors to the building as the kids who had gone off campus for lunch returned in a rush. I wanted to skip school so bad, but I slogged my way back inside, knowing that if I didn't, I'd have to deal with another call for my absent aunt.

24

Chloe

AFTER SCHOOL I RUSHED to the police station. A female officer sat behind the desk. I explained who I was, and she had the envelope ready for me.

"That's $2.50 for the copying fee."

Thank goodness for tip money. I dug into my backpack and pulled out a handful of change, paying her in quarters, dimes, and nickels. Her cool gaze and pursed lips made me think she didn't appreciate that, but hey, money was money.

I tore open the flap, pulled the papers out, and read as I walked toward the diner. A quick scan showed me there wasn't much information. There were no notes about either the cop I disliked or the chief talking to any of the people who knew Dad. It's not like the list was very long. There was nothing in there about my dad's cell phone records either. Maybe things like that weren't part of the police report.

The only thing interesting was a list of evidence collected at the cemetery. Mostly, it seemed like garbage, some cigarette butts and wrappers. The same kind of stuff I'd found on my search.

But then I took a closer look at the fourth item on the list, a blue stone bead, and wondered if it was like the one I found at the base of the angel statue. I really wanted to get a look at it. But it was completely possible that it meant nothing. People lost jewelry all the time. Jewelry broke, and when that happened, the beads usually flew everywhere.

I hurried to change into my work clothes, and as I stowed my bag on an employee hook at the back of the kitchen, I heard someone gasp and turned to find Molly staring down at the exposed section of my legs. I'd been so preoccupied with reading the police report that I'd forgotten to put on the socks that covered up my scars.

"Chloe, what happened?"

"Oh, I'm sorry. I usually wear socks to cover up my scars."

"Were you burned?" Molly's bright red lips were turned upside down.

"It was a house fire. I was really young. My mom died, and I was in the hospital for a long time. I don't remember it at all, but I was left with some souvenirs." I tried to laugh but it sounded forced and fake. I looked down at the puckered skin. "This isn't even the worst part. The scars start above my knees." I regretted saying that when I saw Molly's reaction.

Her hand flew to her heart, and her eyes were glistening like she might cry. "Well, bless your soul. I'm sorry that happened to you, Chloe. You don't have to wear anything to cover those up if you don't want to."

"I don't want to gross anyone out."

"If they have an issue with it, they can just leave."

I stood there, pondering what to do. I rarely let anyone see my legs uncovered, even a portion of them. Sure, my friends saw them once in a while by accident, but usually I changed for sports or phy-ed in a bathroom stall and wore leggings under my shorts. I hated it. It was hot and uncomfortable. Did I have the guts to go partially bare-legged in public? I decided to give it a try.

The shift was busier than normal. It was Friday. I'd almost forgotten the day, because well—everything. Every table was full. *(Yay tips!!)* I loved that I was getting the hang of waitressing. The early crowd thinned out the closer we got to kick-off time for the high school football game. Football was a big deal in our town.

Jarvis came in and took a seat at the counter. I didn't know he was coming, but I was glad to see him. I was about to take his order, when the door banged open and the woman who Molly hadn't hired staggered in. She was obviously drunk or high or maybe both.

"Good Golly Miss Molly, Miss MOLL – EEE," she sang off key. I stood there unsure of what to do. All conversation in the diner had stopped as we all stared at her.

Molly came out from the back. "Good gravy," she muttered, approaching the woman. "Look, I don't want to have to call the police on you. Can you please leave?"

The woman kept shouting, "You'll be s – sorry Molly! You should have hired me."

"Clearly, I made the right decision," Molly said and some of the diners laughed. Two of the guys that were still eating had gotten up to help. Together they moved the woman out the door, where she staggered off down the street still shouting her empty threats.

At least I hoped they were empty threats. I turned back to Jarvis and mouthed, "Oh-my-god." We both laughed. "I didn't expect you here tonight, but I wanted to say thanks again for – y'know – your help. During lunch I went through my dad's calls and found out that he received and made a call to that prison number."

"Oh, about that. It's a woman's prison. I looked it up."

"A woman's prison? I can't believe dad would know any convict let alone a female one. I would really like to know who he talked to there."

Jarvis nodded and ordered a piece of cherry pie a la mode.

It wasn't long before only our regular late diners remained, including Candi. She sure liked the corner booth. It was funny. She was always willing to wait for it if someone happened to be in it. If they just sat down and we knew it was going to be a while, she might settle for the next booth, but she never, ever sat at a table.

To each his own – well – her own. I liked booths, too. Somehow, they felt more comfortable.

I served her the usual pie and coffee and didn't spill a drop of either.

I was enjoying getting to know the regulars. Mr. Massey, the local farm implement dealer, wanted me to top off his decaf coffee. "Too late for the high octane stuff or I'll never get to sleep," he'd joked every single night. It made me smile, and it made me miss my dad. That's exactly the kind of stuff he used to say.

As things slowed, I finally had time to clean up the mess left over from my shake-making extravaganza on the back counter near Jarvis. Ice cream splatters were everywhere, and the shake machine was a disaster. A utensil clattering to the counter made me look over. Jarvis had dropped his fork and was staring at my scars.

"Chloe, what's wrong with your legs?"

Ugh. I hated talking about this, and now I had to tell the story twice in the same night.

I said it all really fast. "I was in a fire when I was little. I don't remember it, but I was in the hospital for a long time. End of story." I said that last part more firmly than I meant to.

Candi usually lingered over her pie, but not tonight. She was waiting at the cash register to pay and heard what I said to Jarvis. She looked down at my legs and her face grew pale. She looked like she might be sick, and nearly threw the money on the counter with her bill. "Keep the change," she shouted behind as she rushed out.

"What's her problem?" Molly asked, coming through the swinging door from the kitchen. "Did you spill something on her again?"

"Very funny. I think my scars might have grossed her out. Jarvis asked me about them, and Candi overheard. Right after she took a good look at them, she told me to keep the change and ran out. Maybe I should wear the socks. These scars are ugly."

"Scars aren't ugly, Chloe." Both Molly and I swiveled our heads to Jarvis. "Outside scars show you survived something. They're part of you. Inside scars are, too, but people can't see them."

Who was this strange boy? I nearly started crying because he was so right—profoundly right. I came around the counter and gave him a hug. This time he didn't flinch, and for just a second his arms came up and hugged me back.

25

The Watcher

CHLOE'S SCARS ARE TERRIBLE. It was hard not to stare, thinking about how badly she must have been burned.

She must have been in so much pain. I never want her to suffer like that again.

I know she's strong—but she needs me to keep her safe.

Danger is all around her. Others watch like I do. Hovering close. Waiting to pounce.

But I'm the one she really needs.

26

Dean ~ 8 Days Before Death

WHEN THE FOURTH CALL came in from the same unidentified number in as many minutes, Dean relented and answered, immediately regretting his decision.

He hoped it was merely someone calling about burial services, but the voice he heard opened a haunting pit in his stomach.

"Dean—well finally. A girl might get her feelings hurt when her calls don't get picked up."

Dean was startled by the laugh that followed and hit the end call button. *How in the hell did she get his number?*

The phone rang again—same number. He could block her, and he was nearly ready to do that, when he thought better of it. He needed to know what she wanted. At least then he could plan his next steps.

"How did you get this number?"

"I have my ways. I'm still connected to some very powerful and very dangerous people."

"Yeah—I'm shaking in my boots. Get to the point. What do you want, Diana?" Dean steadied himself against the door frame between his kitchen and living room. She didn't need to know he was actually shaking, mostly with anger, but there was fear, too.

"You owe me."

"Do I now? For what exactly? This ought to be a good story coming from your fucked up mind."

"Hey, I'm clean."

"Only because you couldn't get a fix in prison."

"Oh, you'd be surprised what you can get inside. No, seriously, I've been clean since my conviction."

"Well good for you, too bad you didn't decide to do that about a year earlier."

"Look, you're right, and I know I deserve all the shit you're throwing at me. Would it help to say I'm sorry—sorry to my core. I know nothing I can say will change what happened."

"I'm hanging up now, don't ever call me—"

"Wait – wait. Dean, they know where you and Chloe are living."

Dean recognized the fear in her voice as her bravado slipped. "Why do they even care?"

"It's Lance, I guess he's known all along. That's who got me your phone number. He was waiting for me when I walked out of the prison. They appreciate that I didn't rat them out, but Lance covered my debt to the cartel—and now he wants me to pay him back."

"I can't help you. You know you aren't supposed to be contacting me for anything, ever. Leave us alone."

"I think they might come for you if I can't pay them back. That's how they're trying to get me to cooperate."

"What did Lance say to you?" After all these years, Dean thought for sure this problem was long gone. It's not like drug cartels were known for their patience.

"Just that if I wanted you and Chloe to stay safe—I need to repay him what I owe."

"When did you ever care about either of us?"

"They've threatened to kill us all."

"Ah – there we have it. You're only trying to save your own hide."

"No – well, yes – I want to save *all* of us."

"So, pay them back, Diana."

"It's thousands of dollars."

"You'll figure it out—you can always work it off. Offer to open another meth lab for them. You were always such a great cook. Don't you dare contact me again."

27

Chloe

JARVIS WALKED ME HOME, but I didn't invite him in. I had to be back at the diner at 6 a.m. for the breakfast shift. We made plans to go through everything we knew the next afternoon. Before bed, I reread the police report. It didn't help me sleep because I got mad all over again. It seemed like the cops had put in zero time to solve Dad's murder. Wasn't it their job to eliminate all possibilities? I laid awake thinking about who could possibly gain from my dad being dead. Maybe he saw something that he shouldn't have. Maybe he was simply in the wrong place at the wrong time. How would I ever unravel the truth? My head spun with unanswered questions, and I didn't relax until the warmth of my guardian angel hugged me close. I hadn't felt him for a couple of days. "Thank you, Leb," I whispered before drifting off to sleep.

I was still mad the next morning while I walked to work after sleeping less than I needed. A school bus rumbled by as I turned the corner onto the town square. With a heart-tugging sting, I realized it was the bus carrying the cross country team to the invitational I was missing. I stopped and stared. Through the window, Emma's eyes met mine, and she pressed her hand to the glass. I gave her a little wave in return and tried not to cry—my mad now turning into something else.

That lasted until the police chief sat in my section an hour later. Fueled by my lack of sleep and overall outrage at the lack of a real investigation, my anger came roaring back.

"Hello, I'm Chloe, would you like some coffee?" I said through clenched teeth. He gave me a funny look because I obviously did not need to introduce myself.

"Sure."

I flipped over his cup with a rattle and sloshed coffee into it.

"Do you know what you want or should I give you a minute?"

"I'm ready. How about two eggs over easy, two blueberry pancakes, and a side of bacon."

Yum! *I know what I want, too. A police chief who does his job with a side of honesty.*

"Coming right up." I tried to make my words as full of sarcasm as possible. It wasn't easy, but I was pleased the chief seemed to get my meaning as his eyes narrowed at me.

I put his order in and made the rounds for coffee before I saw him beckoning me over. *I was ready for this.*

"Are you okay? I know it's really hard to lose a parent."

I swallowed hard before replying. "One, he wasn't *A* parent. He was my *only* parent. Two, you lied to me about being thorough with your investigation. I know you never talked to anyone who knew my dad. I read the police report. You said you were going to do that."

"I did say that." He nodded at me with no further explanation.

"What?! No point in doing your job when you've already made up your mind about my dad?" I said way too loudly.

I felt Molly approach as her skirt swooshed in beside me. "Everything okay here, you two?"

"I know I'm right. And I'm well on my way to proving it, doing the work you haven't done." My fury made me exaggerate my progress, but maybe by the end of the day I would know more.

"Be careful, Chloe," the chief warned in a low voice. "That report is only from the night your dad died. It isn't the whole file on the case. We don't put every detail into the public report."

The chief's words made me pause for a moment, but only a moment. "What do I have to be careful of if my dad overdosed all on his own, like you think. Then there's no one dangerous running around, is there?"

"People who sell drugs can be dangerous. Please be careful."

Molly put her hand on my shoulder. I took a deep breath, holding back tears and expecting to be fired. "How about you take your break now?"

I scanned the restaurant to see if others had noticed my interaction with the chief. I was getting to know the regulars. They were all kind—and they all *appeared* to have minded their own business. Although, I suspected that wasn't true. This was a small town after all. Walking to the back for my break, I saw the crazy lady Molly kicked out the other night. She was hanging around the door on the sidewalk outside. I sure hoped she wasn't going to try coming in again. I didn't have the energy to warn Molly, knowing she could handle it, particularly with the police chief in the restaurant.

When I came back, I was relieved the woman was gone from out front. Molly said she'd never seen her. I hoped that was the last of her.

I made it through my shift. As I clocked out, I stretched my back—the breakfast shift was brutal. I had no idea how hard waitressing was going to be.

"Hey, Chloe, do you have a minute?" Molly called to me from her office at the back of the kitchen.

I had more than a minute actually. Although, I wasn't sure if I wanted to hear what she had to say. I'd never been in her office and couldn't help smiling the second I stepped in. Her desk was constructed from the front grill of a bright red vintage car, complete with headlights.

"Do you like my baby?" Molly smiled, patting the shiny paint. "It's a '55 Corvette in the original gypsy red. There's a guy in Madison who makes furniture out of salvaged car parts. I couldn't resist."

"I love it." I continued to smile, but I knew why she wanted to talk to me and jumped into my apology. "Listen, I'm mad at the chief, but I shouldn't have said anything while I was working. It won't happen again."

"That'd be good, but I don't have a problem with that. If my dad were dead and I knew that the police should be doing something about, I'd be mad, too. Remember, I'm on your side, but I also think the chief is, too."

"But he's not doing anything. He didn't even talk to the people he should have."

"Don't be so sure about that."

I leaned in eager to hear what he told her, but she held up her hand, stopping my question. "Now, he didn't say anything to me specifically, but when I went back to bring him his breakfast, I asked him if he'd truly closed your dad's case. He didn't say anything, just gave me this look. It's one I've seen before."

Molly took a deep breath before she continued. "I want to tell you a tough story – not because I want sympathy or anything, I just want you to know how serious the chief is about doing a good job. About twelve years ago, right after I first opened this diner, I was closing late at night and went out the back like I usually do. Someone wearing a mask jumped me. At first, I thought I was being robbed, but he – he forced himself on me. He – he raped me. I called the police and reported it. They started investigating, but then things got weird. All of a sudden, I'm being asked about my past by the officer in charge of my case. That maybe I knew my attacker and that it wasn't *really* sexual assault. That he'd heard a rumor that maybe I'd been an escort in Madison before I opened the diner. None of that was true, of course, but people started looking at me funny. The police made no progress on finding my attacker."

"Oh my god. I'm so sorry." I couldn't imagine surviving what Molly had, and my heart sank at both the brutality of the attack and the powerlessness of being treated like a liar.

"It's okay now. It wasn't then. But I'm telling you all this for a reason. So weeks go by, and I've given up that the investigating officer is going to find this guy, when Chief Barnett comes in, only back then he was Officer Barnett. He talks to me and goes over all the details once more and tells me not to tell the other officer about our conversation. Not long after, an arrest is made, and you know who my attacker turned out to be?"

I simply shook my head.

Molly was nearly whispering when she answered her own question, "The original cop investigating my case."

"No way. That's horrible." I couldn't imagine what that must have been like for her.

"It was and still is in many ways, but the chief said he had a hunch and worked on the case quietly without letting the other officer know. He has that same look now. Chloe, I trust him. I see why you're angry, but I wouldn't give up on him. I will talk to him about taking another look at your dad's information—that is if he isn't already doing it. But he's right. You do need to be careful. Small towns look safe, but they're often hiding more sinister people than you really would care to believe. I know."

"I am being careful, but I have to figure this out."

"I understand. I'm really glad you're not alone now that your aunt's in town."

"How do you know about my aunt?"

"Oh, the chief mentioned that he wanted to swing by and talk to her."

Oh, no. Not another person looking for my absent aunt.

"You should have her come in some time. I'd like to meet her."

"Yeah, sure." I smiled and nodded agreeably, but my sarcastic brain went into overdrive. *It's a date, say two-and-a-half weeks from now? We'll invite my school guidance counselor and my social worker. And the police chief, too. It'll be a party.*

28

Chloe

JARVIS GAVE ME A look of awe when I told him later about what I had the nerve to say to the police chief. "For once, I said what was on my mind when I was mad."

"I can never do that. Usually, it's only later that I think of what I should have said."

I arranged the meager evidence I had collected in front of us; the list of my dad's incoming and outgoing phone calls, the envelope with his stuff, the police report, and the small bag of things I found while searching the cemetery. We stared at it.

I sighed, feeling like every bit of energy had left my body. Caffeine would be good. When I looked in the fridge, I was reminded that we, no, *I was* out of coke. I planned to shop later today now that I had enough money to buy groceries, thanks to my tips and the small advance on my wages Molly gave me.

Jarvis grabbed the police report and began reading. I made coffee.

The smell overwhelmed me. I missed my dad. He was the one who usually drank coffee each morning and when I closed my eyes, I could almost imagine him here in the room with me instead of Jarvis. What would he tell me to do? I knew the answer. He'd tell me to "get on with it."

Whether he was there with me or not, my dad's voice in my head was right. No one else was going to figure out who murdered him. My investigation skills came from being an avid crime drama fan. *Yeah, I knew that was fiction*. But I figured they couldn't be that far off or people wouldn't watch, right? "We should reconstruct what my dad did for the last two weeks."

Jarvis looked up from his reading and nodded.

I pulled a notebook out of my backpack and wrote the date from two weeks ago on a blank page, filling in the rest of what we knew. It wasn't much—the only thing out of the ordinary was Dad's call to and from the Florida prison. Suddenly, I had a thought. My dad didn't keep his schedule on his phone, he was old school and kept one of those large desk pad calendars. I ran to the living room and removed the September and October sheets from the holder on his desk, bringing it back to the kitchen. I noticed a corner was torn off like someone had used it for a piece of scrap paper.

I was surprised that Dad had an appointment with a lawyer—8:30 a.m. Loyal Law was scrawled in the square for this coming Monday. It was the same law firm he'd made an outgoing call to a couple of days before he died. I'd assumed he made a call regarding burial arrangements because sometimes lawyers handled these things, but now I needed to find out what that appointment was all about. Along with all the calls I tracked from my dad's phone, I added in the five burials that happened in the cemetery in that timeframe, too. Those would have been days when mourners and funeral home employees were coming and going and might have noticed something. I finished up with his usual breakfast on Monday and Thursday mornings at the highway coffee shop—even though I couldn't be sure he'd gone on those days. I'd been at school already. That was it for his schedule.

"Jarvis?"

"Yes?"

"Chief Barnett said he would talk to everyone that my dad knew, and I'm not sure he did. At the diner, he said that not everything goes into this report."

"That makes sense. This report doesn't have much in it. I read it a second time even though I've already memorized it, just in case I missed something. I don't usually."

"Usually what?"

"Miss anything."

"Wait. You really memorized the entire report?"

"I do that with things I read."

"Like word for word?"

"Well, sort of. I see the page as a picture in my head and I can remember everything on it. Eidetic memory."

"That's cool. No wonder you get good grades. So I'm going to have to talk to these people and ask if anyone noticed anything weird with my dad. I mean, even if the cops do have the information, they're not sharing it. I could go out to the coffee shop in the morning. Do you want to come with me?"

"I'm not great with people. I'm much better with research."

"I could do all the talking." I hoped he'd give in because I really didn't want to do this alone. "I'd really appreciate the help." And the company, I realized, although I didn't say that part. Jarvis was becoming a good friend.

"Fine." Jarvis sighed and closed his eyes. "What time?"

"Aaah, how about 8 o'clock," I suggested, not wanting to push my luck with the even earlier time that had first crossed my mind.

"That early on a Sunday?"

"I want to catch the old guys who hang out there before they do whatever else they do on a Sunday. Probably church. And it's a long walk out there."

"I could probably borrow my stepmom's car, so we don't have to leave so early."

"Really? I could give you gas money."

"You don't have to do that," Jarvis said.

"Do you like cinnamon rolls? They have these huge gooey ones nearly as big as a plate."

"I like cinnamon rolls." A smile pulled at the very edge of his mouth. "Alright, it's a deal."

We looked through the other items. I picked up the bag of evidence – er – trash that I collected when I searched the cemetery. "This is all I found when I looked around outside. The police have a small list of evidence they gathered, too. It's mainly garbage like mine. Except for—"

"—the blue bead." Jarvis grabbed the bag from my hand and looked at it closely.

"Yes, but who knows if it's the same kind? Or if it even means anything?"

"We don't, but I want to see the one the police have." Jarvis pulled it out of the bag and looked at it more closely. "Lapis lazuli."

"What?"

"The stone. It's called lapis lazuli."

"Oh, okay. I didn't know what it was. Will they show us the one they have?"

"I don't think they usually do that, but you can try."

One more thing to add to the list. I knew the police station had someone there all the time, but I didn't know if the right person for my evidence question would be there on the weekend. Probably not. One thing I did know was that there was no way I could visit the lawyer during business hours without skipping class.

My phone rang, jarring us. I nearly answered it and then pulled my hand back like my phone was a hot potato. It was a number I didn't recognize. Who knew who was at the other end of that call? I had to remember that my phone was also my aunt's incognito phone.

I let it go to voice mail and listened immediately.

"Hello, Ms. Gill. This is Jonathan at the hospital morgue. We know this is a terrible time for you, Ms. Gill. But we need to know which funeral home will be picking up your brother's remains. Please call us back or have the funeral home contact us as soon as you've made those arrangements."

I tried not to cry as the finality of the word arrangements rolled over me. I'd done my best to erase the image of my dad—well his body—laying in a cold morgue drawer. But I knew he—his body—couldn't stay there forever.

Dad's mostly morbid job gave me more than a working knowledge of the final arrangements that must be made when someone died. We talked about the pros and cons of burial versus cremation in gross and humorous ways, never really thinking about either one of us making these decisions for the other. At least I'd never taken the conversation seriously.

Surprisingly, given his job, Dad was a firm believer in cremation. At least I knew that much. Could I pretend to be my aunt and make these arrangements?

I picked the only funeral home in town that had a crematorium. *How weird was it that I knew that?* My throat constricted at the thought of my dad's body being burned up. That image was way worse than imagining his body in a cold morgue drawer. I had to remind myself that it wasn't him—not really—not anymore.

I swallowed hard and dialed the number. Marcus, the younger of the morticians answered.

I tried on a more serious, slightly deeper voice. "Marcus, this is Maggie Gill, Dean Cowyn's sister. Can I ask you to pick up Dean's body from the mortuary at the hospital? We're finally getting around to making arrangements."

"Please accept our condolences, Maggie. We worked with Dean and liked him very much."

I realized I could at least cross one funeral home off the list since I had him on the phone. "Yes, about that—working with Dean, I mean. We're wondering if you noticed anything strange in the last few weeks when you've been here at the cemetery. Perhaps someone that didn't seem to fit with the burial you were conducting?"

"The police chief asked me the same thing. Nothing comes to mind, but, of course, we're focused very much on the family we're serving during the graveside services."

I was stunned for a second that he'd actually spoken to the chief. Maybe I was wrong about him doing his job?

Marcus cleared his throat before continuing. "So, you mentioned Dean's body is being released from the morgue? We can bring him back to the funeral home today. Would you like us to prepare him for a viewing?"

I almost threw up. Choking back vomit, I slipped out of my Maggie voice for a moment. "No, we don't need that."

There was a long pause from Marcus. Had I been found out? My heart was racing.

"That's fine," Marcus said. "Would you prefer cremation?"

Apparently, I was safe for now and plowed ahead. "Yes, if we could arrange for that now, we'll plan a service for a later date."

"That's completely fine. Could you come down on Monday morning, so we can walk through everything in person?"

I'd managed to compose myself again. "No, that won't be necessary. Can you hold onto the ashes until Chloe and I have the chance to decide what kind of service we want?"

"Yes, but there is - well – er – there's the matter of payment. That is usually handled up front."

I tried out a slightly offended Maggie voice. "Really? I was under the impression that you knew my brother quite well and worked with him all of the time."

"Yes, of course, but still—" Marcus broke off. I could almost imagine him sweating and wiping his forehead.

I maintained my silence, holding back a sad combination of laughing and crying as a Dad memory crashed into my heart. A few years ago, when I went with him to buy his new truck, he taught me that the art of negotiation was never to be the first one to break a silence.

No longer able to hold it back, I start crying. It was just too much. The crying must have carried through to Marcus.

"Well, alright, Ms. Gill, we'll make an exception in this case. When you come down to plan the service, you can pick out a proper urn for your brother's cremains."

"Yes. I'll call back as soon as I can manage and make an appointment." *Probably in a little over two weeks when the real Maggie was scheduled to show up. Oh my god! I was going to be struck dead for all of these lies.*

I put the phone down and tried to even my breathing, wiping my sweaty palms against my jeans. The word cremains stuck in my head. What a horrible word.

Jarvis, who stayed completely silent during this whole hideous conversation, sweetly reached out and covered my hand with his. It didn't really count as holding my hand, but it was a comfort I needed right then.

I stared at my phone like it was an evil thing.

Because it was basically my enemy—and quite possibly my salvation.

I realized that Absent Aunt Maggie (*also known as me!*) forgot to answer the voice mail from the social worker, who according to Jarvis needed to close my custody case by October 6. I decided to try texting her.

FAKE MAGGIE: Thanks so much for helping with Chloe. I'll take over from here. I know that you want to meet, but my work is keeping me super busy as I finish this story. Maybe in a week or two?

The answer pinged back almost immediately. Ameena was a fast texter—even on a Saturday.

AMEENA: Thanks for the reply. Sorry for the inconvenience, but I do really need to meet you face to face.

Sooner rather than later. I promise not to interrupt your day for more than a few minutes.

I had no idea what kind of answer would satisfy her without putting eyes on my aunt. I didn't text back.

29

Dean ~ Week of Death

DEAN KEPT A CLOSE eye on his phone, on the neighborhood, and on Chloe in the coming days. He watched the groups of mourners as they came and went during graveside services to be sure there wasn't anyone lurking around the perimeter who shouldn't have been there. He scanned the crowd at Chloe's cross country races more than he watched her run. Some of the courses went through wooded areas, but with Chloe so often in the lead, he knew she'd be within sight of the four-wheeler that led the way for the runners.

He sat on the porch late at night after he locked the gate and stared out into the darkness of the cemetery. He'd always liked the seclusion of their house. But having next door neighbors – the kind who weren't dead – might have been a better option now that he was worried. He was lucky his job allowed him to work alone, so he could manage sneaking in the occasional nap when he knew Chloe was in the relative safety of school.

He had to believe that Lance's threats were empty ones—just to get Diana to comply with whatever he needed from her.

He'd nearly talked himself into that when he hadn't heard anything in almost a week.

Then during one of his late-night watches, his phone screen lit up with a call, showing her number again. He answered.

"Dean?"

"I told you not to call me again."

"I'm in town."

"What the fuck, Diana! Are you alone?"

"Yes."

It felt like she answered a little too quickly, and Dean assumed she wasn't alone and that bastard Lance was with her. It'd be just like Diana to bring danger to their doorstep again.

"You're going to get thrown back in jail for leaving Florida."

"Yeah, probably. It couldn't be helped. Look, I only need money and I'll go away."

"I doubt it. That's not really your way of doing things, is it?"

"No, I swear, if you help me out of this jam, I'll leave. You'll never hear from me again."

He couldn't believe he'd even entertain the idea, but nearly any amount of money would be worth getting rid of her forever. The problem was that Dean wasn't a rich man. He had some savings, but that was mostly to help Chloe through college. He wouldn't sacrifice that nest egg. "How much do you need?"

"I knew I could count on you. You were always such a good guy." Somehow she made that sound like an insult.

"Diana—this isn't a game. How much will it take to get you to go away?"

"Lance said that I needed to come up with a hundred grand."

"Are you insane? I don't have that kind of money. Why that much?"

"He said that was how much everything was worth that burned up in the fire—cash and drugs."

"That wasn't everything that burned up in the fire, Diana. There were things lost that were worth a lot more than that. You have a lot of nerve coming to me for anything."

"Dean, I don't have anywhere else to go. Can you please think about it?"

"There's nothing to think about. I don't have that kind of money."

"But you have some money saved up, right? I – I don't know a way out of this. He's not going to let this go."

Dean couldn't believe that even after his hard work disentangling their lives from violence and danger, that Diana sucked him right back into her disaster vortex. None of this was his problem, but only now it was—and he couldn't let this evil touch Chloe—again.

"Are you staying somewhere in town?"

"Yeah, the Night Light Motel out by the highway."

"I'll meet you there tomorrow morning in the coffee shop at 8:30. And I know Lance is with you. DO NOT bring him!"

He could hear her saying something else as he pulled the phone away from his ear—but he was done with the conversation.

30

Chloe

I WAS TOO DEPRESSED to do more sleuthing, and really there wasn't much else I could do immediately. However, I needed to grocery shop, which presented a problem. The grocery store was on the far side of town. Technically, I knew how to drive, but Dad and I had been waiting to set the date for my driver's test until the cross country season was over because practices and meets made it hard to schedule with the DMV. I looked sadly at the truck, which would make my chore so easy, instead wheeling my bike out of the garage and sliding on the backpack I emptied to fit the small amount of shopping I could afford with my meager budget.

Halfway through shopping, I nearly banged carts with someone I hoped to avoid—Chief Barnett. *Twice in one day? Really??*

Not knowing what to say, I ignored him and steered around his cart attempting a quick getaway. *What kind of offense was that: fleeing an officer in aisle nine?*

"Whoa there, Chloe, slow down."

I nearly laughed or maybe I should have neighed.

"Sorry. Didn't see you. My mistake."

The chief chuckled. "I think you saw me just fine. Look, I know I'm not your favorite person right now."

Were we really doing this? Here? In Pick N' Save? Oh-kay.
"No. You're not my favorite person. My favorite person was my dad, but he's not here anymore." I stared hard at the chief's face. I could have sworn he flinched.

He took a deep breath and looked around. We were attracting some attention as we blocked the aisle in front of the bacon and lunch meat. He leaned over and said quietly, "There's no evidence anyone else was involved."

"You didn't even look—not really." I'd lowered my voice, too, but my words still caught in my throat as I began to tear up—for what seemed like the hundredth time that week.

"We did. Both Officer Mank and I did." The chief sounded a little sad. His voice wasn't confrontational or angry at all. I wondered if Molly was really right about him. And I wondered if he felt bad enough to help me out by showing me the evidence that the police had collected.

"Molly says I can trust you." He glanced down momentarily, but his ears started turning red. His reaction almost made me like him. "Can I?"

He tilted his head to the side like maybe I was asking him a trick question. "Yes, you can trust me."

"I searched the cemetery too, a couple of days after you did. I found a bead like the one that's on the evidence list. Is there any way I can look at the one you have to see if it's the same?"

His eyes narrowed at me, but he kept his voice even. "What are you playing at here, Chloe? I know you think we're not doing anything, but without much to go on we *are* keeping an eye out for anything out of the ordinary, just in case."

"Just in case what?!" My voice got louder. "Just in case my dad wasn't a drug addict?"

"Yes." The chief's mouth thinned into a hard line. "And yes if you want to look at that bead, you can do that. We can go now if you want."

His honesty and his offer made me wonder if I was hallucinating somehow, but, nope, he was looking at me for an answer. "Yeah, sure." I looked down at the items in my cart, realizing with a panic that it definitely looked like food for one. *Maybe my aunt was on a diet?* Thankfully, the chief didn't seem to notice.

"Meet you out front when you're done?" he asked.

I nodded and steered my cart toward my last stop—frozen pizza. I only had to wait a few minutes with my bulging backpack next to my bike before the chief came out with his purchases.

"Your aunt's not a fan of grocery shopping?"

"Well, she's got a big project she's working on right now, and I wanted to get out of the house."

The chief nodded, gesturing toward an extended-cab truck a few rows into the parking lot. "I can stow your bike in the back if you're okay with that."

I wheeled my bike over so he could heft it into the bed of the truck.

We didn't talk on the short trip to the station. I followed him as he opened the door leading from the waiting area to the offices where I'd never been.

Officer Mank was sitting with his chair tilted back and his feet up on the desk, watching a college football game on his computer screen. Seeing us round the corner, he nearly lost his balance, scrambling for the keyboard. Up popped a spreadsheet in place of the game as he attempted to look busy. The chief didn't say anything to him as we passed, but I silently seethed, staring holes in his back. It was obvious he wasn't working on my dad's case or any case for that matter.

"Sit here." The chief pointed to a chair on the other side of a glass partition and walked into a room at the end of a hallway. While I waited, I peered through the divider at the cop I disliked. He gave me a nod and a sly grin. I looked away immediately. I really didn't like this guy.

"Your dad kept the place up real good." The chief said, laying a clear plastic baggie down in front of me. "We didn't find much. None of it is probably worth anything as evidence, but you never know."

I looked at the bead and rolled it around inside the plastic. My heart sank. It wasn't the same kind of stone. It was turquoise, which I recognized because my aunt had once bought me a bracelet with similar stones from one of her many trips.

"It's not the same. The one I found near where my dad was that – that – night was a darker blue."

"Good to know."

Yes, good to know that the only piece of solid evidence that I had was no evidence at all. *Just awesome.* "Thanks," I choked out.

"Chloe, I understand why you're doing what you're doing. I get it. But like I said, be careful."

"My groceries are thawing, I'd better go." I whipped my backpack on and nearly collided with the other officer who had crept up while we'd been talking. "'Scuse me," I said, sidestepping him and nearly running for the door.

I rode home as fast as I could, enjoying the burn in my thighs, which matched the rest of my burning—my heart, my head—everything was on fire. I used my anger to propel me home. The exertion felt good. I hadn't run lately since I quit the team. I needed some endorphins. I threw my groceries in the fridge and freezer and changed into my running gear. A long run might help me clear my head. It usually did.

31

The Watcher

SHE'S FASTER THAN USUAL. Her shoes seem to barely tap the sidewalk as she runs down the street away from my hiding place.

I don't even try to follow. I can't risk her seeing me, even though there's no way I could keep up.

She's suspicious now of the police—their motives.

I'm glad. It's better for me if she doesn't trust them.

If she has nowhere else to turn, she'll rely on me the most.

32

Dean ~ 3 Days Before Death

DEAN INSISTED ON DRIVING Chloe to school the next morning. He watched her walk all the way to the door as if she were a grade schooler before heading to the coffee shop and the meeting he surely didn't want to have. He'd considered his other option, he could call the local police and tip them off that there was an ex-con violating her parole and a restraining order. But getting Diana arrested didn't get rid of Lance.

At the coffee shop he was immediately greeted by the bunch of retirees who he shot the shit with over coffee on Mondays and Thursdays—funeral permitting. Sometimes death got in the way.

"Hey, Deano, it's Wednesday. Is your calendar broken?" Earl was the comedian of the group, but he always meant well, even if his jokes were stale.

"Just keeping you old coots on your toes," Dean shot back. "I'm actually here to meet someone." Dean quickly scanned the other diners and realized Diana wasn't there.

"Oh, you steppin' out on us?" Lou also thought he was pretty funny most of the time.

Dean really didn't want the guys knowing his business and quickly created a plausible lie. "Nah, I have to meet someone about arranging a graveside service. They don't want to use one of the funeral homes in town—trying to keep it low cost."

The guys all nodded, having now reached an age where they'd planned a funeral or two and knew how expensive it was to say goodbye to your loved ones in style.

Dean slipped into a booth on the other side of the restaurant but with a good view of the main door and the entryway that came from the motel lobby. Betty, one of the regular waitresses, flipped over the coffee mug in front of Dean and filled it up. "You solo today?"

"I should be meeting someone."

"You want your regular?"

"No, I won't be staying long." Dean scanned the patrons again to make sure he hadn't missed Diana. Even if she changed a lot in prison, no one her age was there. No one resembling what Lance looked like fifteen years ago was there either. He'd give her a few more minutes before he took off.

He was doctoring up his coffee with cream and sugar, when he had an awful thought that, once again, he'd been too trusting.

Maybe this was a setup, not the kind where he had to be worried about his safety, but maybe they were trying to keep him busy on the other side of town for another reason. Chloe. His gut sank. Would they try to take her from school to make him give them money?

He threw cash on the table and rushed out.

As he peeled out of the parking lot, he called Chloe's number.

She didn't pick up.

He knew some of her teachers were very strict about cell phones in class. He didn't blame them, but now he really needed to hear her voice and make sure she was okay.

He dialed her again. This time she answered.

"Dad, what's up?"

His heart calmed some. She was fine. Just fine. "I wanted to tell you to have a good day. Love you, Chloe Bear."

"Are you okay? You're being weird. You just told me that like thirty minutes ago when you dropped me off."

"Yup. Getting senile I guess."

"Hardly!" Chloe snorted. "See you after practice."

He'd freaked out for no reason and headed back to the house to get started on his work day.

He parked the truck and went into the kitchen, but immediately heard rustling coming from the living room and found Diana ransacking his desk. His instincts had been right, but he'd misjudged the target—it'd been the house—not Chloe.

Dean reached her in three long strides and, pulling her up by her shirt, he spun her around and pinned her to the wall.

"Jesus, Dean. Let me go."

It was strange to be so close to her. Her eyes were clear and not glazed over like they'd been so often during their marriage. Even with fifteen years of age since he'd last seen her, she looked better than she had then. Being a junkie aged a person. It looked like she'd been telling the truth about not using.

"What are you looking for?"

"Money."

"I told you, I don't have that kind of money."

"But you have a lot more money than you ever did when we were married." Diana held up one of the bank statements and waved it in Dean's face.

"That's not yours. I'm saving it for Chloe's college."

"Well, she can't go to college if she's dead."

Dean slammed her back against the wall, shouting, "What's wrong with you? Haven't you done enough damage to her life?"

"Ouch, calm the fuck down."

"Calm down? Is Lance here? Is he going after Chloe while you keep me busy?"

"He's here, but he's at the motel. I told him I could handle this, and he was willing to let me talk to you."

"This isn't talking. This is breaking and entering. And violating your parole and the restraining order. I'm guessing that would land you back in prison for a while."

"Go ahead and call the cops on me, Dean. But Lance is serious. He wants his pay back, and I don't have any money or way to get any."

"If he wanted his money back so bad, why didn't he come after me in the last fifteen years?"

"I don't know. He wants me to come back and work for him. He thought I would cave. But I can't do that. I can't be near that stuff anymore. So he threatened us, if I didn't pay him back."

Dean wanted to be sympathetic, but he'd lived with the aftermath of her bad decisions for years. Dean let her go.

She smoothed her shirt and stared at him.

Dean backed up a step and stared back, taking in the files she'd managed to rifle through. Not only had she gotten into his financial files. She'd opened the fake tax receipts file and dumped out the contents.

"Did you get a good look at the lives you ruined? Did it bring back some good memories of your trial? They called you the Meth Lab Mom."

"I know that what I did was – is – unforgiveable. How – how is Chloe?"

"You don't get to know that. You gave up the right to know anything when you started the house on fire and didn't even try to get to the crib."

"I did—"

"No, you didn't. You were too high."

Diana clenched her hands at her sides and took a deep breath. "I promise to go away, if you help me with the money I owe."

Dean grabbed his wallet, pulling out all his cash. Then he stomped to the kitchen and grabbed the emergency coffee can and pulled out that stash as well. Altogether it was several hundred dollars. "Here. This is all you're going to get. Take it and get out of here before I call the police."

"But – but aren't you worried about Lance? About what he'll do?"

"I'm done with this! If Lance comes after me, you tell him, I'll be the one taking him down."

"He's going to kill me."

Dean should have cared. But he didn't.

The person standing in front of him—once someone he loved—once someone he trusted—once someone he thought he built a life with—was none of that anymore. "About fifteen years too late in my opinion, you should have died that night. You should have died trying . . ." Dean's throat had closed up on him. Without another word, he led her to the door and shoved her through it, causing her to stumble a little. The slam of the door echoed both through the kitchen and out onto the porch where she stood. Dean watched her hurry away, down the cemetery driveway and to the gate. Before she went through, she stopped and reached around to lift up her shirt to pull out the papers she'd hidden in the waist band of her jeans. With one parting gesture, she flipped him off.

Dean went back to the mess she'd made, determined to figure out what papers she'd taken. He meticulously put everything back in order. He flipped through the small photo album and found two empty slots. "That bitch," he muttered under his breath. The fake tax receipt file felt thinner. He went through it page by page. The old life insurance policy was missing, too. The one he'd been meaning to throw out. It wasn't even valid anymore. He was mostly angry about the photos. She didn't have a right to those toddler pictures anymore.

Then he noticed that the corner of his desk calendar was ripped off like someone used it for scrap paper to write something down. He didn't know what. Did she have time to copy down his bank account number?

33

Chloe

I WOULD HAVE LOVED to sleep in, but the goal was to get to the coffee shop out by the highway before the old guys who were regulars were gone for the day. At 8:30—our renegotiated later start time—Jarvis was waiting. I quickly unlocked the gate, pushing it all the way open for visitors. Sunday was a big day at the cemetery.

Jarvis walked ahead of me to a blue Subaru and opened the passenger door for me. I was so in awe at his good manners that I almost forgot to say thanks.

We didn't say anything on the short drive to the coffee shop. When we entered, most of the people there swiveled their heads to see who had come in. I was glad some of those gawkers were my dad's breakfast buddies.

I went straight to their table and Jarvis stayed a couple of steps behind me. "Hi, everyone."

"Hey, Chloe," Earl said. "We're so sorry about your dad. We're going to miss him. Have you made funeral plans yet?"

"No, my aunt and I haven't decided exactly what we're doing yet, but – um – we'll let you know when we've figured it out. Can I ask you guys some questions?"

"Sure you can, Chloe," Lou said. He was just the sweetest and my favorite in the group.

"Did you notice anything strange in the past few weeks with my dad?"

"No, not really. Maybe he seemed more tired than usual, but we're all tired sometimes," Lou answered.

"Don't forget the Wednesday before last," Earl said.

"That's right." Lou nodded. "Your dad came in, and we were surprised because it was, well, Wednesday. He said he was meeting someone to talk about private burial plans or some such thing, but they never showed and then he sped out of here fast."

"Later he said that he thought there was an emergency at the cemetery but that he'd been mistaken," Earl added.

"Okay. Nothing else you can think of?"

They all shook their heads.

"Did the police ever come and talk to you about my dad?"

"Not me," said Earl. "Any of you guys?"

There were no's all around the table.

I sighed. "The chief promised he would talk to everyone my dad knew, but I think he was only saying that to get me to quit bugging him."

"About what?" Lou asked.

"I know my dad didn't do drugs, so someone had to have done this to him." I was angry, but somehow my voice sounded like I was about to cry.

The men all shifted in their seats, looking uncomfortable. Finally, Earl spoke up. "Well, we talked about this a bit because we were surprised too—you know—when we heard the news about his overdose. Your dad really didn't seem the type, and he never looked like he was on anything. We don't think it's true either."

"You don't? The police don't believe me." A relief that I didn't know I needed flooded through my body. I really didn't want to cry here in front of these men and Jarvis, too. He'd already had to deal with my epic breakdown yesterday when I was making cremation arrangements for my dad's body. But boy, did it feel good to have someone else say that they didn't think my dad did drugs. "I don't think they're doing a thorough investigation at all."

"Chloe, you be careful what you're doing though. If all that's true, there's someone dangerous out there. I'm going to stop down to the station after breakfast and make sure they know we don't think your dad would have been doing drugs either. You call us if you need help with anything, okay?" Lou wrote down his number on piece of paper and handed it to me.

"Thank you. I'm glad I came out here to talk to you all."

I was a little numb as Jarvis and I slid into a small two-person booth at the edge of the dining room.

"They believe me, Jarvis."

"I heard."

"No one has hardly believed me this whole time . . . well, except for you and Molly."

"Chloe, we'll figure this out."

"I wonder if whoever my dad was supposed to meet on Wednesday was someone dangerous? There was nothing on his calendar for the day. It was less than forty-eight hours before he was murdered." I couldn't think straight. I felt like I was missing something, but I didn't know what. I needed food.

Betty, the waitress who I'd gotten to know from coming here with my dad, gave my shoulder a quick grandmotherly pat when she approached to take our order. I appreciated that she didn't say anything, but her actions told me she was thinking of me. As promised, I treated Jarvis to one of the famous giant cinnamon rolls and ordered one for myself, too.

I looked around, thinking how I probably wouldn't come here anymore—with how much it reminded me of my dad. Neither Jarvis or I talked. I was kind of talked out on the main subject for the moment. And Jarvis was definitely the kind of person who wouldn't talk unless he had something important to say. No idle chatter from him—thank God. The clank of the dishes, the murmur of the people, and the steady hum of highway traffic was comforting in a way. I stared out the window at the motel parking lot and wondered about people who preferred motels over the two chain hotels on the other side of the highway. People who didn't have much money probably. People like me, I mentally added.

Just then I saw someone I recognized come out of one of the rooms. It was the odd lady that Molly hadn't hired.

I shifted in my seat as I watched her.

"What are you looking at?" Jarvis asked.

"I recognize that lady. She's the one from the diner who yelled at me for taking her job the first night I worked. She made a scene while you were there."

Jarvis pivoted. "Yes, that looks like her."

"She was outside the diner yesterday when I was working, but she didn't try to come in. I thought that was smart, since Molly had kicked her out. Plus, the police chief was there as a deterrent."

The woman lit up a cigarette and paced back and forth like she needed to keep warm while she smoked.

A guy with shoulder length brown hair came out of the same room and said something to her, grabbed her arm, and pulled her back toward the door. She shrugged him off and threw her half-finished cigarette onto the cement and crushed it out with the toe of her shoe.

"That didn't look like a friendly conversation," I said.

"No, it didn't."

Our cinnamon rolls arrived, and we dug in. It was the kind of comfort food I needed, but I filled up fast. I was surprised when Jarvis finished his, but I wrapped up half of mine for later. There was no way I was wasting food with money so tight right now.

Jarvis pulled his car all the way up to my house when he took me home.

"Thanks for coming with me and for driving."

"Do you want more help today?"

"I – I'm not sure. I don't know what else to do. I guess we can go over everything again. We've got to be missing something." I was grateful when he agreed to come in for a while. The house didn't feel so empty then.

Jarvis and I sat at the kitchen table. I re-read the police report.

"There's really not very much evidence," I said. "I mean we have my dad's call log, so we generally know who he was talking to. But we don't know why. Why was he talking to someone at a Florida Correctional Institute? We've never lived there. Who was he supposed to meet at the coffee shop? This is nothing like solving a murder on TV. We need some fingerprints or something."

"Wait!" Jarvis said and grabbed the file from me. He skimmed it quickly as it was only a page and a half long.

"I thought you had that thing memorized."

"I did, but I didn't want to say anything until I double checked."

"Say what?"

"Chloe, I'm not sure it'd be in this report. Probably not." Jarvis shook his head. "But I just thought of something. You said there was a needle in your dad's arm. I wonder if they got any fingerprints off of it."

"Oh my god, you're right. The syringe. I don't know where that went."

"It's probably at the hospital," Jarvis suggested.

"Would they have thrown it away?"

"I'll bet it was sent to a lab for testing, but I don't know if they would have checked for fingerprints first or not."

"They better have. The only fingerprints that should be on the syringe, if my dad wasn't murdered, would be his own."

"You should ask the chief."

"Like he'd want to take my call . . . but he did give me his card."

"Call him."

34

Chloe

THE CHIEF PICKED UP right away. I could hear the TV blaring some sports game in the background. I cringed a little, realizing I was probably calling in the middle of the Packer game. I knew to keep my question brief.

"Hey, Chief. It's Chloe Cowyn. I have a question. Did anyone check the syringe in my dad's arm for prints?"

"Yes, that was done before it was sent off to the lab to test what was in it."

"So, were there any prints?"

"No, there weren't."

"None? Not even my dad's?"

The chief didn't answer. And I forged ahead with my questions.

"Doesn't that seem impossible that my dad could have overdosed and taken the time to wipe his prints off the syringe?"

All I could hear was the cheering from the game.

"Are you there?"

"Yes. Chloe, I appreciate how smart you are putting all of this together, but you have to stop now."

"Why? Why should I stop? Today the guys out at the coffee shop told me no one from your department ever talked to them. You know the ones my dad ate with twice a week. They told me my dad was out there on a different day than usual and was supposed to meet someone there, but they didn't know who. And that person never showed up.

"And did you ever check any of the phone calls that my dad made or got in the last couple of weeks? Why aren't you investigating?"

"Chloe, you have to stop and let me do my job."

"I'm never going to stop until I find out who did this to my dad.'

"That's what I'm afraid of," the chief said.

I'd had enough and hung up on him.

I took a minute for myself in the bathroom. Angry red splotches colored the middle of my cheeks. I splashed some water on my face in an attempt to calm down.

I heard a car drive in, but people were always visiting the cemetery on the weekends. So I didn't think anything of it until someone knocked on the back door.

I almost came out to answer it, but I waited since I was still avoiding the social worker.

Jarvis answered instead. "Hello. Can I help you?"

"Hi, I'm looking for Maggie Gill, Chloe Cowyn's aunt."

My blood pressure, which had only begun to calm down, shot through the roof again. It was Ameena Alavi, the social worker, making house calls on a Sunday. I had to hand it to her. It was a good day to probably catch people at home if you needed to find someone. Right in the middle of the Packer game, too. Smart lady.

"She's not here."

Oh, bless Jarvis and his brief answers.

"Um, Okay. Is Chloe here?"

"No, she isn't either."

"Do you know when they'll be back?"

"No idea."

"Well, I really need to meet with Ms. Gill. Can you give her this message along with my card?"

"I'll definitely leave that message here for her."

I waited for a few moments and heard the car drive away.

"You can come out now, Chloe. She's gone."

"Thank you, Jarvis. I reached up and gave him a big hug. He stiffened at first and then relaxed a little. "That was an Oscar-winning performance."

He laughed at that.

He didn't do that enough—laugh. But since I'd gotten to know him better, we really hadn't been doing things that were lighthearted enough for laughter.

"I guess you know who that was then." He gestured toward the back door.

"Yeah, I could hear her talking."

"I recognized her too from the guidance counselor's office at school. Good thing."

"Yes, a very good thing." *In a huge sea of very bad things.*

35

Dean ~ 3 Days Before Death

WHILE DEAN CALMED DOWN, he thought about his next steps. How could he keep Chloe away from the monster that was her mother—how could he protect their future?

He'd start at the bank. Even if Diana had his account number, she'd still have to figure out a way into the account. Dean was glad then he hadn't set up online banking even though Chloe had teased him for being a tech dinosaur.

At the bank, they helped him set up a new account—online this time. While he was waiting for the confirmation of the electronic transfer that moved the money from his old account to this new one, he called Trent Walker, the local lawyer he knew handled a lot of estate work. Trent had the afternoon free, which was a good thing, because Dean had a lot to cover.

He only had to walk across the square to get to the attorney's office.

"Dean, good to see you," Trent said.

"Thanks for letting me do this today."

"It sounded important."

"It is." Dean looked around the office at the other staff and asked in a quieter voice, "Can I explain it in your office?"

"Sure, sure." Trent ushered him in and shut the door. "What's up. You've got me worried."

"I probably need to start at the beginning." And for the first time ever, Dean told the horrible story to someone else. He tried to only state the facts and separate himself from the emotion of it all. He did fine, mostly, and Trent graciously ignored the way his voice cracked when he got to the hardest parts. He finished up with Diana arriving in town with Lance and their threats.

"Man, I'm so sorry that happened to you. That's awful. And now she's come back. How the heck did she find you?"

"I guess Lance knew all along. He kept track of us since Florida. Or at least that's what Diana said. Although I know better than to take her word for anything. It doesn't really matter."

"Listen, I think you really should be telling this to the police." Trent shifted in his chair, leaning forward. "I'm not going to be able to do anything about these threats. I mean this is the cartel you're talking about. You don't mess with them."

For the moment, Dean ignored Trent's suggestion. "I know you can't do anything about that, but I do need you to draw up a new will and create a trust for my life insurance policy so Chloe will be protected if – well just in case."

"Okay, I can do the will right away. It's simple. I'm heading out of town tomorrow, but I can get my paralegal to work on the trust document, and when I'm back we can finish that up."

"I also need you to make sure that the restraining order from Florida is definitely enforceable in Wisconsin. The Florida corrections official who called about Diana's release said the one in that state was still active, but now I'm worried that we might need to file a new one here."

"Why don't you just go to the police and get her picked up for violating her parole?"

"I know. That'd be easy, I'm debating about getting the local police involved. I tried so hard to protect our privacy. In this small town, you know how fast all this would become common gossip. Chloe doesn't know the truth, and I never planned on telling her. She's already had enough pain in her life. I've only told you this much because you need to understand the details. And I know you can't talk about this because of attorney-client privilege."

Trent chuckled a bit. "Well, you're right. I can't, but I wouldn't either. But outside this room, nothing stays secret very long in this town. That's for sure. Do you have a copy of your restraining order paperwork?"

"No, but I can bring it in for you."

"I'm back in a week. I can't do anything about it until then. Is that okay with you?"

"Sure. The main thing I was worried about was the will."

"I can't practice law in Florida, but I can do the preliminary work. You might not need someone licensed there anyway. Let me call your original law firm and the court that issued the restraining order. It wouldn't hurt for me to have that correction's office number, too."

"I'd give you that phone number right now, but I've got to grab it from home. I deleted the calls to be sure Chloe didn't accidentally see them."

Dean felt a lot better leaving the law firm. He should have done all of this years ago, but he didn't want to confront it. His will was done, naming Chloe the only heir to his assets. Once the trust documents were complete, the Chloe Cowyn Living Trust would be the sole beneficiary of his life insurance policy with the money to be used only for education purposes after her 18th birthday. God forbid anything really did happen to him, but if it did and Diana tried to get to Chloe somehow and get her hands on the money, this would prevent that. He knew he could count on Maggie to fight back, but it sure helped to have solid legal documents on your side.

He paused, looking out at the town square. Everything seemed so peaceful, so safe . . . and that was so deceiving. The police station was only a block away. Dean could almost see it from where he stood. He took a deep breath and walked that direction. Trent was right, it was time to get the police involved. But once he gave them this information, it was only a matter of time before it trickled out to the rest of the world. That meant he had to plan a conversation with Chloe. A really, really tough conversation he'd been avoiding for fifteen years. He had no idea how he was going to be able to explain everything to her.

Dean opened the station door, approached the young officer behind the desk, and took a deep breath before uttering words he didn't think he'd ever said before. "Hey, man, I need your help."

36

Chloe

I skipped school for the first time ever on Monday morning. I'd never even faked being sick before. I didn't believe that the days after my dad died counted. I *was* sick, my heart was broken.

It was still broken. I tried so hard not to think about my dad being gone forever, but the times that those thoughts slipped past my focus on finding his killer were like the shock of jumping into a too-cold lake. I would double over in pain and gasp for breath. Most times my guardian angel was there to soothe me, if I let him in. Days like this I wished I still had a mom—or anyone really that could give me comfort the way a family member could. I loved Maggie, but she loved her career. I had no idea what my life with her might look like. I'd probably end up in a boarding school somewhere, so she could keep doing her job all over the world.

I unlocked and pushed open the gate as I'd been doing each morning, but I turned to go toward the center of town instead of heading to school. It felt strange but oddly liberating.

The Loyal Law Office was on the same side of the town square as Molly Bell's. A guy in a suit arrived right before me, fumbling for his keys as he juggled his briefcase and an insulated coffee mug.

"Here, let me help," I said, catching his mug before it slipped completely from his grasp.

"Thanks."

"You're Trent Walker, right?"

"Yes, I am."

"I'm Chloe Cowyn. I saw on my dad's calendar that he had an appointment scheduled with you this morning. I wanted to know what it was about."

"Oh, gosh, Chloe. I'd really feel better if you'd talk directly to your dad about it. Attorney-client privilege and all that. He should be here any minute anyway."

He didn't know. My heart thudded and I swallowed hard. "You haven't heard the news?"

"Heard what? Just got back from vacation last night. My wife made me promise I'd go tech free the whole time."

"My dad's dead."

Mr. Walker's face slumped, and I felt a little bad about my abruptness.

"Oh my god. I was afraid of that."

"What?" I had to have heard him wrong. "What are you talking about?"

We simply stared at each other for a second as he continued to process the information. He sighed deeply. "You'd better come in."

He turned on the lights as he held open the door for me. "My staff doesn't start until nine." I followed him past a few desks and into a private office at the back. "Grab a seat. Do you want anything to drink? We've got sodas. Water?"

I shook my head.

He laid his briefcase on the top of the desk and settled into his chair. "Tell me what happened, Chloe."

I explained things as quickly as I could. "I don't believe he did this to himself. So, I'm doing the job that the police should be doing. No one believes me."

I expected him to be like most other adults who would tell me to let the professionals handle it. Instead, he leaned back and rubbed his hand across his face. "Aw, shit," he mumbled and then looked over at me. "Sorry."

"Well, if ever there was an 'aw shit' moment, I think this qualifies. Tell me what you meant when you said you were afraid of that."

He sat there tapping a pen on the desktop as if he were weighing his next words very, very carefully.

"Look, I know my dad called you the day before he died."

"You do?"

"Yes, I have a record of his incoming and outgoing calls."

"But I thought he said— oh, never mind." Mr. Walker shook his head as if to erase whatever he'd been about to say. "He did meet with me, and we redid his will. He wanted to make sure that you were protected as his sole beneficiary. Your aunt will be your guardian. We were drawing up the papers for a trust fund for where his life insurance money would go. That's what he was coming here to sign today."

"But that doesn't answer why you were afraid for my dad. What had him so spooked that he'd come in to do his will?"

"Chloe, I'm not sure how much I should share about that—for your own safety."

"My safety? What's going on? Are you saying you believe that my dad *was* murdered?"

"Let's just say there were things he told me that could lead us in that direction. And I'll go to the police immediately with what I know."

I had another person on my side, but he was someone who knew a lot more than I expected. Should I trust this guy? "Can't you tell me anything more?"

"We can talk more with your Aunt Maggie present. She's your legal guardian, and we can go over everything in the will. The trust fund paperwork can't be filed without your dad's signature, and that's impossible now, but your name is still on the life insurance policy. We can work all that out with your aunt. I assume she's in town."

"Yes." Then a brilliant idea occurred to me. "I'll have her call you today." I'd pretended to be Aunt Maggie before and I could do it again. "You should know that the cops in this dumb town aren't taking any of this mess seriously. You'll see that when you start talking to them."

I was glad to hear that my dad had taken care of me by setting aside money, but that still didn't explain why there was nothing in his wallet or in our safety stash at home. Although, it did partially help me understand why he'd moved money into an online account. What had he been doing? I wished Mr. Walker would tell me the full story, but I guess it made sense that he'd want to talk to an adult. I just hoped I could get him to divulge those secrets to me – er – *Aunt Maggie* over the phone.

I nearly rushed home to call him immediately, but when I saw the glow of Molly Bell's neon sign, I found myself changing direction. I wanted to see a friendly face and didn't think it through that she might question why I wasn't at school.

When I went in, I said hello to the weekday waitress, Justine. We crossed paths each day as she was finishing her shift and I was starting mine. Molly stood behind the counter and her eyebrows raised as I slid onto a stool, but she didn't say anything.

Neither did I.

She set to work making something with her back to me and when she turned around, she placed a mug of hot chocolate piled high with mini marshmallows in front of me.

I smiled for a second. This is the kind of thing Dad used to do for me when I was down. With that thought, missing my dad and knowing I wasn't any closer to solving his murder, I was sure I couldn't get any lower.

"Do you want to talk about it?"

"Not really. I only wanted some company."

Molly nodded and left me to my steaming mug. I slurped a spoonful of gooshy marshmallows into my mouth and stirred the cocoa, willing it to cool off.

She made her rounds, filling up coffee mugs and taking orders from the newest arrivals and came back to check on me.

"So, no school today?"

"Not for me."

"What, you think you're special or something?" I knew she was joking with me.

"Yup. These are special circumstances. In case you didn't know, my dad's dead."

"I heard. You think that makes you special, kid? There's lots of hardship here in this little diner. You've got Gabe over there whose wife died from cancer last month. Marjorie there," she said gesturing to the other side of the diner, "had her husband just up and leave her with no explanation. Now she's raising three kids on her own. In the far corner, ol' Mike's eyesight is getting so bad that I had to cut up his ham for him today. The world is a troublesome place, Miss Chloe."

"That it is, Miss Molly. That it is." I took another sip of my cocoa. "You know what I found out today?"

"Do tell."

"My dad drew up a new will with Mr. Walker only two days before he died. And when I told him my dad was dead this morning because he didn't know because he'd been on vacation this past week, you know what he said?"

"I haven't a clue."

"He said 'I was afraid of that.'"

Molly's eyes grew wide.

"But he wouldn't tell me what he meant, only saying that he'd tell everything he knew to the police right away. And you know what else?"

"I hate to guess."

"The group of people who believe my dad didn't do this to himself is growing . . . the old guys my dad ate breakfast with out at the truck stop coffee shop didn't think so either."

"Well, well, the Chloe's dad-didn't-do-drugs club *is* getting bigger. What does your aunt say about all this?"

It was one thing to play this verbal back and forth with Molly, but I didn't like lying to her. "She doesn't know this last part. I went to the law office on my own. She's really busy with a story. You'll meet her eventually." *In probably about thirteen or fourteen days.* I finished my cocoa and pushed the mug toward her.

"You going to make it in to work tonight?"

"I wouldn't miss it," I called behind me as I pushed open the door. *And I wouldn't. I needed the money.*

I walked past the law office on my way back home and saw that all the desks that had been empty now had workers behind them. I slowed and stared toward Mr. Walker's office at the back and recognized the unmistakably large shape of the police chief occupying the chair I'd sat in earlier.

I was relieved Mr. Walker was keeping his word. At least I hoped that's what he was doing. I wanted to march right in there and make them tell me what they knew. I wanted to confront the chief about not doing his job, *again*. But I took a deep breath and headed home. It probably wasn't a good idea for someone skipping school to have an argument with a cop.

37

The Watcher

SHE'S TURNING INTO A rebel—investigating her dad's murder, taking on the do-nothing cops, and now skipping school. I wonder how much of that is because of me.

I follow her at a distance, the lawyer's, the diner, and home again. She doesn't notice me come into the cemetery behind her.

She really should be more careful—like me.

You never know who could be lurking in the shadows. Today, I'm the only one.

38

Chloe

BACK AT HOME, I dialed the law firm, but was told that Mr. Walker was in a meeting. He was probably still in with the police chief. I should have waited a while longer. But I left my aunt's fake number for a call back.

I decided to do some more snooping around my dad's desk in the living room to see what I could find, and I'd just begun pulling out files when I heard someone knock at the back door. I froze, thinking that it might be the social worker back after her quick visit the day before that Jarvis fielded for me. I waited a minute or so and then crept around the corner careful to stay out of view and saw that it was Frank, my dad's boss. He was taping something to the back door. I walked up and pulled it open.

He jumped with a yelp that he tried to cover up by laughing. "Well, geez Louise, Chloe, you sure surprised me. I didn't think anyone was at home, so I was leaving a note here for your aunt to call me. I realized that I didn't have her number. Say, shouldn't you be at school today?"

"I didn't feel so great."

"Ah, yeah, sure. I can understand that. So, is your aunt around?"

"Nah, she's out running errands, but I can give her the message." I was already dreading what he was going to say. I was sure he was going to give me notice to move out.

"Well, it's like I said. We posted the job and someone is going to start in two weeks."

I nearly breathed a sigh of relief, but Frank continued. "And we always have a cleaning and paint crew come through when we hire someone new. Do you think you and your aunt can manage to move things out of here by Sunday? The cleaning crew wants to get in here bright and early next Monday."

That'd leave me homeless for one week before my aunt was supposed to be back. I stared at him, trying to come up with where I might go.

Frank cleared his throat. "I'm really sorry about this, but there's nothing I can do. See the housing comes with the job and—"

"It's okay," I interrupted. The last thing I needed was for him to question why I was being weird about moving out. But since he seemed to be in an apologetic frame of mind, I hoped he'd agree to my request. "Is there any chance we can leave the truck and some boxes in the garage until we can decide what to do with everything?"

"Sure, sure. That'd be fine. Make sure to leave room for the new caretaker's car on one side."

"No problem."

"And your dad's final paycheck is pending at city hall. I assume you're his beneficiary."

Maybe Frank's visit wasn't all bad news. "Yes, I am. I was just over at Loyal Law Office talking about his will."

Frank looked relieved. "Great. Mr. Walker will know what form to send to the clerk to get that done. You have your aunt let me know if you need help moving anything."

"Thanks, Frank. I'll be sure to tell her."

There was an awful lot that I'd have to catch Aunt Maggie up on when she ever returned from wherever the heck she went where she couldn't even take her cell phone.

I went back to my dad's desk, searching through files and stacking them on the desk top. Nothing here seemed strange so far, but I was being thorough and looking in each file folder and envelope as I went.

My phone finally rang, and I recognized the phone number of the law office. I cleared my throat and quickly tested my hello, lowering my voice by a couple of steps before answering.

"Hello, Maggie Gill speaking."

"Hello, Ms. Gill. This is Trent Walker. I'm your brother's lawyer, and I'm sure Chloe told you by now that I just redid his will for him. I'm sorry that I didn't call sooner, I was out of town, and until Chloe visited me this morning, I hadn't heard that Dean had died. I am so sorry."

"He was murdered."

"Yes, right. I wanted you to know that I talked to the police about what I knew that might help them catch whoever did this to him."

"So you believe he was murdered?"

"After what he told me the week he died, I wouldn't be surprised."

"What did he tell you?"

"Ms. Gill, I'd far prefer us to have this conversation in person. I never like to trust such delicate matters to phone calls."

"Delicate matters? What do you mean?"

"The situation with your former sister-in-law."

Who the hell was that? I played along. "Of course." I had no clue who he was talking about – my aunt's former sister-in-law would mean she had been married. Or was he referring to my dad's wife? As far as I knew, Aunt Maggie had never been married and my dad only had one wife—my mother—and she was dead.

"I know Chloe isn't aware of everything that happened in Florida, but I wasn't sure if you knew that she hadn't been told. And we need to go over Dean's will and your guardianship of Chloe and the life insurance money."

My mind was racing. What secrets had my dad and aunt been keeping? Florida? This had to be something to do with that women's prison phone number.

"Right, yes that's – that makes sense." I had no idea what I was agreeing to and nothing made sense, but still I managed to squeak out that nonsensical line, hoping my voice still sounded as mature as my aunt's.

"Let's pick a date for a meeting."

"I'll have to call back to set that up." *Good delay tactic, Chloe.* "But can you do something?" My mind was reeling from what Mr. Walker had said, so I couldn't believe I remembered about the paycheck. But money was going to be even more important now that I'd be forced to move out. "Frank from the city says you need to send him some form about Chloe being the beneficiary to get Dean's paycheck rewritten to her?"

"Sure, I can get that done."

"Thank you."

"One other thing you should know now. Dean asked me to check on whether a Florida restraining order is enforceable in Wisconsin and it is definitely valid."

"Okay. But I'm a little confused. Dean and I hadn't talked in a few weeks as I've been away on assignment . . ."

"Oh, sorry. Your former sister-in-law is out of prison, and she's violated the conditions of her parole by coming to Wisconsin. If she comes near either you or Chloe, she's also violating the restraining order. Call the police and she'll be arrested."

"Um, wow." *That was a very un-Maggie-like line. Pull it together, Chloe. What would Maggie do? She was a world-class reporter for god's sake. She'd ask a ton more questions.* But all the questions racing through my mind would immediately tip off Mr. Walker that I wasn't Maggie. I needed to get off the phone before I gave myself away.

"I know, this is a messy situation. But I filled Chief Barnett in on the details today, so he knows about her, and he says they'll keep a look out."

"Thank you."

"You're welcome. I'll wait for you to call me back to schedule an appointment."

39

Chloe

MY DAD HAD KEPT secrets—major ones. Who was this person who'd just gotten out of prison, and why were they here in Wisconsin when they shouldn't have been? How worried did I have to be if there was a restraining order against them? But most importantly could this person have killed my dad?

It was possible Aunt Maggie had been married, and it wasn't something she talked about. But as far as I knew, my dad had only been married to my mom, but she died in the fire the same night I'd been horribly burned.

Was it possible that my dad had remarried while I was too young to remember a stepmother? And she was a bad person? Bad enough that we needed to be protected from her?

A chill ran through me.

I was so confused.

Desperate for answers, I tried Aunt Maggie's producer again. The call went to voice mail, and I nearly didn't leave a message. But at the last second, I reminded him that if Maggie happened to check in early that I really needed to speak with her.

A long shot for sure. I tried to find my resolve, but instead of being methodical, I pawed frantically through his files, abandoning my careful search from earlier. Taxes. Receipts. Paystubs. Bank statements. I flung everything out of the desk into one big pile on the floor. The answers had to be here somewhere.

I felt around the cubby hole of the desk for a hidden latch or something like you see in movies that would open a secret compartment. Nothing.

I shifted to the bedroom and made a mess in there, opening books on my dad's shelves and shaking them out. Pulling boxes out from under the bed and only finding old photos. There weren't any of me with my mom, ever. I knew that, but once, when I begged and begged, my dad had shown me a photo of my mom when she was younger, before she had me. I wanted that photo now. I needed to see it.

I'd kept it in my room for a while. But one day I'd come home from school, and it was gone. He said he'd put it away because it was simply too painful to look at after she died.

I'd been mad at him for that, but then I felt bad because he looked so sad.

"Aren't we okay together? We're a team, right?" he'd asked me. I could still remember the way he looked, like he might cry, and as a little girl that had scared me. I didn't want to be responsible for anything that made my dad so sad. I agreed. It was the two of us against the world, but I still liked having the picture of my mom around.

I let the subject drop, glad that he'd at least shown me the photo.

Now, I wondered about all of it.

What was the truth?

I'd always believed my dad about everything.

But in the middle of the floor surrounded by a mess of papers, my heart gave a painful lurch when I realized that wasn't true anymore.

40

Chloe

HIDING MY PUFFY FACE with makeup after I'd bawled my eyes out on the floor of my dad's bedroom almost made me late to work.

"You made it," Molly said. "How was playing hooky?"

I snort laughed. "No one calls it that anymore, Molly."

"Well, they should. It's a great word. But I can see from your face that you perhaps did not have a carefree day after you left here."

"Nope."

"Wanna talk about it?"

"Nope."

Molly pulled me in for a quick hug and then shoved my apron into my hands. "Get to work then. It's busy for a Monday."

I was grateful for that. Keeping track of orders kept my mind from working overtime trying to put together the puzzle surrounding my dad's death. But it couldn't stop the running mantra that whispered, *My dad lied to me, my dad lied to me.*

Except for my swirling thoughts, it was a normal night. Most people on Mondays were regulars. Candi came in and sat in the corner booth she preferred.

"Hi, Candi."

"Hey there, Chloe."

"What can I get you tonight?"

"The patty melt special sounds great."

"I'll put that right in for you. And if you have your eye on a piece of French silk pie, I need to warn you there's only one slice left. I can set it aside for you if you want."

Candi laughed. "You take such good care of me, Chloe. Tell you what. Why don't you bring me that slice of pie right now. I have a mind to eat my dinner backwards."

"Aren't you naughty? I tried to talk my dad into letting me do that a few times, and I never could get him to agree." The weight of my dad being gone crashed down on me again and my throat closed up tight. I pivoted away quickly so Candi couldn't see my face, but I saw her pained look and knew she must have noticed. I fetched her pie and forced a smile as I slid it onto the table in front of her, but I was still unable to speak.

"Order up." The cook boomed, and I headed back to the serving counter to fill up a tray with hot food.

Like I said, it was a normal night. Until it wasn't. I was about to step out into the dining area when the bell rang over the door. I caught a brief glimpse of Ameena Alavi coming in. *Shit.Shit.Shit.* I reversed course and backed all the way into the kitchen and nearly bumped into Molly.

"Honey, the customers are thataway." She smiled and pointed toward the dining room.

"Yes," I said, finding my voice again. "But there's – well – there's –"

"Spit it out, Cowyn."

"Someone's come in who I do not want to talk to. Can you take these to table seven for me?"

"Who is it? An old boyfriend – an old girlfriend?" Molly wiggled her eyebrows.

"Neither. Please, Molly, just do this for me. I'm sure she'll go away soon."

"Okay, but I'll need to know more later."

I nodded and kept out of sight, but close enough to still hear what was going on.

Molly delivered the food and came back to greet Ameena. "Would you like a table?" she asked.

"No, but the food smells delicious. I'm actually looking for Chloe Cowyn. I was told she works here."

"Yes, she does, but not tonight. Can I help you with something?"

Ameena sighed. "I've been trying to get a hold of her – well – her aunt - actually. I'm the social worker assigned to her case. I need to meet with her aunt, so I can close the file. It's a formality really. I've texted back and forth with the aunt, but I've never talked with her in person or on the phone. I have to actually meet her to do my job properly. I'm sure you understand."

"Have you tried their house?" Molly asked.

"I did, yesterday. A boy named Jarvis was there and said that Chloe and her aunt were out running errands."

"I know Jarvis. He's one of Chloe's friends."

Unfortunately, Jarvis took that moment to come into the diner. "Hey, Jarvis." Molly said. "I'm surprised to see you on Chloe's night off." She said the last three words very deliberately.

"But I—"

Molly cut him off. "Why don't you sit down at the counter, and I'll get you your regular."

"Ah, okay." Jarvis seemed to be catching on. He picked a seat far enough down the bar that he noticed me lurking in the shadows. Giving me a quick nod, he grabbed his phone. My phone pinged with a text.

JARVIS: Skipping school and hiding from the law?

ME: U have no idea. Technically she's not the law, but I have crazy things to tell u

JARVIS: Like how you are about to be busted by your social worker

ME: That & more

Ameena must have finished talking with Molly because she was headed Jarvis' way. "Do you know where Chloe is tonight?"

Ameena's back was to me, but I stepped as far into the hallway as I could, ducking down into a squat.

"She should be at home? Have you tried there?"

"Yes, before I came here." Ameena's voice was getting a little sharp. I couldn't blame her for being frustrated. *I was doing a great job at avoiding her.*

"Oh, well they should be home now." *Yes, thank you Jarvis!! Get her out of here!*

"This doesn't feel right. No one should be this hard to meet. Is there anything you should be telling me? I only want to make sure Chloe is safe."

"Oh, she's safe. Really safe."

Gah! He was laying it on too thick.

"Let me dial the aunt's phone and see if she picks up."

In my moment of panic as I watched her punch numbers into her phone, I almost fumbled mine—aka my aunt's fake phone—but managed to put it on silent, cutting off the first chirp of the ring tone. Ameena looked around for a split second, and then put the phone to her ear.

"Ugh. Same automated voice mail message." Ameena jammed her phone into the pocket of her satchel. "Thanks anyway. When you see Chloe next, tell her to call me. Here's my card. I'll try to stop back at her next shift. When is that by the way?"

"Oh, not until Friday." Molly lied as smooth as her French silk pie.

"Okay, then. Bye."

I breathed a sigh of relief, until Molly came around the corner with a seriously angry look on her face. "I do not like lying—well—unless I know it's for a good cause. Is this for a good cause, Chloe?"

"Yes, I swear."

"I need to know the whole story."

"I – I don't know if I can tell you the whole story," I paused, watching her face for any sort of forgiveness and seeing none, added, "yet."

"Good catch. We'll talk more after closing. Go take care of your customers."

I simply nodded and got back to work, checking in on each table and refilling drinks. It was nearly closing anyway.

"Thank you so much, Jarvis," I said when I finally made it back to where he perched at the counter.

"Molly said she was going to get me my regular, but she never did. I didn't know she knew what I liked. You usually wait on me."

I could only laugh. "Jarvis, you order the exact same thing every time. A bacon cheeseburger with cheddar not American, with pickles and tomato but never any lettuce or onions. And a vanilla shake."

"Yup, that's it. I could shake things up and order chocolate." Jarvis chuckled at his bad pun, his eyes sparkled with amusement.

I laughed, just a tiny bit—only because he seemed so pleased with himself over his joke. Who knew serious Jarvis had a lighter side? He sure didn't show it much.

"So, when is your aunt actually going to show up?" Jarvis asked.

"I hope by the end of next week, but I got bad news today—a bunch of it. The city needs me out by Sunday so they can get the house ready for the new caretaker. I'm going to be homeless."

"I wouldn't let that happen to you." Jarvis reached out and touched my cheek. He'd never done that before. It startled me at first, but my skin tingled—in a good way.

Someone cleared their throat behind me, and I pivoted around to find Candi waiting at the cash register ready to pay her bill.

"How was your food tonight?" I asked out of habit.

"It was delicious. I felt kind of rebellious eating my dessert first."

I smiled at her and reached out to give her the change, but she shook her head. "You keep it. There's a little more I left on the table for you, too."

"Thank you." I wasn't one to turn down a double tip, particularly when I needed the money so badly, but it made me wonder if she'd heard me talking with Jarvis about my impending homelessness.

I locked the door after her and, as she stepped off the curb, a car sped around the corner and screeched to a stop right in front of her. Candi jumped back when the driver leaned across the passenger seat and flung the door open. I couldn't get a good look at who it was because Candi was between us, but I heard him yell, "Get in, bitch."

Candi leaned down and yelled something back to him, but whatever she said was muffled.

The man's hand snaked out and grabbed her wrist, twisting it. She pulled free, and I was about to open the lock to let her back in. But the guy said something else that made Candi freeze. She turned her head toward the diner and seeing us, she gave a wave and got into the front seat. The car roared off.

"What the heck was that?" I asked, looking over at Jarvis. "Should we call the police?"

"And say what?"

"Well, he was hurting her."

"And it also kind of looked like they might have been a couple having a fight—I mean—she got in on her own."

"I didn't think to look at the license plate, did you?"

"I couldn't see it from this angle," Jarvis said.

"I don't even know her last name. She always pays in cash."

"Candi seems like the kind of person who can take care of herself, y'know?"

I wasn't sure I agreed.

41

Chloe

AFTER THE BIZARRE SCENE out front with Candi, I was more than ready to leave with Jarvis. He was now chowing down on his 'regular' order. I had so much to tell him about what I learned that day. I needed someone to listen to the details while I tried to sort it out. He always had good ideas, mainly because he was so observant.

Molly watched me clock out. I watched her watching me, but I didn't say anything, hoping she'd let me leave and save her questions for another day. But that wasn't going to happen.

"Okay—come clean with me, now."

I didn't know how much truth I should tell her. I wasn't even sure what the truth was anymore after the confusing day from hell with the crap ton of info that had gotten unloaded on real me and on the fake-Aunt-Maggie me.

"You can trust me. I swear to god." Molly stepped forward and put her hands on my shoulders. "I'm worried about you and what you might have gotten yourself into investigating your dad's murder. But why avoid the social worker?"

All I could think about was her friendship or what I suspected was more than friendship with Chief Barnett. Even if she promised, she might let something slip when they were together. Molly deserved better from me. She really did, especially after lying for me, but I settled on a half-truth. "My aunt is super busy with a work project." *Truth.* "She doesn't like to be disturbed, so she doesn't always pick up her phone or answer the door." *Mostly true.* "And sometimes she is away overnight to get that work done." *Truth – well sort of – that kind of implied that she was here some of the time.* "I just don't want the social worker to think that she's not taking good care of me and – I don't know – try to take me away or something."

"I don't think that would happen. You've both been through a lot with losing your dad. I'm sure there's some leeway on that kind of thing."

"And I didn't say it before, but thank you for telling her I wasn't here tonight. And thanks for telling her I didn't work until Friday. You didn't have to do that."

"No, I didn't. Don't make me regret it. I'm guessing there's quite a bit more to this story. You can talk to me whenever you need to. I'll keep whatever you say confidential."

It was almost like she had read my thoughts about her and the police chief.

"I'll tell you more when I can," I said. "I had a really strange day. You know part of it, but I learned a lot of things that make me wonder if my dad was always truthful with me."

"Promise me this – if you think you're getting close to knowing who might have done this to your dad, you'll take your evidence to the police. You don't want to end up in the same situation."

A chill ran down my spine as I remembered what my dad looked like, leaning against the angel statue when I found him in the cemetery. I definitely didn't want to end up like my dad.

Jarvis walked me home. On the way, I caught him up on my day. I started with how Mr. Walker reacted when I told him my dad was dead.

"Oh, that's wild. I wonder what your dad told him that would make him say that. Maybe someone had been threatening him?"

"Maybe. He wouldn't tell me, but I did learn more when I called back as Aunt Maggie. He said that Aunt Maggie's sister-in-law was out of prison and that the Florida restraining order keeping her away from us was valid in Wisconsin."

"So that explains the Florida prison phone calls."

"Right, but I still don't know who this person is. Either it's the sister of someone my Aunt Maggie was married to or it is someone my dad was married to. I don't think Aunt Maggie was ever married, and I thought my dad was only married to my mom. Unless he got married again after my mom died and I was too young to know. Or, I suppose, he could have been married *before* he married my mom, but he would have been really, really young for that—like not even twenty years old."

"Did you get a name?"

"No, I wanted to ask, but he didn't offer, and clearly I'd know the name of my sister-in-law if I was Aunt Maggie. I couldn't ask without giving myself away."

"True."

"Well, we could try to do some searches on your last name in Florida to see what court cases came up. It's not a common last name. If your dad did remarry, then maybe this woman would have the same last name. And your aunt is kind of famous. If she'd been married, there's probably a record about it somewhere online showing her husband's last name, so we'd probably be able to figure out if it's her sister-in-law who's the convict."

"I suppose." I felt defeated. There was so much I didn't understand. Even when real Aunt Maggie showed up, she might not want to tell me. Mr. Walker had mentioned to me (as fake Aunt Maggie) that my dad had kept things from me. The whole conversation was making me sick to my stomach, so I quit talking.

Jarvis got the hint, letting that subject drop. "So what are you going to do about your living situation?"

"I'll figure something out. Maybe I can get a hotel room. It looks like they'll give me my dad's last paycheck once the lawyer gives them some form. That'd be enough to get a room for a week. I need to get everything packed up and moved out to the garage though. At least Frank was nice enough to let me use the space for storage."

"I've got a little money saved up. I can help."

"Thanks, Jarvis. That's sweet. I hope I'll have enough."

As we neared the cemetery gate, I pulled Jarvis back into the shadows. "What if the social worker is waiting for me?"

"We could walk around the back way and make sure that she's not parked by your house."

We retraced our steps to the corner and walked on the sidewalk outside the cemetery fence. The cemetery was the size of four city blocks—one big square. Once we got to the next corner we turned again and could see the back of my house.

No social worker. I breathed a sigh of relief.

Jarvis was pointing to another small gate. It was actually more like a door that was part of the wrought iron fencing. "Why don't you ever use this one?"

"I don't know. We just never did. More convenient to go out the front. Maybe it's rusted shut or something?"

"I don't see any rust," Jarvis said. He then grabbed my arm and pulled me closer. "Check out the lock. It has scratches all over it."

I stepped closer to see for myself. "When people try to pick a lock do they leave scratches?" I asked.

Jarvis laughed. "Seems like you wouldn't if you knew what you were doing. This kind of looks like someone was having trouble lining up the key with the lock."

"Weird."

I looked back toward the house one last time before we headed to the main gate and gasped.

"What—"

I pulled Jarvis backwards warning him to shush.

A man was now standing on the grass right outside our house and looking in the living room window. He went from window to window, peering in. I didn't think there'd be much for him to see. I hadn't left any lights on. Just then a small point of light became visible as the man used it to look inside. It reminded me of the light I saw the night my dad died, sending a shiver down my spine.

I was frozen while I watched him, but when he went around to the other side of the house, I sprang into action. "C'mon, Jarvis." I ran back toward the main gate. "We can't let him leave without knowing who he is. He might be my dad's murderer." I probably should have been scared, but now I was simply determined to catch him or at the very least get a good look at him.

I assumed he'd keep going around the house and we'd catch sight of him again as we turned the corner, but no one was there.

We stayed partially hidden behind one of the big oaks and waited. From personal experience I knew how easy it was to hide behind tombstones. There was also the garage, the little chapel in the middle of the cemetery, and the house if the person didn't mind breaking in.

It took a minute for the fear to catch up with me. Now, I was scared to go home, imagining my dad's murderer hiding in any of those places.

We waited a few more minutes but didn't see any movement.

"What do you want to do, Chloe?"

"I'm not going to be able to sleep if we don't look around to make sure he's gone."

"Where do you want to look first?"

"The chapel. It's the closest."

I'd been in the chapel right after my dad died, searching for clues. As we approached, Jarvis reached down and picked up a rock for defense. I was about to go up the leaf-covered steps to the doors, when I stopped. "Look," I said to Jarvis, gesturing at all the leaves covering the entry stairs. "He didn't come this way. If the door had been opened, the leaves would have been swept away from here."

We headed to the garage next. There were more hiding spots here, and we had to look around equipment to make sure no one was there.

That only left the house.

Turning on lights as we went, we searched. The kitchen was empty, so was the bathroom.

Jarvis stopped short as he surveyed the papers strewn all over the living room. "Um, Chloe. I really hope you made this mess and whoever it was didn't get in here and do this."

"It was me. I was looking for any info my dad might have that would help me unravel things.

"Okay, good. Well, not good, but I'm glad it was you."

We looked under the beds and in the closets, which in my dad's room was easy because I'd pulled so many boxes out from those two spots earlier. Jarvis didn't say anything about the mess this time.

I was very grateful that we didn't have a basement. Not sure I would have wanted to go down there even if we did.

"So where did the guy go?"

"I can't believe that he had enough time to get out of the gate without us seeing him."

"He must have. He's definitely not here."

"Let me walk you out, so I can lock the gate behind you."

Jarvis held up the rock. "Do you want to keep this in here?"

"No, I've got a baseball ba—" What I saw on the rock had me stopping midword. I grabbed it from him to get a closer look. There was a large dark spot on the rock that looked very much like dried blood. "What do you think this is, Jarvis?"

"I don't know. It kind of looks like blood to me. But it could be paint. I picked it up near the chapel. When was it last repainted?"

"Last summer, but this doesn't look like that paint to me."

"Are you thinking this is your dad's blood? Was he bleeding when you found him?"

"Not that I saw. But doesn't that look like old blood?" I thought about what I was holding and now creeped out, set it down quickly and went to the sink to wash my hands.

"What are you going to do with it?" Jarvis asked.

"I don't know. The police should have found it. This shows me again that they didn't look too hard."

"Or maybe they thought it was paint," Jarvis offered.

"Maybe. But they should be able to test what it is, right?"

Jarvis nodded. "Hey, are you going to be okay here alone tonight?"

I said sure, but I wasn't positive I meant it.

"I could stay if – if you want me to."

"You want to stay?" I thought his offer was simply a kind one, but, with the focus on my dad's death and solving his murder, I hadn't really thought about what this was – this – this thing with Jarvis and me. I mean, was it a thing? I didn't even know.

He must have noticed something in my expression as these thoughts flew through my head, and he rocked back and forth on his feet. "I – I mean not like – that. Just so you're not alone."

God he was so sweet. "I'd like that, Jarvis, but won't you get in trouble with your parents?"

"No, my dad's on a business trip. I'll call my stepmom. She probably won't even pick up, but at least if I leave a message she won't wonder where I am if—"

"If what?"

"Um – if – if she even notices I'm gone."

Now I had a ton of questions, but I didn't want to pry. Jarvis never talked about his parents, but nearly all the ones I knew would have an issue with their son out all night. I went into my room to change into pjs while he was making his call.

42

The Watcher

I AM GLAD TO stay vigilant—to keep her safe. She takes unnecessary risks when she's upset.

She's torn the house apart, looking for clues.

She's frightened, but she doesn't know of who. I see it in the way she looks around now. Wary—of everyone.

43

Dean ~ Day Before Death

DEAN'S LACK OF SLEEP was catching up with him. He liked to think he was always aware of his surroundings, but his new hyper alertness was driving him crazy. Outside, every time the wind picked up, the motion of leaves dropping startled him. Inside, every little sound in the old house made him whip around in defense.

He'd nearly tackled Chloe the other night when she'd gotten up to get a drink of water.

"Dad, you scared the crap out of me." She laughed and mopped up her spilled water by dragging a kitchen towel across the floor with her foot.

"Nice, Chloe, real nice."

"What? The floor's kind of clean. Well at least now it is in that one spot."

Dean just shook his head.

"Dad, you look tired. You should go to bed."

"I haven't been sleeping well." Dean should have said he hadn't been sleeping at all, staying up at night to guard the house and sneaking the occasional nap when he knew Chloe was safe at school.

Even though he was dead tired, he made it to breakfast with the guys at the coffee shop the next morning.

"Mornin' Deano," said Earl. "What the heck had you tearin' out of here so fast yesterday?"

"Ah, it turned out to be nothing, but I thought I had an emergency back at the cemetery. False alarm."

Earl looked at him and gave a little shake of his head, like he didn't quite believe him, but he let it slide. The other three guys arrived by then, and Betty filled their mugs and confirmed orders.

"So what's new?"

Lou jumped in with some news that his long-time neighbors were moving to Florida permanently. "They've been good to live next to. Who knows what kind of people the new owners are going to be? I only hope they're not loud."

"I don't have to worry about that. My neighbors are very quiet." This earned Dean a good-natured chuckle around the table.

"So, boys, did you hear about all the cars broken into last night out in the subdivision by the golf course?"

"No. Was much of anything taken?" asked one of the guys.

"Chief Barnett stopped in for a coffee right after I opened," Betty said. "He was coming back from taking the reports. Seems like it was mostly wallets and cash that got snagged, except for the poor kid who left his backpack in his car with his computer inside."

"Well, you don't expect that in a small town like this," Dean said.

"Did they say if they had any idea who it was?" Earl asked.

"No, but they've got a partial plate picked up on one of them doorbells with the cameras," Betty said. "Sometimes I think all this technology is too much, but if it helps to catch the bad guys, maybe not."

After breakfast, Dean hung back as the guys left and scanned the cars parked in front of the motel rooms for any with Florida plates but didn't see any. He pivoted toward the motel office and was glad he didn't recognize the middle-aged woman working behind the desk.

"Welcome, are you looking for a room?" Her bright smile made Dean smile back.

"No, actually I'm looking for my friends who are staying here, but I don't know their room number."

"Oh, we can't give those out, but I can call their room for you. What's the name?"

"Diana Johnson."

"I don't think we've got anybody here by that name." The woman slid her finger down the computer screen facing her to double check. "Nope, no Diana."

"I suppose the room could be under Lance Riggs."

"Nope, nobody by that name either."

"Maybe they checked out already?"

"I'm not seeing anyone with those names recently. Why don't you just call them and see where they're staying because they're not staying here." Dean felt the woman's suspicion wash over him.

"I'll do that. Thanks for your help." He should have realized that they'd use fake names.

Dean wanted to hang around, but now the lady at the desk was watching him, so he got into his truck and drove it out of the lot. But instead of leaving altogether, he found a spot on the street, out of view from the office windows but still with a good view of the rooms. He waited and watched for an hour and finally gave up, hoping they'd left town.

That conversation about doorbell cameras at breakfast had Dean stopping at the hardware store on his way back to the cemetery. There were all sorts of video security systems available that connected to an app on your phone. Of the two the store had in stock, Dean picked the one that seemed most reliable. He mounted it to the side of the house facing out toward the gate. Installing the dang app on his phone proved slightly more difficult. But once it was connected, he was pleased with the view it showed. It was triggered by motion and sent a notification to his phone. It wouldn't eliminate his need to keep watch entirely, but it would tell him if anyone was snooping around that shouldn't be. In fact, he figured he could expense it to the city as a way to catch the occasional group of kids who decided sneaking into the cemetery was a fun night's activity.

He spent the rest of his day doing tasks that came with the job; mowing the grass, maybe for the final time of the year, and maintaining the small backhoe that fit between the rows of grave markers. So far this week, there'd been no burials planned . . . a slow week for deaths was fine with him. Dean was even able to catch a short nap before Chloe got home from cross country practice. His app worked great and woke him with a chime when it detected Chloe coming through the gate.

It was a low-key evening. He had a chance to check once more when he went to close and lock the gate for the night.

The camera caught his motion and alerted his phone, exactly like it had when Chloe came home. Dean felt more relaxed knowing that.

Chloe was eating a bowl of cereal in the kitchen when he came back in and he slid into a chair across from her.

"Did you get your homework all done?"

"Yes, Dad," she mumbled around a mouthful.

"Don't talk with your mouth full."

"Then don't ask me a question when my mouth is full."

"Sassy pants," Dean teased. "No, seriously, how are classes going? I haven't asked you since like the first week of school."

"Pretty good. Chemistry's hard. I knew it would be. I liked biology better. I have a really smart lab partner though. I got to class late on the first day and was paired up with a kid I don't know. He doesn't talk much, I'm not sure he likes me, but he catches my mistakes, so my lab report grades have been good."

"Sounds like it's turning out okay."

"I guess."

"So when's your next meet?"

"We actually don't have anything until next week. It's the big invitational in Watertown."

"If I don't have a burial to take care of, I'll definitely make the trip over."

"Awesome." Chloe rinsed her bowl in the sink. "G'night."

"Hey, you're not too old to give me a hug."

"Never." She leaned down for the embrace and gave him a quick peck on his cheek.

44

Chloe

EVEN WITH JARVIS ON the couch in the living room, I couldn't settle down to sleep. I'd offered him my dad's bed, but he turned me down, explaining he wanted to be closer to the doorway.

When he'd said that, a wave of emotion crashed through me. I was so grateful to have him on my team. I knew the current situation was my own fault. I mean, I could have been safe in a nice bed in Emma's house, but that wouldn't be getting me any closer to solving my dad's murder. I knew I had to be here . . . where it all began . . . the scene of the crime and all that.

I willed my guardian angel to keep me company and felt his presence wrap around me, but it didn't do the normal job of lulling me to sleep. I missed my dad. I wanted to hear his voice. I dialed his cell phone and waited for his voice mail message. I did that twice, and it didn't help the pit in my stomach. In fact, it made it worse.

It also made me realize I hadn't kept my dad's phone charged. Even though it was right there with me, it'd never rung. I thought at first it was because I put it on silent mode in Chem class, but it had since run out of battery. I plugged it in now.

As it charged, I slid to the floor in front of the same window I'd heard the wailing through the night of my dad's murder. Only now the window was closed. It was getting too cold to keep it open for very long, but I pushed it up a few inches to breathe in the cool fall air that smelled like wet leaves and wood smoke. Someone had their firepit going. It actually was a perfect night for that.

Before I could stop myself, I'd tiptoed past a sleeping Jarvis and out the back door, sitting down on the top step to slip on my tennis shoes. I figured whoever'd been scoping out the house was long gone, and I wanted to go to the place where my dad had died. Well, I guess he technically was declared dead at the hospital, but I knew that he'd died right here—that's what his flat eyes had told me when I'd found him that night.

I made my way over to the avenging angel statue and stood in front of it mimicking its pose with one arm flung up to the heavens holding a sword with the other grasping a shield. If only I felt that brave or looked that imposing. I tried to imagine my dad's last moments. What had happened here? Had someone hit him on the head with the rock?

The distance from here to the front of the chapel wasn't that far. Someone could have dropped the rock there as they left.

"Dad," I whispered. "Dad, you gotta give me some help here. Help me figure this out, so I can prove you didn't do this to yourself." I sank to my knees, feeling the dampness through my pj pants.

"Chloe, Chloe."

I jerked up thinking it was my dad answering me, but quickly realized that I wasn't getting a message from "the beyond."

Jarvis was coming toward me, holding a phone.

"Your phone was making noise and woke me up. I'm sorry, I meant to stay awake to keep watch."

"That's not my phone, Jarvis. It's my dad's. I plugged it in because I'd let the battery die."

"It's got some sort of alert pinging."

I grabbed it from Jarvis and typed in his security code. "I don't know what this is," I said, finding an app hidden in a folder with a notification icon showing. I tapped it and saw what looked like security camera footage of the drive and the area where the drive split to our house. What it showed was a video of me walking past a few minutes prior.

"Wow, look Jarvis. My dad must have put up some sort of camera. He never told me."

Jarvis peered over my shoulder. "If he saved the videos, we should be able to go back and see the night he died."

"And tonight, too. We should be able to see who was looking in the house. How did I never notice he had this?"

"Don't feel bad, Chloe. I never noticed this app either. It only activates when someone walks by."

"I wonder when he put this up. I wonder *why* he put this up—probably for the same reasons he told Trent Walker."

We rushed back in the house and used my dad's phone to access the recordings.

There weren't any from the night of my dad's murder. The first recording was me coming toward the house the day I'd pretended Aunt Maggie had arrived.

"It's weird that I never saw this. I've kept his phone with me nearly the entire time since I got it back from the police, but I guess it's either been powered off, in silent mode, or the battery's been dead."

We continued watching the videos that recorded all the people who came in through the gate and up the drive past our house. There I was coming and going, Jarvis as well, a few funeral processions. Ameena Alavi had also been there three times. *Phew – no wonder she was mad.*

We waded through the footage until we got to the prowler. It was a guy in a baseball cap. I didn't recognize him. He wore dark jeans and a black leather jacket, but other than that I couldn't tell who it was. The camera caught him jogging down the drive toward the main gate—about the time that we started running on the street behind him. We'd just missed him. He was moving like something had spooked him.

He was my prime suspect.

I had a ton of new evidence to give to the police chief.

"Jarvis, there had to have been video of the night my dad was attacked. And then the next day, the police chief said that one of the officers had come back to search. So that video should be here, too. Wouldn't he have told me if he had video of that night?"

"Maybe not, but would they have erased it?"

I looked through the set up on the app. "This shows it's set to save video for thirty days. You have to actively go in and delete files. I don't know why they would have deleted any even if they'd downloaded them. Looks like the police chief is going to have even more questions to answer."

"We can save these videos to another location, Chloe. To keep them safe." In a few minutes, Jarvis had them downloaded to my computer.

It was late, and I had a feeling I'd be missing more classes in the morning. I urged Jarvis to get some sleep, and I went back to bed. Jarvis insisted on keeping Dad's phone close so he would hear the camera's alarm if it went off again. My guardian angel wrapped me in his safety, and I sent a silent thank you to him for that comfort. The last I remembered was the clock reading 3:33 a.m. before my alarm jerked me awake at 7:00.

I shuffled out into the living room and found Jarvis folding the blankets. "I've got to run home to get ready for school."

"Thanks for staying," I said, yawning.

"I wouldn't have felt right about leaving you here alone. Can you let me out of the gate?"

"Sure." I slipped into my running shoes without tying the laces, and we hurried down the drive. I unlocked the gate and debated about just leaving it open for the day, but as Jarvis walked away, a wave of unease came over me. It felt like I was being watched. I glanced around, but the street was quiet.

I turned the lock and felt better hearing its reassuring click.

45

The Watcher

THE LIGHTS GO OUT. She's tucked in for the night. The man from earlier hasn't come back.

I can relax for a few hours. But before I leave, she surprises me by going out into the cemetery—alone.

What is she doing?

She's both brave and foolish. I admire her bravery. I feel like I might have something to do with that. I hope I do.

Even so, I stand guard all night.

This morning she's more watchful than ever. I can tell she's looking for anyone who doesn't belong.

46

Chloe

BACK IN THE HOUSE, I dialed the number for the chief that I used before.

"Chief Barnett," he barked.

"Um, hi, Chief. This is Chloe Cowyn."

"Chloe, are you okay?" He sounded worried and for a minute I wondered what Molly might have said to him.

"Yes, but I've found some strange things that I need to show you. Can you come over here to the house?"

He assured me that he'd be right over. By the time he arrived, I reopened the gate, knowing he'd arrive soon, and waited for him on the porch dressed for school.

"So, what's going on, Chloe?" He asked as he exited his squad.

"I'm doing your job for you again." I knew I should have backed off, but the minute I saw him all this anger oozed out of my pores and came out in the most sarcastic way. I wanted to believe Molly and give him the benefit of the doubt, but really all I had was doubt, doubt, doubt.

"Okay." He chuckled a little but that only made me madder.

I gripped the white wood railing so hard that paint flecks came off and stuck to my palms. "Do you think this is funny?"

The chief cleared his throat and hooked his thumbs on his belt loops. "Of course, I don't."

"I hope you at least talked with the guys my dad ate breakfast with."

"I'm meeting them later today. Look, Chloe, you have to know that I'm doing my job here, and there are things I can't tell you right now."

"I'm just supposed to believe that?" I crossed my arms in front of me and walked to the top of the steps.

"Yes, you can trust me. I swear."

I needed that to be true.

"I have a bunch of stuff to show you. Inside." I held the door open for him. In the kitchen, my dad's phone, now fully charged, was squawking with the notice from the video camera.

"What's that?" the chief asked.

"That's evidence."

He looked at me, tilting his head in question as I opened the app and showed him the video of his arrival.

"Whoa. Your dad had one of those security cameras?"

"I guess so. I would have thought you guys went through my dad's phone for evidence."

"Yes, I thought that'd been done." The chief's brows pulled together making a serious crease down the middle of his forehead.

"I didn't realize it until last night. And you know the date of the first video? The day that I came home from the Phillips' house the Tuesday after my dad died. So where are all the videos that came before that? When I go into the set up on the app, you can see that the videos are set to save for thirty days."

"Okay."

"And, all the other days after, every time there's motion in the camera's range it gets recorded. So someone had to have deleted those videos."

"Can you give me the log in to the app so I can take a look at these more carefully?"

"Sure." I grabbed a pad of paper and a pen and wrote down the info. I'd already downloaded the videos from the archive, so there was no reason not to let him into the program. "But you need to look at last night's video. Jarvis and I were walking along the backside of the cemetery, and we saw someone looking in the windows of the house. We ran as fast as we could to the front to see if we could cut him off before he came out of the gate, but he beat us to it. I cued up the video and played it. See him run down the driveway?"

"We only get the side of his face as he turns. I'll see what my tech can do with this."

"I think he might be the guy who killed my dad. Who else would be prowling around here?"

"Chloe, where's your aunt? There are some things I need to discuss with her."

It was only then that I realized who he wouldn't see if he looked through all the videos. There wasn't a single one showing my aunt, for good reason. As I mulled over my huge mistake, the chief had to ask his question again.

I finally answered with a panic-induced, spur of the moment lie. "She left to go into Milwaukee for the day. Some television thing." *That barely made any sense to me. But the chief seemed to buy it.*

"Okay, I really need to speak with her. Can you give me her cell number again? I thought I had the right one, but it keeps going to an automated voice mail."

I read the number to him, and he nodded. "That's what I have."

"She's really bad about returning calls." *Especially when she's on assignment in some war-torn foreign country without her dang cell phone.* "Does it have to do with what Mr. Walker told you yesterday?"

The chief coughed a little before he answered. "I know you met with him, and he said some things that perhaps he shouldn't have when he was shocked to learn about your dad's death."

"Yeah, he said he wasn't surprised that my dad was dead. Y'know, I'm sixteen. I'm old enough to be let in on some of this stuff. Particularly if you think I'm in danger. I need to know who to watch out for."

His eyes narrowed, and I could tell he was wondering what I might already know. I wanted to ask him about everything. I suppose I could have tried bluffing my way through, pretending that Aunt Maggie had filled me in. But truly the things I learned when I was pretending to be Aunt Maggie weren't very clear, and I'm sure I'd fumble the conversation somehow and make him suspicious.

"I'd be happy to sit down with you both and go through what we know."

I wasn't going to get any further on that track. He turned for the door.

"Wait—you still need to see what my friend Jarvis found in the cemetery." I pointed to the rock in front of me, so out of place on the kitchen table I was surprised the chief didn't mention it before. "Do you think it – it's blood?"

He looked at it from a couple different angles. "I don't think so, Chloe. Blood does dry dark brown like this, but I think it's paint. Can you show me where you found it?"

I took him outside to the spot where I thought that Jarvis had leaned down to scoop it up for defense the night before.

"I think it was about here."

The chief searched around the area and then took a couple of big strides toward the chapel. Here more small rocks bordered the beds where the shrubs were planted. A couple of them had stains like the one Jarvis found. "I'm guessing this is paint – like the stuff that matches these rocks and the chapel. Maybe it just got kicked out this way. Let me grab an evidence bag and have it sent into the lab for testing to see if it might be blood." He hurried to retrieve one from the trunk of his car and flipped it inside out, using it like a glove to avoid touching the rock as he put it in the bag and sealed it shut.

"Do you know if my dad had a head injury?"

"I didn't see that in any report. I would have remembered that, but I can double check with the doctor on duty."

"Wouldn't they have done an autopsy?"

"Well, no, that's not automatic. Autopsies are expensive, Chloe. And we knew what killed your dad. Well mostly. I know that blood samples were sent to the lab to confirm what drugs were in his system—the syringe too, but if he had any sort of head trauma, that would have been noted by the ER doc. I'll double check on that, but the report in the file didn't mention any sort of wound. I can always have them take another look at your dad's body."

My heart sank. "No, you can't."

"He's still in the morgue, Chloe."

"I don't think so. On Saturday they called and asked what arrangements we'd made, and I told – I mean – we told Marcus to pick up his body and bring it back to have it cremated. I think they probably have done that already."

A muscle in his jaw twitched and two spots of color bloomed on his cheeks. "I didn't sign off on the release of his body. They're not supposed to do that until I do. This is an active investigation."

"Wait! What? How could that happen?"

"I'm not sure but *I will* find out." Anger flared in his eyes, but then he took a deep breath and turned to me with a calmer expression, one that looked like he'd worked hard to put there. "Isn't it time for you to head to school?"

I checked the clock on the kitchen wall. "Past time actually. I'm going to be late."

"I can give you a ride."

"No, it's fine."

"I'd feel better if I dropped you off. In fact, can you make sure you're not alone right now, in case your theories have been right all along." The fact that he was now basically agreeing with me, made my blood run cold.

"You believe me," I whispered.

"I've got some hunches. Let me drive you to school, Chloe."

I nodded and grabbed my backpack. I hadn't opened it all weekend. I knew that in the big picture, my lack of studying wasn't going to make a huge difference, but I still felt a pang of guilt. I knew my grades were going to slide. And I knew how disappointed my dad would have been with me. I had to figure he'd forgive me if my effort led to finding his murderer.

The police chief opened the door to the front seat.

"You're gonna let me sit up front. Is that allowed?"

"Yes, it's allowed." He chuckled.

That was the complete opposite of the way Officer Mank treated me, making me sit in the back seat as we followed the ambulance to the hospital the night my dad died.

We pulled up at school a few minutes later and before I hopped out the chief asked me if I had to work right after school.

"Four p.m. until closing."

"Will your aunt be home by the time you get home?"

"She should be," I lied.

"And will you promise to ask Molly for a ride home. I'm sure she'd give you one."

"I'm sure she would, but my friend Jarvis has been walking me home lately."

"Okay, good."

As I walked toward the door, I veered to the office to get a pass since I was tardy, but that reminded me that I'd ditched the entire previous day. I'd meant to forge a note from Aunt Maggie. I quickly sat on the bench just outside the office door and tore out a sheet of notebook paper. It seemed like any time I brought up anything to do with my dad's death, there was less scrutiny. So while it was sort of horrible, I did it again and scrawled my message in what I hoped look like a busy reporter's handwriting:

Please excuse Chloe from school yesterday.
We took the day to plan her dad's funeral.
Thanks, Maggie Gill

47

Chloe

THE SECRETARY PATTED MY hand in compassion after reading my note, and I only felt the tiniest twinge of guilt. I signed myself in and she handed me a pass to chemistry.

I was only a few minutes late, but the class was already hard at work on an experiment.

"Nice of you to join us today, Ms. Cowyn."

My teacher was a bit of a jerk.

"Good thing Jarvis can handle these experiments without you."

No—*amend that*—my teacher was a big jerk. I mean I wasn't the best at chemistry, but I wasn't the worst. It was true, though, that Jarvis was probably earning the best grade in the class.

"Hey Chloe," he said as I approached our lab bench. "You okay? I saw Chief Barnett drop you off."

I hadn't thought about the classroom windows that faced the front of the school where the chief had parked.

"They probably brought her in for questioning." One of Jarvis' frequent bullies, who was likely getting the worst grade in the class, laughed at his *brilliance.*

Jarvis' jaw clenched and his hands tightened into fists. That surprised me. I'd never seen him do anything more than keep his head down when things like this happened. Before he could step forward, I grabbed his shoulder, leaning in to whisper. "Stop it. He's not worth it." I tried to be quiet but the idiot in front of us heard.

"Oh, no, Jerkis is going to defend his girlfriend. I'm so scared." While the insult hurler had been paying attention to us, his beaker began to spew white foam down the sides and onto the lab table.

"Mr. Anson, you might want to pay attention to the caustic chemicals in front of you, given your failing grade in this class."

Most of the students laughed at that. This time I almost admired my teacher's cutting comments.

"I'll tell you after class," I whispered, and started filling out our lab report.

When the bell rang, we hung back so I could tell Jarvis about the meeting with the police chief. "He seemed really mad when he saw the video footage. He had no idea that there was a security camera recording that view of the cemetery. And he's definitely worried about me. I think he's starting to believe that we do have a killer out there."

"Finally."

"I know, right? Anyway, he made me promise to have Molly drive me home after my shifts, but I told him that you had been walking me home. If you can't, let me know and I'll be sure to ask Molly. The more I'm learning the more I'm not sure about being alone."

"I'll be there."

I saved the worst thing for last. "There's more. When we were talking about the rock, he told me that the medical report he got on my dad didn't include a description of any head injury but that he could ask the morgue staff to take another look at – at my dad's body." I swallowed hard because it was so incredibly awful to think of my dad as a body and not a person. But he wasn't even a body anymore, he was just ashes.

Jarvis brushed his hand down my arm lightly. "You okay?"

I nodded, fighting back tears. "He didn't know that the morgue released my dad's body to get cremated. He said that's something he's supposed to sign off on."

"That's weird."

Students were filing in by now, and we had to hustle to get to our next classes.

"See you at lunch," I called after him.

The rest of the morning went by as well as could be expected. I'd forgotten there was going to be a quiz in AP Lit, and I muddled my way through as well as I could. I hadn't had time to pack a lunch that morning, but I'd thrown an apple and some cheese sticks into my backpack. It'd have to see me through. The sun was shining, and Jarvis and I decided to eat out on the picnic tables. I was nearly to the side door when Coach Brooks stopped me.

"Hey Cowyn, how're you doing?"

"Okay, Coach. Thanks for asking." That wasn't the truth. I was far from okay.

"You don't have to pretend for me, kid. I'm guessing you're not okay. I know I wouldn't be if I was in your shoes."

Emma walked by on her way to lunch and saw me talking with the coach. She paused, like she wanted to say something but changed her mind and kept going.

My stomach sank. I missed my friend.

"Did you hear what I said, Cowyn?"

"No, sorry Coach."

"You can still come back and finish up the season."

"I can?"

"Sure, you need to put in some practice time before the sectional meet—that's a little more than two weeks away. But if you wanted to, you could."

"I – I have my job after school. So – I don't know."

"Look we could make an exception if you wanted to run in the morning. I'll bet a couple of your teammates would switch things up and keep you company."

I sucked in a big breath and let it out. "I don't know about that. They all seemed pretty ticked off at me for quitting."

"I think they were just mad in the moment, y'know? Everyone wants you back." Coach patted me on the shoulder before continuing down the hall.

I hoped that was true, but mainly I assumed they wanted me back on the team to help the chances for qualifying for state. But even so, I missed running. I missed so much . . . I missed my friends . . . I missed my dad . . .

I shoved the door open so hard that it bounced back and nearly caught me in the face as I went out. *Graceful move!*

Jarvis was already there at one of the tables, and a few other kids had decided the day was mild enough to sit outside, too.

Jarvis didn't say anything as I sat down and neither did I. I grabbed my apple and took a huge bite and chomped on it loudly while lining up the two cheese sticks in front of me.

"Is that all you brought?"

"I was a little busy this morning."

Jarvis handed half of his sandwich to me.

"You don't have to do that."

"You have to eat more than that."

"Thanks." It was a good sandwich, ham and Swiss with tomato and plenty of mayo but no lettuce.

Even though our lunch period was short, it was nice to simply sit and not talk about anything.

"I'll see you at the diner later, and then maybe tonight we can do some searching for Florida court cases. I'm good at that kind of stuff," Jarvis offered as he held open the door for me.

I wasn't surprised that he'd be good at that. But I was no slouch when it came to finding things on the internet. There had to be some evidence somewhere of who this person was. I knew Wisconsin had a court case system that you could search. I assumed Florida would have the same thing. I wouldn't have even known about that kind of records search, but Emma's parents talked about it once at dinner when they were discussing a case and what was available for the public to see.

At the diner, the little sleep I had the night before was catching up with me. I was glad for the free drinks benefit and drank enough coke to keep me caffeinated and alert.

I was still worried about Candi and the guy she left with the night before, and when she didn't show up like usual, I was even more worried. She was nice to me, and I didn't think she had any friends in town. I'd never seen her with anyone, but obviously she knew someone enough to get in their car—at least I hoped so.

"Molly, did Candi come in before my shift?"

"No, haven't seen her today."

"Last night, as she left, a guy pulled up in a car and yelled mean things to her, and then reached across to the passenger side where she was standing and kind of grabbed her. It looked like she didn't want to go, but then she turned toward Jarvis and me and waved. So, I think she was okay going with him, but . . ."

"I'm sure she's fine. She'll probably be back tomorrow, or maybe she's gotten sick of eating here every night for ages."

I hoped that was true. I stared out the window toward the town square. Someone was sitting on one of the benches in the dark. Kind of odd. I walked closer to the window to get a better look and realized it was the woman who Molly had kicked out. I waved Molly over to show her, but by the time she got there the woman had vanished. I questioned whether I'd actually seen her at all. *Was I so tired I was hallucinating?*

The night ended up being slow. Molly let me go early, so Jarvis didn't have to wait at all.

As we left the diner, I looked for the woman I thought I saw earlier, and then as we got closer to my house, we approached carefully, keeping watch for anything—or anyone strange. Nothing seemed out of place.

We set up our computers on the kitchen table.

"I'm not going to be able to do this very long," I warned. "I'm super tired."

"Me too, but let's at least give it a try."

I typed in Florida Court Case Searches and an online records search system was one of the options. On that website, you could choose a county name from the pulldown menu.

"I was hoping there would be a statewide search option. I'm not sure what county to choose. Wait where was the prison?" I rifled through the papers with my notes and found where I'd written down the info on the prison number I called. "When the person answered there, I asked where they were, and they said Pinellas County." I looked for that name, and there wasn't a match in the list.

Jarvis was looking over my shoulder. "That list is really short. In a state as big as Florida there have to be more counties than that. Wisconsin has seventy-two."

"How do you know that?"

"I don't know. I learned it in 4th Grade, and I just never forgot it. I'll bet some counties have their own database."

I typed in Pinellas County Court records and sure enough, Jarvis was right. They had their own search system.

I clicked through to where I could input a name. I typed in Cowyn. A few cases came up. The lone woman with that last name had a court record from twenty years earlier for speeding. I looked at her birthdate and did some quick math – the lady would have been in her late 80s when she received that ticket. She had to be dead by now.

I sighed. "I knew there was no way it'd be that easy. Now what? Do we keep searching counties one by one?"

"That's probably what we have to do," Jarvis said.

I groaned and shoved my computer forward on the table, leaving enough room for me to lower my head onto my arms. "I'm so tired. I need to do this, but I just can't do it tonight."

"Do you think your dad's files would have anything in them that would help us?"

"I didn't find anything to do with Florida. I'll look again. I'm going to have to pack everything up anyway, so I can go through them one-by-one when I do that."

"Right, you have to be out this weekend."

"Don't remind me."

"Do you want me to stay over again?"

Did I? I wanted to be tough. I wanted to be brave and say, *No, I've got this.* But I found myself lifting my head and nodding, quickly adding, "But not if you're going to get in trouble. Won't your parents have a fit, two nights in a row?"

"Nah. My dad's still out of town on a business trip and my stepmom's . . . kind of a hands-off parent. She doesn't care much what I do." Jarvis was quiet for a moment. "You know, I should probably check in with her. I'll be back in twenty – thirty minutes tops. I can lock the gate behind me and then come back in on my own." He snagged my dad's set of keys off the counter on his way out.

Letting my dad's keys out of my sight felt wrong, but this was Jarvis. I trusted him. It's not like I didn't have my own set for the gate, even though I'd taken to using my dad's exclusively. I was being oddly possessive. They were just keys.

"I'll be right back. Keep your phone with you and lock the door behind me."

It was weird how Jarvis had suddenly turned into my only friend. I hardly talked to anyone at school. No one knew what to say to me anyway. Emma wouldn't accept my apology, although it looked like she might have wanted to talk to me earlier. My other friends were all runners, and since I wasn't running, well, running for sport anyway, I only saw them in class. They smiled and said hi, but that was it. I suspected they were still mad (even though the coach didn't think so). I mean, how would he know? It's not like they were going to talk to him about that.

I liked Jarvis more and more every day, but I wasn't sure what our relationship was. He was a friend . . . but it was becoming more than that. I'd gone on dates once in a while and to the school dances, but I'd never really had a boyfriend—I was always too busy training for whichever sport season it was or studying.

Too tired to really ponder anything more deeply, I got ready for bed. I made sure both phones were charged—mine and my dad's. That way if the security camera was activated, the notification would (probably) wake me up. I left the porch light on for Jarvis and curled up on the couch, scrunching the pillow Jarvis used the night before under my head and pulling one of the blankets over my scarred legs.

I'd already fallen asleep when the camera app on my dad's phone chirped. I was very glad to see that it was only Jarvis returning. A few moments later I heard him use the keys to get in the back door. I stretched as I stood up and met him in the kitchen, glancing at the clock, surprised that it had been more than an hour since he'd left.

"That took you a while."

"Yeah, my stepmom was – was being – ah – a little difficult."

I wasn't sure what to make of his evasive answer. "I don't want you to get in trouble because of me."

"No, that's not it. I don't really like talking about her."

"Okay." I was curious where his mom was in all of this. He'd never said anything about her, but I wasn't going to push him to talk about something he didn't want to. I knew what that felt like lately. People wanted to talk about things I didn't want to talk about, but then when I needed answers, everyone was like, "Oh, no, you're not old enough. We need to talk with your aunt first."

Jarvis and I were standing awkwardly in the kitchen. He'd yet to slide his backpack off. "So, the blankets and stuff are still on the couch where you left them."

"Thanks," he said, but he didn't move toward the living room.

"You good?"

He didn't answer. We just stared at each other. I didn't know what *he* was thinking, but *I* was trying to figure out whether I should do something I'd wanted to do for a while. Before I could talk myself out of it, I stepped forward and pressed my lips to his.

It was quick but it had a spark that I hadn't felt with anyone before. I gasped and pulled back.

Jarvis put his hand on my cheek, and I tilted into it a little, anticipating a second kiss, but that didn't happen. His gaze went from intense to distant in a split second. He dropped his hand, said goodnight, and went into the living room, leaving me standing there wondering what had happened.

I had to walk through the same room on the way to my bedroom. I did so slowly, but Jarvis didn't look up. He kept his head down as he rummaged in his backpack.

"Goodnight, Jarvis," I said at a near whisper before softly closing the door to my room.

Even though my mind was spinning with . . . everything . . . fatigue blanketed me along with the comforting presence of my guardian angel as I slid into sleep.

The next morning when I woke up, Jarvis was gone, having neatly folded the blankets again. He put my dad's phone on top, and I checked the app to see that I'd only missed him by a few minutes.

When I went to open the gate for the day, I realized Jarvis had kept my dad's keys, and the frantic search for my set, which I hadn't used since my dad's death, nearly made me late to school again.

48

Chloe

THE WEEK WENT BY—NOT quickly, not slowly—it just went. Maggie didn't call, and I finally gave up hope of her returning earlier than the three weeks her producer had said. There were fewer and fewer days before I had to move our things out of the house, but still I hadn't packed. When the mess of files on the living room floor began to annoy me, I finally organized them into stacks. I'd looked at the names on every file and envelope. There was nothing there that could help me figure out what the heck was up with this person from Florida and the restraining order. I needed Aunt Maggie to fill in the gaps as none of the other adults who knew the truth were talking to me.

Jarvis and I scoured the internet for people with the last name Cowyn but had very little luck, even when we expanded our search to other counties in Florida. We couldn't find any records to show that Maggie'd been married, so that was a dead end. But on Thursday night I got my hopes up when I found an obituary.

"Jarvis look at this." I pointed at the screen for an obituary for a Verna Grace Cowyn, the same lady who had gotten the speeding ticket so long ago in Pinellas County. "She died a few years before I was born." I read the short notice. "She was ninety-two when she died, seventeen years ago . . . from Sun City, Florida." I gasped at what I saw next. "Look, oh-my-god look! She's survived by her grandchildren Margaret Gillian Johnson and Dean Archer Johnson. What are my dad and aunt's names doing here with a different last name? This has to be them."

"Margaret Gillian, Maggie Gill," Jarvis murmured.

"I knew she used a shortened version of her middle name professionally, but our last name is Cowyn, not Johnson. But my great-grandma was a Cowyn?" I slumped back into the sofa cushions and drew my knees up to my chest. "Would my dad have changed our last name?"

"Maggie would have had to change her name, too," Jarvis said.

"I suppose, but maybe not. I never called her anything but Maggie, and anything I've ever seen with her name on it has always said Maggie Gill. I can't say that I've ever seen her name with either Cowyn or Johnson attached to it. This is crazy."

"But it explains why we weren't able to find anything under Cowyn. We've been searching for the wrong last name."

"Johnson is so common," I moaned. "We're never going to figure this out."

"It definitely makes it a lot more difficult, but I wouldn't say impossible." I could practically see the gears turning in Jarvis' mind by the expression on his face. He definitely liked a challenge.

I snapped my laptop closed. "I'm done for the night. Is your dad back from his business trip yet?"

"No, tomorrow."

"So..." I let my voice trail off because, again, I felt like a big baby for not wanting to stay at home alone. But still, I knew there was a killer out there.

Jarvis reached over and grabbed my hand. "Don't worry. I can stay tonight. Not sure about after tomorrow, though, when my dad's home."

"Okay." My voice was a little squeaky, and I hated it. I hated that I wasn't able to be as tough as I wanted to be.

Jarvis inched over on the couch and put his arm around me. This was as much physical contact as he'd ever initiated. I leaned into him and laid my head on his shoulder.

"We'll figure this out," he said against my hair.

We stayed like that for a moment more. Jarvis kissed my forehead, and I tilted my face up, wanting more. His eyes were darker than ever, his pupils dilated, his face unreadable. Did he want more?

He abruptly shifted away from me and stood up. "Go to bed, Chloe. I'll lock the gate."

I was left standing there as he went out the door.

I was so confused, but clearly Jarvis wasn't interested in more. I didn't think he'd appreciate a deep conversation about his emotions—what guy did? I hurried through my bedtime routine and said a quick goodnight to him when he came back in before shutting my door for the night.

Luckily, my guardian angel was there to lull me to sleep. I'd tried to explain this presence to my dad, but I'd never been able to make him understand. In the end, I let him think that it was just my over-active childhood imagination. I quit talking about it as I got older because I could tell it made him uncomfortable. After a certain age, people do not have "imaginary friends." But this presence wrapped around me in a hug that made everything better—at least for the moment. Even though I dreamed about a different set of arms being wrapped around me.

I expected Jarvis to be gone before I woke up, and he was, but somehow the neatly folded stack of bedding made me sad this morning. I picked up the pillow and hugged it, breathing in deep. It smelled like him—in a good way. Ugh! What was I doing. I threw the pillow back on the couch. *Knock it off, Chloe.*

It was Friday morning, and with less than three days before I'd be homeless, I needed my dad's last paycheck. But the news on that front wasn't good when I called Frank.

"I'm sorry, Chloe. I know you and your aunt can probably use that check sooner rather than later, but they won't put that out until the next payroll a week from today." Frank added with a rueful chuckle that there was no way to get city bureaucracy to move faster. Luckily, it was payday for me. Even though I wouldn't be getting a huge check, every bit helped.

Where was I going to go? Jarvis offered to help me, but he'd already been doing so much. I didn't want him to use up his savings on me. And, I didn't want to be too far away, not if I was going to continue the hunt for my dad's killer.

As I headed to school, I passed the garage and wondered briefly about sleeping in the truck that would remain in storage there. That might work, but the garage would also be used by the new caretaker, and, before that, the painting/cleaning crew might go in and out. It was also where the grave digging equipment was stored. I quickly dismissed it as a place with too much traffic.

But then I passed another building on my way to the front gate. The chapel. It was hardly ever used. It wasn't gross . . . I mean other than the lower level being an old crypt. I was relieved to have a plan that would work for a few days.

Until – hopefully – Aunt Maggie turned up.

The more I thought about it, the more I liked the idea. I didn't need to take more help from people, like Jarvis, who had gone out of their way already. No one would expect me to be in the chapel. It was probably safer than staying in the house. As long as I came and went after the painters and cleaners were done for the day, there'd be no one to notice. And it put me in a perfect location to watch who came and went from the cemetery.

I was a few blocks from school on a residential street that I walked down all the time, when I saw the cop I didn't like in an apartment building parking lot. He was arguing with another man. Well, at least I thought they were arguing. I couldn't hear everything they said, but the way the cop was standing with his hand on his holstered gun seemed threatening to me. I didn't know why, but something was telling me to hurry by so I wouldn't be noticed. When I turned my face away from the lot, I saw something else that had me really wondering what was going on.

Chief Barnett was in regular clothes in a regular car, watching the other officer. Or was he? Maybe he was watching the other guy? Maybe he was the other officer's back-up.

When he saw me, his eyes widened and he waved me on, like I was in his way.

Happy to comply, I skedaddled to school, where my day got even more fun.

I really wanted to tell Jarvis about what I'd just seen, but he didn't come to school. A pit of worry clawed at my stomach. My imagination was running wild, and all I could think was that when he left my house early that morning, maybe he ran into the people who murdered my dad. I texted him but didn't get a reply.

As I slipped the phone into my bag, the same insult-hurling idiot was at it again. "Where's your boyfriend, Chloe?"

I ignored him, and luckily, Mr. Hughes intervened and made everyone get to work. Which was great, until it wasn't. I did my best, but I'd come to rely on Jarvis—possibly too much. Finally, class was over, and I could check my messages, so relieved to see one from Jarvis.

JARVIS: Sorry, I should have texted. My dad came home early and it was a shit show this morning - tell you more later.

ME: I'm so sorry! Can I do anything to help?

I waited and waited, but there was no reply.

My other classes were just as awful. I think the teachers had a meeting and collectively decided that my sorry-your-dad-died reprieve was over. I was given an ultimatum about my (many) missing assignments as we were approaching the midpoint of the semester. It kind of made me laugh because any midterm reports sent home weren't going to be seen by anyone but me. But still, I was typically a good student, so I did my best to focus and turn in as much as I could. I hadn't really admitted it to myself, but deep down I knew I needed to keep my grades up so I remained eligible to be on the cross country team. Although the season was slipping away, I'd been thinking about what the coach said the other day about allowing me to practice in the morning.

Mrs. Hartman, the guidance counselor, added to "Chloe's Great Day of Fun" when she spotted me before my last class of the day.

"Chloe, I've been meaning to catch up with you. Can you come to my office?"

"Mrs. Hartman, I don't want to be late to class. I'm kind of behind and . . ."

"That's one thing I want to talk with you about. C'mon." Her tone was warm but firm. I wasn't getting out of this discussion.

"Don't worry. I'll give you a pass to class when we're done."

Once in her office, she offered me a seat. I perched on the edge, keeping my backpack on one shoulder.

"How're you doing."

"Um, okay."

Mrs. Hartman smiled. "I'm not sure I believe you."

Well, Mrs. Hartman, you are very astute. I'm not fine . . . I still haven't found my dad's murderer, someone is lurking around my house—possibly the killer, somehow my last name is not my real last name, I will be homeless in three days—scratch that 2.5 days, I have basically no real money, and my aunt is somewhere far, far away.

"You know you can talk to me—about anything."

When I didn't say anything else, she straightened a few papers on her desk. "Okay." She sighed. "I'm getting a phone call every day from Ameena Alavi with the county. You remember her, right? The social worker. Anyhoo, she's saying that she hasn't been able to meet with your aunt. What's going on?"

Shit. "Oh, um. I thought Aunt Maggie had taken care of that. She's been so busy."

"Let's take care of this right now." Mrs. Hartman picked up her phone and referenced a number on a file folder and dialed.

I thought maybe she was calling the social worker, but my heart lurched when the phone in my backpack started to ring and vibrate—my fake Aunt Maggie phone. I ignored it and hoped Mrs. Hartman would, too.

Nope.

She pulled the phone away from her ear and looked at me, squinting and leaning across the desk toward me. "Is that your phone ringing?"

"Mine? Oh, maybe."

I unzipped the front pocket and pulled out the still buzzing phone.

Mrs. Hartman hung up and the phone in my hand quit ringing. She narrowed her eyes at me.

Think fast, Chloe. Think fast.

"Oh, no. I have Aunt Maggie's phone. I must have grabbed hers from the counter by mistake this morning. We have the same phone case."

Mrs. Hartman tilted her head at me. She wasn't buying what I was selling. I used my dad's negotiation trick and stayed silent, projecting every bit of innocence to my face that I could.

"Chloe, I don't think you understand how serious this is. The social worker can't close your case until she has a meeting with your guardian."

"I promise to make sure Aunt Maggie contacts her today. I swear." I even did the little cross your heart gesture. "Can I go to class now?"

"Of course," Mrs. Hartman said and wrote me a pass.

Thank God it was nearly the end of the day, I was actually looking forward to my shift at the diner—even though it was Friday, which would be a busy night.

Friday.

Until that moment, I'd forgotten that Molly had told Ameena that my next shift was Friday. She'd be sure to show up at the diner tonight.

I still had my fake Aunt Maggie phone in my hand and started texting.

FAKE MAGGIE: Hello, Ms. Alavi. This is Maggie Gill, Chloe Cowyn's aunt. Sorry I've been so busy. I know you need to meet with me.

AMEENA: Thanks for texting. Yes, I do need to meet with you. Today if possible.

Today!!??

FAKE MAGGIE: So sorry, today won't work. Sometime next week?

AMEENA: Today would be better. But I absolutely must file this paperwork by the end of the day on Monday.

Monday!!?? What choice did I have?

FAKE MAGGIE: Okay, Monday.

AMEENA: Let's make it early? Say 7:30 am? At your house?

FAKE MAGGIE: Sure.

I'd have agreed to anything to stop Ameena from showing up at the diner tonight. I didn't know what would happen on

Monday when no one was going to be at the house to meet her. I wouldn't be living there anymore. And the shit was surely going to hit the fan when no one answered the door.

For a brief moment, I stood in the hallway. The outer door looked like a great escape hatch from my craptastic life. I seriously needed a break. But my conscience won, and I went into class, handing the pass to my teacher.

I walked by Emma's seat, and today she was actually looking at me, and she smiled, making me glad I hadn't skipped the last few minutes of school.

After the bell, she waited for me.

"Hey, Chloe. You okay?"

"Kind of. You're talking to me again?"

"Looks like it. I'm still mad at you for what you said."

"I said I was sorry. It was a crappy thing to say. You didn't deserve that."

"No, I didn't, but I forgive you. What are you doing tonight? Do you want to hang out?"

"I would love to, but I can't. I have to work."

"Oh, that's right. How's that going?"

"Pretty good. I like Molly. I like earning money."

Emma chuckled. "Yeah, but do you need the money? Isn't your aunt taking care of you?"

I hated lying to Emma, but it couldn't be helped. "She is." *She will.* "I just want to pull my own weight, y'know?"

"I can understand that. Maybe this weekend? What about tomorrow? We could go for a run."

"I would really like that. I have a lot of work to do this weekend. It's been hard to – to concentrate." *And, I've got to*

pack our things and keep working to solve my dad's murder.
"There's a lot I should catch you up on."

"Call me tomorrow?" Emma asked.

"I will. I'll try to get everything done in time for a run."

49

Chloe

JARVIS NEVER TEXTED ME back. I hoped he'd stop by the diner at some point during the evening, but I thought maybe he was grounded if his dad was super mad about him not being at home at night.

I was happy it was a busy shift. It went fast, and I made a lot of tips.

When the police chief came in, I was actually glad to see him—for a change.

"Hi, Chief Barnett. What can I get you to drink?" I slid the menu onto the table in front of him.

"Coffee would be great, Chloe."

When I came back with a mug, I sat down across from him. "I saw you this morning."

"I noticed."

"Were you on a stakeout?"

"I can't talk about that, Chloe."

I ignored him. "Did it have anything to do with my dad's murder?"

"I *can't* talk about that," he repeated.

"Alrighty. Can I ask you something?"

He gave me a pointed look.

I sighed. "Something *else*."

"Sure."

"Aunt Maggie told me about the restraining order, but she wouldn't tell me much," I lied. "I'm nervous about who I should be watching out for. I don't know what she looks like. Do you have a recent picture or anything?"

"Is there a reason why your aunt hasn't come in to talk to me yet? I'm a little surprised."

"I know. She's been busy." People were probably as sick of hearing this excuse as I was of giving it. But it wasn't exactly false. She was simply being busy on a different continent.

"I can give everything I have on this to your aunt. Technically, it's her decision what to share with you because she's your guardian." He scratched his head and sighed. "Chloe, I'm sorry about this. Are you staying safe?"

"Yeah."

"You sure?"

I nodded and changed the subject. "So, what can I get you to eat?"

I took his order back to the kitchen and grabbed the food ready for another table. Refilling rounds of drinks, taking new orders, and around and around we went.

Molly was ringing up the chief's bill at the cash register when Candi came in. She veered away from the dining room toward the bathrooms before I could even say hi. I was glad to see her. I wanted to make sure everything was okay, but I wasn't sure how to bring it up. She had to know that Jarvis and I saw the scene with the guy earlier in the week.

The chief leaned in and whispered something in Molly's ear, which made her laugh. A blush tinged her cheeks, and she swatted his arm.

As he left, she called out to him, "Thanks, Chief. You have a good night."

"Oh, I will." He chuckled on his way out.

Their flirting made me grin, and Molly looked over at me and smiled back, before flicking her hair and turning toward the kitchen in a sassy swirl of poodle skirt.

Candi emerged from the adjacent restroom hallway at the same time.

"There you are," Molly said.

"Me?" Candi asked, her eyes wide.

"Yes, you. We missed you."

"You did?"

"Yup. Your regular spot is open." Molly nodded toward the corner booth.

I followed close behind Candi with a menu.

"I was worried about you after I saw how that guy treated you on Monday night. He wasn't being nice. Are you okay?"

Candi fiddled nervously with the chunky beads on her necklace.

"Oh, him. He's an old friend, well sort of." She forced a laugh.

"But I thought you were new to town."

"I am. Never been here before in my life."

I opened my mouth to ask how she had an old friend in town then, but she beat me to it with her own question.

"Look, I'm fine, but I'm worried about you. How are you?"

It was my turn to be surprised. "Me?"

"I overheard you the other day, talking to that boy about how you have to move out of your house and were going to be homeless. Is that true?"

So, she *had* been able to hear our conversation the other night. "I'm fine," I said quickly. *I was getting an 'A' for my acting skills . . . or maybe not.* Candi was giving me what I'd officially call "the look."

"There's no shame in needing help. Cuz if you don't have somewhere to stay, you could stay with me. I'll be getting an apartment soon. I've been looking for the perfect one. But right now, I'm at a motel. There's an extra bed."

"That's really nice of you, but I'm good, I swear." It *was* nice of her but also a little weird. I didn't really know her well enough to move in together. I would feel more comfortable camping in the chapel.

"Okay, but if you change your mind, you let me know. Let me give you my phone number." She held her hand out for my order pad and scrawled her number on it. As she wrote I noticed that she didn't have her normal bracelets on. I guess she swapped them for the necklaces.

As she handed the pad back to me, I again noticed the tattoo of the watch on her wrist now that it wasn't covered up with jewelry. The face of the watch design didn't tell a specific time. There were no hands pointing to the hour or the minute. It didn't look like a fresh tattoo, but maybe it never got finished? "I noticed your tattoo. It's kind of clever doing that with a watch on your wrist. But it's not finished, there's no hour or minute hand."

Candi pulled her arm back like I'd burned her, hiding the wrist with her other hand.

"Oh, I'm sorry, if it's something super personal. I – I just happened to notice it."

Candi seemed to recover. "No, I'm sorry. I forget it's there sometimes. I had it done when I was waiting for something—something that was going to take so long that it didn't pay to count the minutes or the hours. If that makes sense."

"I – I guess so."

We suffered through an awkward moment of silence before Candi gave me her order, and I left to put it in for her.

Standing at the pass-through window to the kitchen, my eyes were drawn to the small television that was sometimes on in the back—mostly tuned to sports games that the kitchen staff didn't want to miss. Molly didn't mind. But this Friday the cook had it tuned to a news station.

"You interested in international news all of a sudden?" Molly joked with him.

"Not usually, but there's something going down where I was deployed in the Middle East, and I've still got buddies there."

The station was announcing a live update from the middle of the conflict zone.

"We're going straight to our own Maggie Gill who's been embedded with the Kurdish fighters in Turkey for the past three weeks. "Maggie, what's happening there on the ground?"

"Tom, it's a chaotic and dangerous situation as the Kurdish Opposition Group attempts to hold their territory against an aerial bombardment from the Turkish government."

I stared at the screen. Molly kept looking back and forth from me to the TV where the banner under my aunt's name boldly stated in red letters "Live from Turkey." I gripped the serving tray in front of me like a shield as blood pounded in my ears and my legs got wobbly.

I was so screwed.

50

Chloe

"You don't happen to have two aunts, do you?"

I shook my head.

"And that woman is your aunt?" Molly pointed to the TV screen.

I nodded.

"So who have you been living with?"

I knew she wasn't going to like the answer. I hated to even say it out loud. But Molly was staring me down, with hands on her hips and her cherry red lips in a pissed-off pucker.

"No one. I've been living alone. Well, except for Jarvis. He's stayed over the past few nights since we saw a guy peeking in the windows of my house."

"Whaat?" Molly shrieked. "You have a stalker?"

I looked toward the dining room where heads had swiveled our way.

"I don't know who it is. I'm afraid it might be my dad's murderer."

"Are you out of your ever lovin' mind?"

I rushed to my own defense. "I told Chief Barnett about it. He says they're keeping watch. He made me promise not to be alone, and I haven't been alone—much—since then. Jarvis walks me home and stays the night, and then otherwise, I'm either at school or here."

"Okay, so where's Jarvis tonight? It's nearly closing time." With her eyes wide and serious, she was a force I didn't want to go up against. I'd never seen Molly this livid. I'd seen her annoyed and a little short tempered. But this was fuming mad, and it was directed at me.

"I don't know where he is. I think he's in trouble because of me. This morning he went home to get ready for school, and then when he didn't show up, I texted him. He said his dad came home early from his business trip and was mad that he'd been over at my house. I don't know why he wasn't at school, but since he didn't show up tonight I think he might be grounded. He's not returning any of my texts."

"So, what are you going to do tonight?"

"I'll be fine."

"Oh, no—you're coming home with me."

I didn't argue with Molly, but I also didn't agree. I knew she felt protective of me, and I appreciated that. I really did. But while I would feel safer at her house, I also was sick of running scared. I *would* find my dad's killer.

I had customers to take care of and moved away from Molly into the dining room, surprised to find that someone sat with Candi in her booth. I wondered if it was the guy from the car the other night. I wasn't sure I wanted to meet him, but I needed to deliver Candi's drink.

"Here you go, Candi." I placed the large glass of cola in front of her and pulled a straw out of my apron pocket. "Your food will be up soon."

I turned toward the man sitting across from her. "Can I get you anything?" I asked.

The guy let out a short bark of a laughter before answering. "No, I'm keeping Candi company." He smirked while he said this, and I wasn't sure Candi wanted him there, but I didn't know what to do.

He pulled a toothpick from the corner of his mouth and pointed it at me as he spoke. "So, you're Chloe, huh?"

"No, I just like to wear random nametags that don't belong to me."

He grinned then, but it wasn't friendly. "Candi has said a lot about you."

"She has?" I looked at Candi and then back at the guy. I was missing something, and I wasn't sure what.

"Can you change mine to takeout?" Candi asked, glaring at him.

"Sure, no problem." I didn't blame her for wanting to get away from this guy. I cleared a few tables on my way back to the kitchen, dropping the dirty dishes off by the sink. Molly was still watching the ongoing news coverage along with the rest of the kitchen staff.

"This is bad, Chloe." She gripped my arm. My aunt was still on the screen, giving her live coverage, but now bright explosions were visible behind her as the sound of bombs zinging past and then exploding pounded through the tinny speakers. Suddenly, we heard a scream and the camera bounced wildly, tilted, and fell at an odd angle before the screen went dark.

"Maggie, Maggie, can you still hear us?"

When there was no answer, they cut back to the reporter sitting behind the anchor desk in the studio here in the States. "Folks, it looks like we lost our feed. We hope to get it back soon and assure you that everyone's okay."

A numbness spread through my body. *Had a bomb just hit my aunt and her camera man? Had my only living relative just been killed on live television?*

I didn't tell Molly about the creepy guy that was with Candi as I'd meant to. I didn't tell anyone Candi needed her order to go. I didn't say goodbye. I didn't say anything. I went to the locker where I stowed my coat and bag and walked out the door without looking back.

"Chloe, Chloe wait," Molly called.

I kept going.

I knew she wouldn't follow me. She couldn't. She still had to close up the diner. That gave me a head start to do what I needed to do.

51

Chloe

I WALKED HOME IN a daze. I wasn't keeping watch. I wasn't picking the busier streets. Instead, I'd taken a short cut through a neighborhood that didn't have sidewalks or many streetlights. The pavement met gravel before the edge of people's lawns.

I didn't know how long I'd been followed when I finally noticed the footsteps crunching behind me. I didn't dare turn around to confirm that someone was there. I wanted whoever it was to think that I was oblivious to them.

I listened carefully. They hadn't stopped or veered off but were steadily coming up behind me.

I sped up. The person sped up.

I turned the corner and with the cemetery in sight, I did a full out sprint. My legs burned. But I made it and slammed the gate closed. Fumbling for my keys, I turned the lock.

Safe.

Only then did I dare look down the street to see who was running after me. It was a guy, and he was limping along like he had a side ache. *Good*. He stopped to lean against a streetlight and in the glow I realized it was Jarvis. And he didn't look well—at all.

As quickly as I'd locked the gate, I unlocked it and ran toward him.

"Oh, my god, Jarvis. Are you okay? Are you sick?"

"Not sick. In pain. Why'd you take off like that?"

"I didn't know it was you. Why didn't you call out to me?"

"I was going to when I got a little closer, but then you started running."

"Did you fall? Is that why you're hurt?" I scanned what I could see of his body for injuries

"No. I'll tell you, but can we go inside? I'd really like to sit down."

"Of course."

He took a few steps, grimacing with each movement. I put my arm around his waist to help support some of his weight, and he hissed at the pressure on his ribs.

I quickly let go. "Sorry."

"No, it's fine. Go slow and I can make it."

"Looks like both of our lives have gone to shit today," I said as we made our way up the cemetery drive to my house.

"What happened?" Jarvis spoke through gritted teeth.

"Harvey, the cook, had the TV tuned to some news station tonight, and my aunt was doing a live report from Turkey. Molly recognized her, and now my cover's blown—with her at least—and with anyone else who saw the coverage. But something worse than that happened. While we were watching, a bomb exploded really, really close, and the camera went dark.

I have no idea if my aunt is even still alive or not. I need to call her office."

I helped Jarvis hobble up the three steps to the porch and inside where he collapsed into a kitchen chair.

"Tell me where you're hurt."

"Bossy much?" Jarvis tried to laugh, but it turned into a moan.

"Let me see." I carefully lifted his shirt and sucked in a breath. His entire side was a mass of purple and red bruising. It continued down his lower back and onto his hip and below the waist of his jeans. "Do you think your ribs are broken?"

"Not broken, I don't think. Bruised. Hopefully."

"How would you know the difference? You need an x-ray."

"I know the difference, Chloe. I've had broken ribs before."

"You have? Who did this to you?" I asked even though I suspected who it was.

"My dad."

"Your dad? What the fuck. Does he do this often?"

"Not too often. Only when I really piss him off."

"He was mad you weren't home?"

"I guess. I think what set him off was that the house wasn't clean. There were dirty dishes and stuff. I meant to clean up before he got back."

"Why is that your job? What does your stepmom do with her time?"

"She drinks. She's really, really good at it."

"Well, that's peachy."

"You could say that."

I grabbed an ice pack from the freezer, wrapped it in a towel, and handed it to him. "So how much trouble are you going to be in when your dad figures out you're not home?"

"He already passed out tonight. He drinks, too. I snuck out because I didn't want to leave you alone."

A strange feeling passed over me. That this boy, who I'd written off as an indifferent loner, had done so much for me. Without me even asking, he'd stepped up when no one else did. And even after being horribly beaten, he was still willing to risk his dad's anger to help me. Tears started falling, and I didn't brush them away.

Searching in the papers on the table, I found the number of Maggie's producer and dialed it. Voice mail picked up almost immediately. I dialed back again and again, hoping for a different outcome, and finally a woman picked up. "Slade Jenning's phone."

"Is Slade available, I really need to talk to him about Maggie Gill."

"Yeah, you and everyone else. He's not going to have time to give any information. Right now, he's—"

"Look, I'm Maggie's niece, and I need to know if she's okay."

"You're who?"

"Maggie's niece. Slade knows who I am. Just put him on."

"Hang on."

I could hear lots of commotion through the phone and then muffled talking, like someone had their hand over the microphone. Finally, Slade came on. "Chloe?"

"Yeah, it's me. Is Maggie dead?" My voice squeaked. Everything had grown taut as I braced for his answer.

I heard him sigh. "I don't know. I'm trying to figure out what happened by talking with other media that were in the area. No one has confirmed anything. I've got to go, but I'll call you back as soon as I know more."

"You promise?"

"Yeah, kid, I promise."

I was frozen in place. Jarvis reached over and took the phone out of my hand and placed it on the table and tugged me over to where he sat, pulling me into the space between his thighs.

I looked down at his face.

He looked up at mine.

We were a mess. His body was as broken as my heart.

"I think I'm all alone in the world now," I whispered.

"No, you're not. You've got me." His voice hitched a little at the end, betraying the emotion he was feeling.

Careful to avoid his bad side, I leaned down and kissed him.

His lips were soft and warm, but what started sweet quickly turned into something more.

Jarvis reached up to cup my cheek but pulled back with a hiss from the stretch.

"Sorry."

Jarvis laughed and then held his side and moaned. "You don't have to be sorry. I liked that. A lot."

My phone vibrated on the table, and I grabbed it fast, both hoping it was and wasn't Slade calling me back. It wasn't—it was Molly.

"Shit."

Jarvis looked at the caller ID and raised his eyebrow questioningly. "She's just gonna keep calling."

I knew he was right, and I pressed answer, cringing in anticipation of what she'd say.

"Chloe? What the heck, girl? I understand you're upset, but that was not cool to run out on me like that. Especially with all the crazy stuff going on with your dad's murder. Are you safe? Are you home? Are you alone?"

"I'm home. I'm fine. Jarvis is here."

"Okay, I'm glad about that at least. I'm coming over."

"No, don't do that."

"You really shouldn't be alone. I'd feel terrible if something happened to you, now that I know you're not being chaperoned by your aunt."

"I'm not alone."

"I meant an adult."

"I've been doing fine on my own. Adults are overrated."

Molly snorted. "Well, I can't fault your logic, but I feel responsible for your safety. So, what about your aunt, you hear anything?"

"I called her producer, and they're trying to figure out from the other reporters that were in the area if she's okay or not. He said he'd call me back." I was trying really, really hard not to start crying again as I told Molly this. I knew she genuinely cared.

"Okay, I won't come over tonight, but expect me in the morning."

"Don't close the diner on account of me."

"I'm not. I already asked Harvey and Justine to cover."

"Um, okay." Molly was always, always at the diner when it was open. I knew it was a big deal to leave her "baby" in someone else's hands—even people she trusted.

"And promise to call me if you get news . . ." Molly's voice trailed off and I knew she was afraid of the same thing—that the news I was going to get wasn't going to be good news.

"Okay, thanks Molly, for – for everything. See you in the morning."

"You hear all that?" I asked Jarvis.

"I heard most of it. You're lucky to have someone like her around." Jarvis shifted slightly in the straight-backed kitchen chair, wincing again.

"Let me help you to the couch, so you'll be more comfortable while you ice that. Have you taken any Tylenol or ibuprofen?"

"Nah, I stayed in my room after my – after – because I didn't want to risk ticking him off more. Once I was sure he was passed out, I realized how late it was, but I decided to try to catch you at the diner before you had to leave on your own. You left early."

"I couldn't stay once I saw what happened to my aunt. And Molly was asking too many questions."

I grabbed painkillers and a glass of water for him. Arranging the pillows on the couch to tuck the ice next to his ribs, before I settled in on his uninjured side. I leaned in close and he very, very slowly put his arm around me.

"Our lives suck," I said, still sniffling.

"A little bit."

"I'm pretty sure Maggie's dead."

"You don't know that for sure."

"It looked and sounded bad."

I reached for the remote and turned the TV to International News Day. We watched for a while, but they still didn't have any information. The breaking news banner across the bottom of the screen said, "Maggie Gill and cameraman Mick Dawson missing after attack on Kurdish forces."

I muted the ongoing coverage and stared at the image of my aunt that filled half the screen. I closed my eyes for a minute, but that minute turned into a few hours. I woke to Jarvis nudging me awake.

"They found her," Jarvis said.

I waited for him to say the word "body" too, but he didn't, and I was fully awake in a millisecond.

"Look." He pointed to the TV screen where the banner now read that they'd been found. I scrambled for the remote and turned up the volume. "Maggie Gill and cameraman Mick Dawson were found a few hours after the bombing destroyed the apartment block they were reporting from in Turkey. Both have been airlifted to a hospital in Istanbul. Early reports say they were conscious but their injuries appeared extensive. We'll bring you an update as soon as we know more."

"She's alive," I whispered.

"She's alive," Jarvis repeated as he pulled his arm more tightly around my shoulders.

"She's probably not going to be able to come here for a while."

"Depends on how bad she's hurt, but, yeah, she might not be up for a long flight right away."

"That's going to make my life really, really difficult. There's no way people"—*and by people I meant all the adults who'd want to take charge of my life*—"aren't going to know she's not here after all that news coverage." Thank God she was okay, but now in addition to needing to pack up my belongings and my dad's too, I had to hide out from the social worker and maybe even the police, and still find my dad's murderer.

52

The Watcher

I SEE THE NEWS coverage. Chloe's aunt—if she's even alive—won't be home anytime soon.

I don't like seeing her sad or in pain, but she'll need me more than ever now.

I've planned it out. How I'm going to tell her everything soon.

Then we can be together forever. The way I've dreamed.

53

Chloe

IT WAS MOVING DAY. Well, more like pack up and go into hiding day. I thought I'd be working at the diner for the morning and then have half of Saturday and all day Sunday to pack up, but now I had to assume that my Aunt Maggie lie was common knowledge, and I expected someone in authority to show up sooner rather than later. I wanted to keep the cemetery gate locked, mainly to prevent those people from coming in, but I knew that would only draw more attention to me if cemetery visitors couldn't get in with weekends being popular "visit your dead" days.

Jarvis left in the early hours of the morning, not long after he'd nudged me awake to see the news on the TV that Maggie'd been found. His plan was to slip back into his bed before his dad noticed he'd ever been gone. He promised to come back and help me pack as soon as he could get away.

Molly would be here soon anyway. I was operating on very little sleep, but I had no choice but to power through. I splashed some cold water on my face and made a pot of coffee with the last of my dad's supply. It felt oddly final to throw the container in the recycling bin, the last coffee my dad ever bought.

While it brewed, I went to the gate and dutifully opened it for the day, scanning the area for anything that looked unusual.

Back in the house, I made sure my dad's phone was fully charged so that the camera app would give me an early warning of anyone pulling past the house. That was going to be a necessity today. I sure hoped Ameena Alavi took her weekends off seriously and didn't spend time watching the news.

I made myself coffee with a lot of creamer because I couldn't stand it any other way. But then I just stared at it, kind of zoning out. I laid my head down on my arm on the kitchen table, letting the smell of coffee help me pretend my dad was still here. I imagined him off doing some chore and that he'd be back in a moment.

But that wasn't true, and no amount of pretending would make it true.

A warmth enveloped me that was better than the familiar smell of my dad's coffee. My guardian angel was there and comforting me. *Thank you, Leb.*

I must have dozed off for a few minutes but jerked awake when my phone rang. At first, I thought it was my dad's phone telling me someone had triggered the camera app. I grabbed his first and then realized it was my own that was ringing. I fumbled with it in my hurry and nearly answered without checking who was calling. I'd have to be more careful, luckily it was Slade.

"Chloe?"

"Yes, I'm here."

"Sorry it took me so long to call you back. I'm guessing you saw on the news that Maggie and Mick were found. I wanted to have more info for you before I called."

"How is she, Slade?"

"She's okay. Bruised up. Concussion. A couple bad cuts from flying debris, but probably no broken bones. They need to check about internal injuries, but they don't think so. They're out of the combat zone, and she's now at a hospital in Istanbul. If she's okay to fly, we'll bring her back to New York late tomorrow or early Monday."

"Does she have a phone? Does she know I need to talk to her?"

"I didn't have time to tell her that there was a family emergency. She was working out of the Istanbul bureau before she went undercover, so one of the staffers is heading to the hospital right now with her things. Next time I talk to her, I'll tell her to call you—unless—unless it's something that can wait. She's had a terrible—"

"No, Slade, this can't wait. I need her back home now—" my voice broke, and I swallowed hard before I could continue. "I needed her two weeks ago."

"Can you tell me what's going on?"

Right as he asked, the alarm on my dad's phone chirped and I went to the window to see who had triggered it. Thank God it was Molly in her vintage Ford Thunderbird. It was hard to miss as it was, of course, bright red.

"Chloe, hey, you there? Can I tell her what the emergency is back home?"

"No, it needs to be me." I didn't know if I could trust him not to tell Maggie her brother was dead. That wasn't right. That news should come from family, no matter how much I dreaded doing it.

"Okay, got it. I've got to run. I'll have her call you as soon as she can."

"Pardon my French, but you look like merde." Molly let herself in and placed a large bakery box on the table.

Molly's bluntness was nothing new, and this time it made me smile and even choke out a small chuckle, but it was like an unhinged kind of laugh that I felt could easily get out of control and turn into a full-on sob fest. "Didn't get much sleep," I managed to say while trying to hold on to my sanity.

"I can understand that. I didn't sleep well either. I don't like keeping this secret, particularly from the chief. Eventually, he's going to know that I knew your aunt wasn't here."

"Thanks for having my back."

"Can I have some of that?" She nodded toward the coffee pot.

"Sure. Can I have some of that?" I pointed at the box that I could smell contained some sort of divine sugary dough.

Molly lifted the lid ceremoniously. "Help yourself. I figured you could use a pick me up this morning."

As she took a seat across from me, I gorged on a chocolate covered custard filled donut. I could tell from her serious expression I was in for a major inquisition.

"Start at the beginning, Chloe. How is it that your aunt is half a world away when everyone thinks she's been living here for the last ten days?"

"She was on assignment, and they told me that she didn't have her phone with her. It was on purpose because she was undercover or something. I don't know. But she was going to be out of touch with her producer for three weeks while she chased this story. And then you saw her last night, just like I did, for the first time. She doesn't know that my dad's dead yet. I'm going to have to tell her that whenever she calls."

"Where is she now?"

"At some hospital in Istanbul. She's coming back to New York in a day or two for sure though."

"So, why did you pretend she was here?"

"You know why. There's no way that Mr. and Mrs. Phillips would have allowed me to investigate my dad's murder. And even if they did, I knew I needed to be closer to where it happened to unravel why someone would have wanted my dad dead. And it worked."

"Wait – what worked? Do you know who did it?"

"Well, no, not exactly, but I learned a lot of things that'd I'd never have known if I'd stayed at the Phillips'."

"And the other night, when you were avoiding the social worker?"

"Oh, that."

"Yeah, that. You lied to me."

"Mostly I just didn't tell you the whole truth."

"Cut the crap, Chloe. If you want to be treated like an adult, then act like one."

"Okay, fine. I lied, but I didn't want to. It's because I know that you and Chief Barnett are – are close."

Molly chuckled. "You could say that, but he doesn't tell me everything—he obviously can't in his line of work. I know for a fact that he hasn't closed your dad's case and lately, I know there's more to it. I'm not sure what, but I can tell he's been worried about something, and he's been working a lot longer shifts than usual, too. So my relationship with him is also an asset. You can believe me when I say that he's a good guy."

"Okay, but there's still a bunch of stuff that's really weird with my dad's case that he won't tell me. He says he needs to speak with my aunt and that it'll be up to her to tell me those things. I know that there's someone from Florida that has one of those court orders to stay away from me and my dad."

Molly sucked in a breath. "How did you find that out?"

I didn't think admitting more of my lies was a great idea, but there was no getting around it. "I pretended to be my aunt, and I called the lawyer back. He said, 'the restraining order against your sister-in-law from Florida is enforceable here in Wisconsin.' But I don't know who he means. Maggie's never been married as far as I know, so then whoever he was talking about has to be someone who was married to my dad. My mom's dead, and if my dad remarried, it would have been before I was old enough to remember it. Or maybe he could have been married really young before he met my mom. And even weirder is that my dad's *never* mentioned Florida."

"Okay, so did that lawyer give you any other information? Like this person's name or what they look like or anything?"

"No, I wanted to ask, but I couldn't because I was pretending to be my aunt, and she'd know all that, right? He said he was going to tell the police everything, so I sure hope they know who they're watching out for. It's making me so angry that no one will talk to me because I'm sixteen instead of eighteen, like those two years make that big of a difference.

I actually feel like I'm about a hundred these days. But that doesn't count for anything."

"I know it sucks, but everyone's just trying to protect you."

"I'm probably in more danger from not knowing the truth. It's ridiculous. Everything I've learned, I had to figure out myself – well – or with Jarvis' help. I went through my dad's things, I found that he'd gotten a phone call and made one to a prison in Florida a couple of weeks before he died. So there's definitely a connection to Florida."

I waved toward the stacks of files on the floor in the living room by my dad's desk. "I've searched through everything."

"I see that, maybe we can look again. I'd be happy to help."

"Great, because that's not the only issue. By the end of the weekend, I need to have all of our personal stuff out of here, because bright and early Monday morning there'll be a painting crew coming in to get the place ready for the new caretaker. And given the news of my aunt, I'm thinking that I need to hurry and get this all done today." I made a sweeping gesture toward the living room.

"Wait, what? You have to move out today?" Molly's face was pure shock as she looked around the space.

"It looks worse than it is. The furniture and a lot of the kitchen stuff isn't ours. And my dad's boss said we can store things in the garage with my dad's truck."

54

Chloe

IT WAS NEARLY NOON before Jarvis limped up the driveway. I saw him from my bedroom window where I was packing my summer clothes. I'd also carefully made up a bundle of bedding with my sleeping bag and kept that separate for using in the chapel. I didn't know how I was going to convince either Molly or Jarvis that I had to stay here, or at least near here, because I was so close to figuring out who had killed my dad. I was pretty sure I was going to have to lie to both of them. Even though I really didn't want to do that. I was getting sick of lying to everyone.

I met Jarvis out on the back porch. "Hey, you doing okay?"

"Yeah. I'm stiff, but it hurts a little less today."

"Your dad didn't mind you coming over?"

"He didn't say anything when I left. I just walked out the door. I guess I'll know when I get back."

"Jarvis . . ." I stopped there, unsure of what else to say. Clearly, his dad's abuse had been going on for a long time.

"This is so wrong. Isn't there anyone who can do anything? You don't deserve this."

"Well, bad shit happens to a lot of people, Chloe. You included. Life isn't fair."

"Yeah, but you could report your dad to the police."

"And then what? I go into the foster care system. I didn't see you jumping at the chance to be a foster kid—even temporarily."

"Hey, my situation is different. I needed to be free to figure out who did this to my dad."

Jarvis shook his head, shutting his eyes briefly. "Sorry," he croaked out. "That was mean. But I figure my dad is gone a lot for work, and as long as I avoid him when he's home, I'm good. I have less than two years left, and then I should be able to get a scholarship into college. I only need to survive until then."

"But will you? Survive? Look what he did to you."

"I know this is bad. Usually, I can see it coming and minimize the damage."

"What about your mom? You talk about your stepmom but you never mention your mom."

"She died when I was younger. My dad remarried when I was twelve. Can we not talk about this?"

I sighed, understanding the desire to *not* talk about things sometimes. I held the door open for Molly, who was on her way to the garage with the last kitchen box.

"Yay, reinforcements," she said as she passed us.

"I'll do what I can but I'm not sure with my ribs that I'll be doing much lifting today. I can pack though," Jarvis said quietly just to me.

"I'm just glad you're here."

"Did you find out anything new about your aunt?"

"They took her to a hospital in Istanbul, and she's doing okay. She might be alright to travel back to New York as early as Monday. She's supposed to call me once she can."

"That's good, right?" Jarvis touched my cheek.

"Yes – no. I have to tell her about my dad."

Jarvis pulled me to his uninjured side for a hug. "You'll be able to do it. I know you will."

After a few seconds, I pulled back. I felt like crying with all the sympathy everyone was offering. There wasn't time for that. I sighed. "Let's get this packing done. I'm working on my room. Can you start in the living room? All the furniture stays but the television and couch pillows and everything that's either in my dad's desk or all over the floor needs to go in a box."

"Do you want me to go through those files again, looking for clues about this person from Florida?"

"Sure. I didn't go through every single file. I mainly looked inside a few of them to make sure the contents matched what was written on the outside."

Molly jumped in to help Jarvis, while I emptied my bookshelf. I jammed everything I needed for the next few days into a large duffle and then pulled all the art off the walls. My closet was nearly empty, all that was left were shoes and a bunch of junk I would have to sort later. I began to randomly pitch stuff into open boxes, trying to hold back the way it made me feel emptier and emptier inside. I was so lost in my own head that I didn't hear Molly calling for me, until she was in my room waving her hand in my face. "You okay?"

"Sorry. Ah, memory lane, I guess," I said, gesturing to my life sticking out of open boxes.

"Hon, you've got to see what we found." Molly gently guided me out of my room and to the couch, where I took the spot that had most recently been occupied by the stack of files. She was holding a big envelope that I'd already seen. It read tax receipts on it. "I doubt my dad's tax receipts hold any deep dark secrets."

Jarvis and Molly shared a glance.

I didn't like it. Their expressions looked like they'd rather be anywhere but here.

"It's not tax receipts. Your dad used that to hide – well – what he was hiding from you."

"What is it? I squeaked. "Does it actually prove my dad did drugs?" It was my worst fear that I'd been so very wrong about someone I loved so very much.

"No, it's not that. Just – just look." Molly shoved the envelope into my hands, like she couldn't get rid of it fast enough.

The top was open, and I upended it onto my lap. A cheap plastic photo album fell out along with a bunch of papers. The photo that showed through the oval on the cover was of two babies. I grabbed it and stared. My heart began to beat faster and faster. The babies looked a lot alike.

"Who is this?" I asked, but deep in my heart of hearts, I knew. I knew. I knew.

I opened the book and the plastic crackled with age. I flipped to the next page. Another picture of two babies together. And another and another. The babies got older. The babies became toddlers. I saw myself in the face of the little girl with the big grin and first birthday cake, frosting smeared from ear to ear. The little boy looked the same – the same smile.

I was Alice down the rabbit hole.

I knew, I knew, I knew.

More pictures, a man in uniform, it was my dad holding the two toddlers. A strangled cry escaped my throat as I turned the page. A photo of the little girl swathed in white bandages from the waist down in a hospital bed. She was holding a teddy bear.

I frantically turned the pages for more but they were blank – all blank.

There were no more.

But I knew.

My heart always knew, but my brain had kept me safe from secrets.

Until now.

"I had a brother," I whispered. In a great rush of air the best of hugs from my guardian angel enveloped me and the panic that seized me subsided enough for me to say it again. "I had a brother. His name was Caleb."

"Your dad never talked about him?" Molly asked gently.

"No, it was only the two of us. He said that after my mom died, it had always just been the two of us."

"Maybe it was too painful," Jarvis suggested.

I nodded. It was painful. Too painful to process.

I flipped back to the first birthday photo. "Look how happy we were."

"You need to look at the other papers," Molly nudged.

I looked through them and found an official looking document that proclaimed that Chloe Jane Johnson and Dean

Archer Johnson would now legally be known as Chloe Jane Cowyn and Dean Archer Cowyn.

My original birth certificate was there along with the birth certificate with my new name. There was another birth certificate for Caleb Christopher Johnson and another official looking certificate. A death certificate with same name . . . I looked at the death date. He'd been fifteen months old. "He must have died in the fire, too."

I sobbed and my hands couldn't grip the papers anymore. They fluttered to the carpet.

Lies. Lies. Lies.

My dad hadn't ever talked about my brother, even when I would talk about my guardian angel Leb – of course – short for Caleb. No wonder my dad cringed when I mentioned him. It had to be strange to have a daughter talking to her dead brother.

"Chloe, there's more," Molly said.

"More?"

"There's more from the envelope," Jarvis said, picking up a few newspaper clippings.

I shuffled through, reading the headlines.

St. Petersburg Meth Lab Explosion Kills Child

Woman Faces Negligent Homicide Charge for Son's Death

Meth Lab Mom Convicted in Son's Death

Mother Will Serve 15 Years for Son's Death and Daughter's Injuries

I reread the headlines again and again . . . finally stopping to read a full article on the conviction.

Diana Marie Johnson, age 27, was under the influence and unable to rescue her 15-month-old twins when the meth lab in the home exploded, starting a massive fire. Johnson was found in an intoxicated state when firefighters arrived and rescued her and her children from the burning home. The boy was pronounced dead upon arrival at the hospital. The girl was in critical condition with severe burns over half her body. She survived and is slowly healing from her injuries. The children's father, Dean Johnson, a member of the U.S. Marine Corps, was deployed to the Middle East at the time of the explosion. Johnson was present at his now ex-wife's sentencing but did not give any comment. Diana Johnson will serve at least two-thirds of her sentence before she will be eligible for parole.

None of the articles included any photos. It looked like the spaces where a photo might have been were torn away. The papers crumpled in my hands as I hugged myself to stop my body from shaking.

I couldn't breathe.

55

Chloe

"CHLOE, CHLOE." MOLLY'S VOICE was again far, far away. While my brain was going 1000 miles a minute, the rest of me felt frozen.

I stared down at those old newspaper clippings. My dad had saved them. *Why? Why would he keep such horrible reminders?* I finally found my voice. "My whole life is a lie."

Neither Molly nor Jarvis said anything. Jarvis pulled my hand into his, and Molly squeezed my shoulders. What could they say?

"My mom is alive."

"Seems that way," Molly said.

"My mom is alive and she's the reason my brother's not."

I stood up. The newspaper clippings fell to the carpet with the birth and death certificates. A mess of ugliness on ugly brown carpet. I walked to the bathroom. Quietly flipping the lock on the door.

Leaning on the pedestal sink, I felt sick. Was I going to throw up?

I lifted my head to stare at the girl in the mirror. She looked a little like me, but not the me I was . . . I'd never be her again. Something broke then and a wail came from deep inside—its sound inhuman. I pounded on the mirror with my fists shattering the image of that stupid girl who looked back at me. I cried and cried and cried.

The doorknob jiggled. "Chloe, let me in."

It was Jarvis.

I rubbed my hands across my cheeks, wiping some of the tears away and used a tissue for the snot dripping onto my upper lip.

My dad lied to me about so many important things. What's worse, he made me feel crazy for having my guardian angel when he knew who this angel was all along. My Leb. My Caleb. Now that I could really acknowledge who or what he was, I felt his presence even more strongly.

"Chloe, let me in," Jarvis called again.

"In a minute," I finally said.

I rinsed my face in cool water and dabbed it with a towel before opening the door. Jarvis was standing right there. I could only stare at him.

"It's okay." Jarvis bit his lip, waiting for my reply.

"Is it?"

Jarvis tilted his head. "No. But it might be – eventually."

"I don't get why he had to lie or why we needed to change our names. I mean, wouldn't moving away have been good enough?"

"You might never know the answer to that."

"Oh, yes I will."

"How?"

"He's not the only who knew the whole story. These are secrets that my aunt knows the truth about, but she can't tell me right now because she was too busy getting blown up." I'd only begun working up a full case of fury against Aunt Maggie when my phone rang. I dug it out of my pocket and saw her phone number—her real one. I nearly didn't answer, knowing what I was about to do to her world, but also being so, so mad at what had been done to mine.

Before it could go to voice mail—the fake Aunt Maggie voice mail, I jabbed the answer button. "Hello."

"Chloe? It's Maggie."

"I know."

"You don't sound like yourself. I'm sure it's been scary watching the news coverage, but I'm okay. Well . . . I will be. Just a little banged up. I'm heading back to New York on Monday. Slade said there was some sort of emergency while I was gone. What's happening?"

"It's bad, Mags."

"Geez kid, you're scaring me."

I hated that I had to tell her this . . . but I needed to get it out fast. So, I did. "It's dad. He's – he's dead."

"Oh my god! Dean. What? When?"

"More than two weeks ago."

"Was there an accident?"

"No, Maggie, I think he was murdered."

"Murdered? You think!? What do you mean?"

"It was a drug overdose in the cemetery, but I know I heard other voices out there, and the police aren't doing much of anything, but I know he didn't do drugs, and I don't think they believe me. And now there's this thing with the fact that my mom isn't dead like you and my dad pretended. And I had a brother who died who no one ever mentioned—"

"Chloe, slow down. How did you find out about your mom and your brother?"

"I'm packing up our stuff today and there was an envelope . . ."

"Oh, shit." I could almost hear the gears grinding in Maggie's head as she decided what to say next. And it made me angry all over again.

"Yeah, there's been a ton of stuff going down while you were off chasing your story."

"I'm so sorry about that. I needed to travel under the radar, and I couldn't afford to be stopped with anything that linked me to my identity as a reporter. It was drastic, but necessary. I'm sorry that you couldn't reach me when you needed me. I'm sorry you found out about your mom and brother that way."

"It's even worse than that. Maggie, I think she's out of prison. Was there a restraining order against her?"

"Yes, there was one that was enforced when she was out on bail before her trial and that kept getting extended. She tried to visit you in the hospital, and Dean wasn't going to allow that. Then after her conviction, she kept writing letters and trying to call collect. Eventually your dad changed your names and moved to Wisconsin. I didn't realize that they kept renewing the restraining order. I guess your dad knew that one day she'd get out."

"Was she that dangerous? I mean could she have come here to murder my dad?"

"Oh, honey, I don't know." Maggie paused before continuing. "No, I'd have to say no to that. She was a mess, and the whole thing with the meth lab and the fire . . . that wasn't intentional. I think mainly she got in with a really bad group and made super bad decisions. She was an addict, and she wasn't always rational. Really, the drug dealers she was hanging around were probably more dangerous than she ever was, but her relationship with them made her dangerous by extension. Those guys are ruthless. If she's out of prison now, hopefully she steers clear of them."

"I don't even know what she looks like. The photos in the newspaper clippings my dad saved were ripped out. There aren't any pictures of her here. Dad showed me a picture a long time ago, but he put it away after a while. I'll keep looking for it. And she's out of prison, but I don't know what she looks like, so I can't watch out for her if she is in town." I was trying not to cry again, but my throat was closing up, and I had this harsh pain right in the middle of my chest that was like I was being stabbed.

"Chloe, I'd send you photos, but I don't have any with me here. I'm sure I do back in my things in New York. Tell me more about what happened to your dad."

I couldn't find my voice.

"Chloe are you there?"

I finally croaked out a quiet yes.

"Take a deep breath. You're okay."

I did what she said, breathing in an out, shakily, but I was far from okay. It was so hard to relive the whole horrible night from finding him in the cemetery to the ride to the hospital and how they worked on him in the ER. I went through the evidence that we'd uncovered and the issue with the cops and how they didn't seem to be investigating like they should. I sank to the floor of the bathroom as I spoke.

In the middle of all of this I saw a call come in from Emma, which reminded me that I'd told her we might go for a run this afternoon. *I don't know why I thought I could do anything remotely normal like going for a run with a friend.* I'd have to call her back.

"So where are you living? You're not living alone are you?"

"Not exactly. It's complicated."

"Chloe—"

"I have to get going. Can you come here soon? I mean are you okay to travel that far?"

"It'll be fine. I'll get to you as fast as I can."

"Love you, Mags." And I did even though I was mad at her for keeping secrets, too.

"Love you too, Chloe."

I walked out of the bathroom to find Jarvis and Molly weren't in the house. I found them arranging boxes in the bed of my dad's truck in the garage.

"How's your aunt? How'd she take the news?" Molly asked.

"She's upset, of course. She said she'd get here as fast as she could."

"Thank God. You can stay with me until then, so you're not on your own anymore." Molly shoved some of her curls out of her face and bent down to heft another box into the pickup, where Jarvis slid them together.

I didn't respond. Jarvis shot me a look. He knew how much I wanted to stay close to the cemetery where I felt like I had a better chance of figuring out who killed my dad. Maybe it was irrational, but didn't they always say that killers returned to the scene of their crimes? I assumed that the killer already had stopped back the night we saw the man looking into the windows of the house.

Emma called again and I stepped out of the garage to take it.

"Hi, I know I said we could go for a run, but things got way too complicated here today, and I'll—"

"I wasn't calling about that. My parents saw the news coverage about your aunt, Chloe. They know that you lied about her being in town. They're mad and now they talked with that social worker from the night your dad died . . . anyway I totally listened in, and she's coming to our house soon, and then they're coming over by you to make sure you stay with us until your aunt can get here."

"Oh, shit." I knew this was going to happen. It's one reason I'd been so paranoid about keeping watch with the security camera app on my dad's phone. But then other things became more important when I found my dad's stash of lies. It was a good thing that they hadn't decided to come earlier when I wasn't paying attention.

"Would it be that bad if you just came back and stayed with us until your aunt gets here?" Emma asked. "I'm worried about you, Chloe."

"Thanks for the heads up, Em. I know I owe you an explanation, but I'm getting close to figuring out who killed my dad. I'm missing something, but I learned a lot of new stuff today. I can't explain right now, but I will. I promise. I need to do this—for my dad. Do you think you can text me when they leave your house to – to give me a head start?"

I heard her huge sigh through the phone. "Yeah, I'll do that."

The only room left to pack up was my dad's. I rushed through it with Molly and Jarvis. It was a good thing anyway. I didn't want to dwell on the horrible process. The good news was that as we were putting his things into boxes, we found the picture of my mom under a bunch of sweaters in his bottom drawer. I stared at it before showing it to Molly and Jarvis. As tense as I'd been all day, well—all week really, I felt some relief when none of us recognized her face.

I slipped the photo in my backpack. Together we put the last of the boxes in the garage, and I carefully slipped my bundle of bedding in an easy-to-reach spot.

Right as I stepped back into the house to make one final inspection, Emma's text came through. I had ten minutes before I'd be trapped by Mr. and Mrs. Phillips and Ameena Alavi. They meant well, but I couldn't do what I needed to do with the tight supervision I'd be under now that my lie was exposed. Unfortunately, it was time to do a little more lying.

"You guys, thank you so much for the help. And Molly, thank you so much for your offer to stay at your house. But that was my friend, Emma. She's the one I stayed with for the first few nights, and I'm going to head over there. Can you give me a ride?"

Molly searched my face, I'm sure for signs of deceit. But I kept my expression as bland as possible. "Sure, no problem, but you can definitely stay with me if you want."

"I know. It's easier this way with school and everything." *I was nearly as good a liar as my dad.*

"Jarvis, do you need a ride home?" Molly asked.

"That'd be great." Jarvis looked at me with an odd mix of worry and confusion. I hadn't told him that Emma and I had partially made up on Friday. But he knew how I felt about her parents and how they talked about my dad after his death.

I grabbed my duffle and my backpack, and we piled into Molly's gorgeous car. I flipped the passenger seat forward and climbed into the back to spare Jarvis' poor body from that torture. It was easier to hide in the back anyway. We left just in time, passing the social worker and Emma's parents as they pulled into the cemetery.

56

Chloe

WE RODE IN SILENCE. I had nothing more to say. Molly and Jarvis were probably scared to say anything at all by this point.

We idled at the curb in front of Emma's house.

Jarvis let out a low whistle. "Nice neighborhood."

He helped me climb out, wincing again as he did. I went up on my tiptoes to brush my lips against his and he leaned in, making the kiss more than I had anticipated. I pulled back and stared into his eyes.

"I'll text you later," I finally whispered.

"You'd better."

I leaned into the car. "Molly, I think I'm going to have to ask for the next couple of nights off."

"No problem, hon. I kind of figured."

"Thank you for your help today—well for the past two weeks. You're a lifesaver. I'm so sorry I lied to you." *And I'm still lying to you.* I really hoped my lies wouldn't ruin our friendship.

Emma had the front door open before I reached it. "Oh my god, I can't believe I just saw you kiss Jarvis Keen. And what are you doing here anyway? I tried to help you avoid my parents. Are you going to stay here after all?"

"I had to lie to Jarvis and Molly—you know her from the diner, right?"

"I recognized her car. Everyone knows that car."

"Yeah, it's hard to miss. Well, I told them that I was staying here."

"But . . . you're not staying here?"

"No, I'm not, but I thought I could slip out the back once you see your parents come home from *not* finding me at my house."

"Ah, got it. But about Jarvis . . . you have to give me the details."

"I will, but there's not time for it now. It's a super long story. There's so much to tell you." Tears were threatening again and Emma (of course) noticed.

"Oh, Chloe. God, I'm so sorry. I've been such a jerk."

"No, it's fine." I waved my hand in the air. "I was a jerk first. Things are just such a mess."

"Can I help you?"

"No, I don't need to drag you into this, too."

"Too?"

"Well, like Jarvis and Molly. I hope I don't make them so mad that they don't want to be friends with me anymore."

"Jarvis looks like more than a friend, Chloe."

"I guess he is."

Emma laughed, muttering, "You guess," under her breath. "Go down to the side door in the basement, and I'll yell to you when I hear my parents open the garage door."

I was halfway down the stairs when Emma called after me.

"Wait. Where are you going anyway?"

"Back to my house." *Sort of.* That didn't technically qualify as a lie.

A few minutes later, I heard Emma shout, "They're here. Good luck. Call me if you need help."

I went out the back door and through the gate that led to the service entrance to their yard, schlepping back across town. . . the same way I did the day I'd made up my mind to solve my dad's murder.

Partway back, my heart nearly stopped when a squad car drove past and then pulled to the curb up ahead. I could turn around and go back the other way, but maybe it was only a coincidence that the car had pulled over at that moment. I decided to play it cool and kept walking. Hopefully it wasn't the chief.

I stared straight ahead, striding fast, but not too fast to be suspicious—or so I thought. My heart was thudding loudly in my ears, when I saw the window roll down.

The minute I heard the voice I knew it *was* the chief. "Hey, Chloe. Stop for a second. I need to talk to you."

I stopped. *Seemed like a good plan to do what the police said.*

The chief got out and stepped around to the sidewalk. "Where you headed?"

"To my friend's house."

"You staying there tonight."

"Yup."

"We all know that your aunt isn't in town now. I'll give you a ride."

"No need. I'm fine. But thanks for the offer." I was going to leave it at that, but this patronizing offer of assistance, without giving me the real help I needed or the justice my dad deserved had me frayed. "I learned something interesting today—but I think you already knew it." My voice was as sharp as I could make it.

"What was that?" The chief looked at me with a slight grimace like he wasn't sure he wanted to know.

"My mom didn't die in the fire where I was burned."

He let his breath out with a woosh. "Your aunt told you the truth?"

"Not exactly, but she confirmed a few things for me when we talked."

"How's she doing by the way. She okay?"

"She's not great, but her injuries won't leave permanent scars." *Unlike mine.*

"I had a brother, but you probably knew that, too." It stung so bad that so many people around me knew more about my life than me.

"I do know that. Now. I didn't at first. Once I looked up the info about your mom getting out on parole and the restraining order that prevents her from coming near you, I saw what she'd been convicted of. I'm sorry, Chloe. That's a lot to learn on top of your dad's death. But your aunt will be here soon, yes?"

"Yes. But my dad's killer still hasn't been caught."

The chief cleared his throat. "I'm working on it."

"Mmhmm," I said, eyeing him up. "Doesn't seem like you're any closer to figuring it out."

We stared at each other for a second, and then the chief shook his head. "I am closer, actually . . . But it's due to you—your help I mean."

"What? If you're only going to say I-can't-give-you-details, I'm out of here."

"Wait—you should know this. You were right about that rock. Not only was it dried blood, but we've also confirmed it was your dad's. We were able to match it against the samples taken to determine what drugs were in his system."

I gasped, hardly able to comprehend what I was hearing. "This – this proves it. It proves without a doubt that my dad was murdered."

The chief nodded. "There's more. The ER report noted your dad's head injury, but that page of his medical report never made it into the police file. I don't know how that happened—yet. But that means I can't let you walk around like this. It's not safe. Get in and I'll give you a ri—"

The radio in the car chirped, interrupting our little chat with a request for all police in the vicinity to head to a multi-car accident out on the interstate. The chief acknowledged the call and then demanded, "Tell me whose house you're headed to."

"I'm going to the Phillips'," I lied. *They were probably already furious with me, what was one more lie?*

As he jumped in the driver's seat, he shouted to me, "After this call, I *will* come back and check that you're there. Don't even think about going anywhere else!"

And just like that he drove away with his siren blaring and lights flashing. I had to assume that if he hadn't been so distracted that he would have realized when he first stopped to talk to me, I'd been walking away from the Phillips' neighbor-hood.

Now that my dad's head injury proved without a doubt that he wasn't alone in the cemetery that night, I was scared. Well – more scared – I'd already been operating from a baseline of fear for days. *Maybe I should just go back to the Phillips' house.* I stood there for a minute unsure if what I was doing was too dangerous. But then my thoughts turned to my dad and how unfairly horrible this had all been and decided to see my plan through.

I approached the cemetery with caution and decided not to use the main gate and circled around to the seldom-used back gate. It was closer to the garage anyway. And that's where I waited until night fell, sitting in the cab of my dad's truck and avoiding phone calls from Emma's parents and the social worker. I had no idea if they were calling me or Aunt Maggie – but either way, I wasn't going to answer. There were no windows in the garage, so I turned on the truck's dome light to go through my dad's envelope of lies again. The photos of me and my brother together hurt my heart. I felt him there with me, and there was a comfort in that—one I didn't know how badly I needed. But it calmed my soul and made me feel more whole, now that I understood the truth.

I didn't really care to read the newspaper stories again, but I made myself do it. I pulled out the framed photo, scrubbing at the grime on the glass, but that only made it worse. Flipping it over, I pried off the backing and pulled the photo free. Once out of the frame, I realized the image was printed on thin paper—not a real photograph at all. The paper was bigger than the frame and all four sides had been folded back so it would fit.

When I smoothed out the edges, words became visible below the woman's image: 5x7 photo frame $9.99

It wasn't my mom at all. It was just some random model used to make picture frames pretty in the store.

Another lie that stung possibly worse than some of the others. I crumpled the paper into a tiny, tiny ball in the middle of my fist until my knuckles turned white. My dad had let me keep that picture in my room for a few months, until he put it away. I guess I knew now that it wasn't because it was so hard for him to look at his dead wife's picture. I hoped he started to feel guilty about his lie and how I'd stare at that image and wonder what parts of my mom's face I'd inherited. There'd never been any talk around our home of how I had my mother's nose or her eyes, and now I knew why.

I felt sick. I was so mad at my dad, yet here I was still trying to find his murderer. To make sure that people didn't remember him as something he wasn't. That there'd be some justice for him.

Maybe one day he was planning on telling me everything, but he didn't get the chance.

I was so, so tired.

I closed my eyes for a moment, but then shook myself awake. I was afraid if I fell asleep in here that I wouldn't wake up until morning. I needed to be in position to watch the cemetery, and the best spot was in the chapel.

I waited long enough.

I made a quick pitstop in the house for a bathroom break, frowning into the demolished bathroom mirror that showed my fractured reflection. *I was probably going to have to pay for that.*

At least no one would expect me to be in the chapel, and I could observe without putting myself in harm's way—hopefully. I had no idea if my stakeout of the crime scene would come to anything. But with my aunt arriving as quickly as she could make travel arrangements, this was my last chance to catch my dad's killer.

I grabbed my bedding, backpack and duffle, and lugged everything up the steps to the chapel doors. Quickly unlocking them, I hustled inside, using the light on my phone to see the interior. I made my bed near one of the windows that faced my house—*not my house anymore* I mentally corrected.

I was in for the night, but then realized I'd left the front gate open. I gripped my dad's keys tightly, thinking how I probably was supposed to turn them back into Frank soon. Hesitating just inside, I willed myself to open it and do my chore.

Taking a deep breath, I made a mad dash for the gate. Something had me spooked. Well more spooked than usual. Nervous tingles crawled up my back to my neck. In my panic, I pulled too hard, and the metal clanged loudly. So much for being sneaky. I clicked the lock, pocketed the keys, and ran back to the chapel. Once inside, I drew a deep, but shaky breath.

I was sure someone was watching me, and I wondered if I *had* made a big mistake staying here alone after all.

57

The Watcher

CHLOE'S CRIES THIS AFTERNOON carry out to where I hide. I am so worried for her.

What is she thinking? What will she do?

Later, when she leaves, I feel lost.

I wait—and I'm glad I do. She doubles back.

I'm not surprised. I should have guessed that she'd return to the cemetery.

She's alone now.

Except for me.

I'll keep her safe. It's the most important job I've ever had.

58

Dean ~ Day of Death

ONCE CHLOE WAS IN bed, Dean had to decide if he was going to keep watch or trust the camera. Tiredness won out, and he slipped into bed fully clothed.

It felt like he hadn't slept at all when the vibration and chime of the app woke him.

As he came fully awake, he squinted at the screen. Someone was coming up the drive, the gate he'd locked now open behind them. It was Diana.

He put on his boots, grabbed his keys, and quietly slipped out the door, making sure it was locked. He sure as heck wasn't going to let her get into the house this time, especially with Chloe at home.

He came around the corner of the porch and expected to find her still walking on the driveway but she was nowhere in sight. Where had she gone?

He stopped and let his eyes completely adjust to the darkness. In one of the rows of larger headstones he saw her, staring out into the cemetery too, like she was looking for something.

"Did you pick the lock?" Dean asked.

Diana shrieked and jumped, spinning around but recovering her composure quickly. "I did, but it's not what you think."

"Oh, really."

"I think Lance is here somewhere, too. But I - I came to warn you."

"You've already warned me—or should I say threatened me."

"I wasn't threatening you. Lance is the one with the threats. I think he's here to hurt you tonight. He thinks that if he kills you that I'll get the life insur—watch out!" she shrieked.

Something slammed into Dean's skull and his world tilted sideways as he tried to pivot and fight back, but darkness overtook his vision, and he grabbed the closest headstone for support, sliding down to sit at its base.

He struggled to maintain consciousness as he watched Diana fight with Lance. She got the rock away from him and pitched it into the darkness.

"Stop, Lance, just stop. I'll do what you've asked. I'll come back and work for you. I'll work off my debt. Leave Dean alone."

Lance laughed. "Why would I do that? Now that I know I can get the money that much faster with this bastard dead?"

"There's no way I'm still the beneficiary on that policy."

"I don't believe you." Lance moved closer to Dean.

Dean tried to get up, but he was seeing double and unable to make his limbs respond.

Diana stood protectively in front of him. Now crying, she begged, "Don't do it, please."

"So now you're going to be a good wife and protect your family? Don't worry, it'll be painless. I've got just the thing to send good ol' Dean on to his next life." Lance waved something around in his hand.

"Noooo," Diana wailed and grabbed on to Lance's arm. He clamped down hard on her wrist with his other hand and twisted it viciously, sending her to her knees as the beads of her broken bracelet flew over the ground.

Lance lunged forward, and Dean felt the sting of a needle, looking down at his arm in time to see Lance push the plunger on the hypodermic, sending god knows what into his system. Dean tried to reach over to pull out the needle, but an odd warmth and numbness bloomed through his body. He couldn't make his hand work properly.

"Jesus, Lance." Diana moaned as she got a good look at the needle sticking out of Dean's arm. "What have you done?"

"Heroin with a fentanyl kicker. You can't save him from that cocktail."

"Oh my god." Diana sobbed. "The cops are going to figure this out and come looking for you."

Lance laughed. "You think I don't have people on my side in this podunk town? They don't pay these guys enough. You stick around if you want. See if they believe it wasn't you. Once you get that life insurance money, you know what you need to do."

Dean was having trouble focusing, but he heard what Lance said and saw him leave. He wanted to tell Diana that the life insurance was Chloe's, but he couldn't make his mouth work right.

Diana leaned in close. "I'm so sorry, Dean. I'm so sorry."

Dean's heart was pounding, and his vision was narrowing, it took all his effort to whisper, "It's Chloe's."

His mind slid through images of his life like one giant kaleidoscope.

Happy, sad, good, bad. He flew.

Diana's wail pierced the night.

Dean could see her kneeling there, but he could also see himself.

He heard the giggle of a toddler, and his beautiful towheaded little boy ran toward him at full speed, his arms outstretched for a hug.

59

Chloe

THE WINDOWS IN THE chapel were low, only a foot or so off the floor. I went to each one to look out at the cemetery in all directions. No one was visible.

Perched on my temporary bed, I plugged my phone into the charger that I was grateful I remembered to bring with me. I checked my dad's phone battery and saw that it was getting low, too. I only had the one charger and hoped my dad's phone would stay on long enough for me to get mine fully charged.

Dumb mistake, I knew, but keeping my phones charged hadn't been on the top of my list with all the other craziness my day held.

My lack of sleep the previous night had me struggling to stay awake even though it wasn't late. It wasn't fully dark yet, and there was still some traffic on the street this early in the evening. It seemed safe to assume no one would show up when there was a risk of being noticed. I set my alarm for two hours, relying on my dad's app to alert me if anyone showed up before then. I'd swap his phone into the charger once mine was done.

Instead, I was awoken by my guardian angel – my brother – calling my name. I came awake as though someone had been right there with me, and I guess, in a way, someone had always been.

Grabbing my dad's phone for the security camera footage, I saw it was dead as I'd worried would happen, but mine was now fully charged. I quickly swapped them out, hearing voices from somewhere outside.

It was frustrating to not hear them clearly.

I wiped my sweaty palms on my jeans before I grabbed the handles at the base of the window and pulled up. The wood squealed in protest, causing the voices to stop.

I waited, holding my breath and hoping I hadn't given myself away.

"I saw you coming out of the house. You better not have hurt her!" said a woman's voice.

The man only laughed.

"I'm serious. I'll go to the police – about – about everything."

"You're not going to the cops. If you do, you'll be right back in prison for violating your parole."

I didn't recognize either of the voices. But whoever it was, she was worried about me.

"I don't care."

"Oh, I think you do care. I think you care a lot. You were always good at saving yourself before anyone else, weren't you?"

The woman seemed to choke back a sob.

"Oh, relax. She wasn't home anyway. The place is kind of bare. Looks like she moved out."

The little slice of the cemetery I could see did not show these two people. I was desperate to know who they were. With the mention of prison and probation, I had to assume the woman was my mom.

My dad's phone pinged back to life with an alert from the security camera app. It was loud, too loud with the window open. I frantically hit the button to silence it.

"Did you hear that?"

"Yes," said the woman.

I simultaneously watched what was on the camera app on mute, while I listened to them. Even on the video, their faces weren't fully visible.

"Someone else is out here. We should go."

"And you'll leave her alone?"

"No, I won't leave her alone. I'm going to get my money."

"You know I'm not the beneficiary on that life insurance anymore. I tried to tell you Dean would never have kept me on, so you can't hold that over my head."

"Oh, but I can. That policy, even if it was old, shows you had a motive to kill him." The man's harsh laugh seemed even louder now.

"But – but I didn't kill him. You did, Lance!" My mom shrieked.

I gasped and held my hand over my mouth. If I believed what my mom was saying, this man named Lance *was* my dad's murderer.

"Who's going to believe you, a felon? Not the cops. Not your daughter. She's way smarter than you. Anyway, that was the old plan, honey."

"What do you mean?" My mom was nearly sobbing.

"Chloe is definitely worth more. I just need to grab her and wait for that rich bitch of an aunt to pay up to get her back. Once I have my money, I'll return her—I just haven't decided if that'll be dead or alive."

"Noooo," the woman screamed.

On the app I saw her lunge at Lance. He easily deflected her, sending her flying. She went down hard, hitting her head on the sharp stone corner of a grave marker. She was still, not making any sound. All I could think was that I'd just watched my mother's murder—on the same day that I learned she was still alive.

But I realized I was in no position to fight this guy.

If he would just turn toward the camera, he'd be captured on the video file and I could take it to the police.

A flash of headlights made the man leap behind one of the larger tombstones, out of camera range while a squad car slowly rolled up the driveway and past my open window, stopping between the chapel and the house.

I've never been so grateful to see a cop car as I was then. It had to be the police chief, making good on his promise that the investigation wasn't closed.

The officer opened his door and got out. In the dim glow of the interior car light, I could see it wasn't the chief. "You dumb shit, Lance. You can come out now."

Oh, my god, what?

It was the cop I hated—Officer Mank. The one who grilled me about my dad's drug dealers. And he knew my dad's killer.

"The kid is hiding in the chapel."

The kid was me. And my options for hiding or fleeing weren't great. If I tried to go out a window, I wasn't sure how far I'd get with the two of them after me. I wondered how long it would take them to get through the locked doors. They were solid, but they wouldn't hold forever.

I needed a hiding place, but with only a few pews and alcoves, choices were limited. Then I remembered the entrance to the crypt below the chapel. Maybe they'd miss seeing it if they got through the doors.

I briefly considered going out the window again but thought about all the shows where people pretended to do something to throw someone off their trail. I gave a huge tug on the window to open it wide enough so that I'd fit through, but instead of jumping I snuck down the cement stairs to the crypt. Upstairs there'd been some light coming in from the street but here it was completely dark. Even in my earlier search, I'd only peered in from the staircase—never entering fully. I'd only ever been in here with my dad. Never alone. Never in the dark. And never with a dirty cop and a killer after me.

I felt my way along the wall, walking into a bunch of cobwebs.

One of my least favorite things were spiders. Shuddering, I kept my cool. I had no choice.

I heard someone kicking at the door upstairs, followed by the cop yelling, "Don't be stupid. I've got a key."

My heart, already racing, stepped it up a notch as I realized the door was no obstacle.

My hands were so damp with sweat, I nearly dropped my phone. I hesitated—I couldn't dial 911 and give away my location—Officer Mank would be clued in immediately. I quickly scrolled through my previous calls and found the police chief's number and hit redial.

The big doors squeaked open upstairs.

The phone went to voice mail, and as footsteps made the wooden floor creak directly above me, I knew I didn't dare to whisper a message.

I froze in place.

"Look here's her stuff. She was in here," my dad's murderer said.

"Idiot. Do you think I wasn't watching? I'm smart enough not to trust you to get the job done. I've been watching all day."

"The window."

"Yeah, I see it."

"She probably went out when we were coming in the door."

"She left her phone behind."

No, I didn't. I touched my phone and nearly groaned. I'd left my *dad's* phone behind. And it was open to the app that showed the security camera footage.

The cop likely knew all about the camera already since the footage from the night of my dad's murder had been deleted—and we suspected he was probably the one who did that. But now, the video would show I hadn't gone out the window.

"Check it out, man."

They were quiet for a moment, but I knew they didn't leave.

To me, my breathing sounded loud, as though I'd run a race. I was sure they could hear me . . . my mind was screaming, *please leave, please leave.*

"Smart kid. She didn't go out the window, but she made us think she did," said the cop. And looky looky, you're on here too assaulting that *poor* woman. Now I'm glad I didn't disable this camera . . . yet."

"You can't tell that's me on there."

"No? Well, I can always testify that I found you assaulting her, while I continued to investigate a murder in this same location. Just think of the points that will earn me with the chief."

"Delete it."

"I might. If you help me catch this kid, and we can finish your plan to get the money. She's still in here and there's only one more place she can be."

Oh, crap. The cop knew about the crypt. *Of course, he did.*

I frantically felt along the floor and the wall for anything I might use as a weapon.

I touched something wooden and pulled at it. It was heavy and as it came off the wall, I struggled to hold it up. I realized I was wielding a cross as a weapon. If ever I needed some help, it was now. I didn't think Jesus would mind.

"Chloe, come out, come out, wherever you are." The cop's sing-songy voice was impossibly close.

I nearly vomited from fear but choked up on that cross like I was at bat waiting for a pitch.

Light flooded the room when the switch was flipped. In the blinding glare, I saw Lance step through the archway. I swung as hard as I could, making contact and sending him flying to the floor. The momentum of the heavy cross pitched me sideways, and I didn't have time to swing back around to hit the cop.

He grabbed me and pushed me to the floor, my chin scraping along the rough cement. He knelt on my legs and yanked my arms behind me. I heard the zip of the plastic cable ties as he painfully tightened them on my wrists.

Out of the corner of my eye, I saw him flick a cap off a hypodermic syringe and bring it down to my arm.

I screamed as the needle sank into my bicep and the cop pushed the plunger down.

I was going to die the same way my dad did.

The edges of my vision went blurry.

60

The Watcher

MY HEAD IS POUNDING. That asshole knocked me unconscious. I should have seen it coming, but I didn't get out of his way in time.

I try to get up.

My bruised ribs scream in pain.

Chloe needs me.

But I can't make my body cooperate.

61

Chloe

I was cold, so very cold. But my shivering meant I hadn't died. At least I didn't figure the afterlife included that sort of discomfort.

I laid on my side on a cement floor, trying to make sense of what happened.

My hands were still zip tied behind me, and I remembered my attempt to defend myself with the wooden cross against both Lance and Officer Mank.

Could I still be in the crypt? Or had they moved me after knocking me out with whatever was in that syringe. At least it hadn't been the deadly stuff given to my dad.

A low moan nearby made me realize I wasn't alone.

In the nearly complete darkness, the only sliver of light came from the bottom of what I assumed was a door, but it wasn't enough to see anything inside the room.

I wanted to call out, but I was afraid that whoever it was might still want to do me harm, particularly if it was Lance in here with me.

My arms ached from the wrenched position they were in, and I remembered the self-defense tips my dad had taught, including how to break zip ties. I had teased him at the time about what danger he thought I'd ever be in, and he had said that it paid to be prepared. *Well, Dad, I guess it did.* But now I wondered if he was thinking about the part of my life he had hidden from me, anticipating it might catch up with us one day.

I scooched into a sitting position as quietly as I could, the plastic sharply digging into my wrists. I wriggled my hands under my butt and brought them around in front of me before awkwardly standing up.

Using my teeth, I maneuvered the tail of the tie holding my hands together to the center. I didn't think they could get any tighter, but I bit down on the zip tie to pull it. And it didn't move. I suppose a cop would know how to secure zip ties tightly.

If you raised your hands up high and then came down with your forearms against your hip bones, that force was supposed to be enough to break the tie.

I gave it a try. It didn't work. I only succeeded in knocking the wind out of myself as I hit my abdomen more than my hips. I adjusted my stance and tried again. This time, I hit my hips in the right position but the plastic tied only dug deeper into my skin. I could smell the blood and feel it too as my wrists became slick.

I leaned against the wall, not sure if I could stand the pain of trying again. Then Caleb was there, around me and in my mind, encouraging me to not give up.

I stood up tall, took a deep breath and lifting my hands over-head, I brought them down with all my might. Miraculously, the tie broke. And I cried out with both the searing pain and the relief that I was free. I tore two strips off the bottom of my T-shirt and tied them around the cuts on my wrists.

I couldn't tell if that tiny sliver of light was daylight or electric light, but if it was daylight, I'd been unconscious for at least eight hours. I felt along the wall toward the light and confirmed there was a doorway. I tried the knob, it turned but it wouldn't open—clearly locked. The walls were somewhat smooth and cool, like stone or cement. I touched a ledge and let my hand roam over its surface and back into the alcove. It was a long shelf. I was in the same place I started. I hadn't been taken from the crypt at all. The shelf was one of the six available for storing coffins.

I kept exploring, shuffling carefully, knowing another per-son was probably laying on the floor. The room wasn't that big, eventually I tripped over the cross and reached down to feel if it was still intact. Part of it had broken off and now made a decently sharp spear. I was grateful for the weapon.

A half cry came out of the dark, and I whipped my head toward the sound.

Then a woman's voice asked, "Is anyone there?"

My heart thudded extra hard in my chest. I thought I was cooped up with my dad's murderer, but that's not who it was.

I whispered my mom's name, "Diana?"

"Chloe? Is that you?"

"Yes."

"Oh my god. I imagined this reunion so many times, but I never expected it to be like this."

"Yeah, this isn't such a great way to meet. I thought for sure that guy killed you when he shoved you into the tombstone. Are you okay?" *I chastised myself for even caring—she was the cause of so much pain.*

"I'm fine—a little headache. I'm more worried about you. Did Lance hurt you?"

"I'll be fine." I choked out, swallowing hard as emotion tightened my throat, and I held back tears. I wanted to have a mom my whole life. I mourned her death. I imagined what life would have been like if she'd lived. I made up stories in my mind about what we might have done together. Fairy tales that were never going to be real. Now, here she was and I hated her—for everything she'd done and not done. I hated her like I'd never hated anything else in my life. I had to know if she'd really been telling the truth outside with Lance and finally choked out, "Why did you come back? Did you help Lance kill my dad?"

"What? No? I didn't help him. I was trying to stop him."

I stayed quiet as so many thoughts swirled in my mind. This was a bizarre, unbelievable situation.

"Chloe? I went to your dad for money, but I didn't want him dead. I – I wouldn't do that to you or to him."

"I don't know if I can believe you."

"I know. I'll admit I'm partially to blame even though I didn't kill him. If I hadn't had the stupid old life insurance paper in my hotel room, Lance wouldn't have thought your dad's death would make me rich."

"You brought him here. It *is* your fault."

"No. He already knew where you were. He's the one who told me where you were living. I've been watching you—trying to keep you safe. I was just waiting for the right time to introduce myself. I tried to stop him, but I was too late. I'm always too late."

"You know, until a day ago, I thought you were dead. It would have been better if it had stayed that way. My dad didn't deserve to die."

"No, he didn't. Dean was always the good guy. He gave me more chances than I deserved. I screwed up so badly."

"Is that what you call it? A screw up?! When one of your babies dies in a fire and the other one is permanently scarred?"

She didn't answer immediately, but I could hear her crying.

"I'm sorrier than you could ever believe, Chloe. I'm sorry about Caleb. I'm sorry about your scars. I'll live with that guilt forever."

"Will you?"

"Yes, I've seen your scars. I know how bad they are."

"You have? Where?"

"I've been around for a while now. Like I said, I've been keeping watch, trying to figure out how I could get close to you."

"Well, we're nice and close now."

"I owe Lance money. And he found me after I got out of prison. I'd run out of options, and your dad was my last shot."

"You weren't supposed to come near us. You're also not supposed to leave Florida."

She laughed again. And the sound was so oddly familiar. Could I possibly have some childhood memories of her laughing?

"Well, that ship has sailed, Chloe. Because here I am."

"If they catch you, you'll go back to prison for violating your parole."

"You're right. If I'm caught, I will go back to prison. But I don't intend to get caught. We have to get out of here. Where are we, anyway? Do you know?"

"Why? Do you have a plan?" The bile rose in my throat and I picked up the cross. My mother was not a good person.

"We need to get out of here before Lance comes back."

"I'm more scared of the cop that he's working with—I didn't like him from the start of this disaster."

"Cop?"

"Yeah, I saw the whole thing. After Lance knocked you out, this cop showed up, and he's definitely part of this."

"Lance said he had some local help. I figured it was someone that the cartel works with. Well, it still might be. They often pay cops to look the other way."

"This is more than that. This officer is way involved. He gave me some drug to knock me out."

"Chloe, we really need to get out of here then before they come back. There's no way they're not going to kill us before this is over. Especially, now that you can identify them."

"I only saw the cop. I never saw Lance's face."

"Oh, you saw plenty. I know Lance wouldn't hesitate to kill again. The only way to stop this is for you to get away and let your aunt know you're safe. Then Lance's plan goes to shit. Now, do you know where we are?"

My mother was most definitely _not_ a good person, but together we might be able to get out of this predicament. That is, if I didn't think she was going to double cross me. I didn't know if I could trust her. As I weighed my options, Caleb joined me, calming me, helping me think more clearly and peeling away enough hate so I could function.

"We're in the crypt below the little chapel in the middle of the cemetery," I told her.

"Can we get out?"

"Maybe." I tested the heft of the cross in my hands. "We'd need to break open the locked door that's keeping us in. I tried the handle and tried shoving against it."

"Could we shout for help? Would anyone hear us?"

"Maybe. If it is daytime, it should be Sunday, and people always visit the cemetery on Sunday. But these are cement walls. We'd be better off trying to break out."

I made my way over to the door, lugging the heavy and partially splintered cross.

Without being able to see, aiming was going to be hard. I felt the door knob, and took a step back. Holding the cross out in front of me, I checked my distance tapping the metal door knob once to see if I'd make contact. And for the second time in less than twenty-four hours, I swung a cross as a weapon with all my might. The impact vibrated up my arms and made my wrists throb badly.

I checked the knob to see if it was still intact. It was, but it had bent. I backed up to try it again.

This time both halves of the doorknobs clattered to the cement floor. I held my breath and choked up on the broken cross in case the noise brought one of our captors running.

The chapel stayed silent. I set the cross down and hooked my finger into the circle of light where the doorknob had been so I could pull. At first nothing happened, but then the door sprang free.

I opened it all the way and turned to get a look at my mother for the first time since I was little. And realized that wasn't true. She was someone I already knew.

"You!" I whispered.

62

Chloe

MY MOTHER LEANED AWKWARDLY against the wall, her hands tied behind her just like mine had been. Her hair was matted with blood from where she hit the tombstone. Her face was smeared with a mixture of dirt and melted eye makeup. But she was still recognizable.

"Your name's not Candi," I said in disbelief. I'd been serving dinner to my mother nearly every night since I took the job at Molly Bell's, and she'd never let on. Not once.

She smiled weakly at me. "Hello, Chloe."

We didn't have time for more because the chapel door banged open and heavy footsteps crossed the wooden floor above us. I held my fingers to my lips, before I bent down to help Candi stand, pulling her into the darkest part of the room. With the door ajar, maybe they'd think we'd gotten away and wouldn't come any farther in. I picked up the cross, which was in even worse shape than before, and backed into the corner with Candi, ready for a fight.

I hoped it was only one of them coming to check on us. I'd have a chance then to do some damage and get away, unlike the night before.

"Damn, looks like they broke out." Lance's shout was close. Too close.

He was yelling to someone. Probably the cop.

"Are you sure?"

My heart sank when I recognized the cop's voice.

"Yeah, look, the door's completely busted."

"Weren't you watching?"

"I swear, I was, all day."

"Then they have to still be in there."

An arm pushed the door open wider. Lance's leather jacket sleeve was obvious. He slowly stepped one foot into the room.

In an odd repeat from the night before, I tightened my grip on the cross, but this time I felt Caleb with me, giving me more strength. It was now or never. I thrust it forward like a spear and slammed the splintered end into his gut.

He screamed, collapsing on the floor, clutching the wood that went straight in below his rib cage with the tip protruding out his back. *Thank you, Jesus. And thank you, Caleb.*

"Lance?" the cop called.

Lance tried to speak but all that came out was a sick gurgle. I stared at him as his face went slack. I should have been horrified. I knew that. But all that I could think was that my dad's killer got what he deserved, and I was glad I was the one to do it.

"Lance, I'm going to kill you if you're messing with me."

Too late.

The cop pushed into the room. In the split second he was distracted by Lance's skewered body, I shoved him as hard as I could. As he tumbled back, I pulled Candi out of the room and propelled her up the steps. Her gait was awkward with her hands still tied. It cost me a few precious seconds to help her, but it didn't feel right leaving her behind.

We were halfway to the door before the cop made it up the same steps.

Candi and I turned.

He'd drawn his weapon. We both knew what came next. He wasn't going to leave any witnesses behind.

I dove for the floor, expecting Candi to do the same.

But instead she jumped in front of me, taking the bullet that would surely have hit me.

I braced for another gunshot, but the doors of the chapel burst open. Chief Barnett entered, shouting, "Drop it, Mank."

He didn't comply. Instead, shifting his aim to the chief and pulling the trigger.

The chief returned fire—three quick shots rang out, and the bad cop staggered back before slumping to the floor.

I only remembered bits and pieces of what happened next. Later they told me it was because of the shock of everything. Chief Barnett bent over me and asked me if I was okay. I remember thinking I was glad he hadn't been hit as he led me out.

Jarvis and Molly were there and together they pulled me to a stone bench. That's when I began to shake.

More police arrived and ambulances. An EMT tended to my wrists and checked me out. I saw my mother being carted out of the chapel and loaded into another ambulance. It pulled away with its siren blaring and lights flashing in a weird replay of the night my dad died. If they were rushing to the hospital, it meant she wasn't dead—at least not yet.

She'd saved my life. I was still so angry with her—and overwhelmingly sad—but as Caleb enveloped me in his warmth, a strange feeling of hope hit me. I – no – *we* – didn't want her to die.

63

Chloe

THEY KEPT ME IN the hospital overnight—for observation, they said. Medically, that was unnecessary. My wrists were cut but didn't need stitches. Whatever sedative the cop had given me was out of my system. I think they were worried about my mental health after I admitted that I was the one who killed Lance.

Chief Barnett asked me to go through my entire time in the chapel. I explained it all . . . how I'd been subdued by the officer after hitting Lance with the cross, how I'd woken up groggy from the drug the cop had injected and gotten out of my zip ties and found out that my fellow captive was my mother.

"So what argument led to Officer Mank killing Lance with the cross?" Chief Barnett asked.

"What?"

"Were they fighting over the split of the ransom money they hoped to get? I'm curious. They're both dead, and we want to piece together what happened."

"No! *I* stabbed Lance!"

The chief's pen paused and he looked up at me and then over to Molly and then to Jarvis, who'd both stayed by my side. "You're telling me that you were able to hit him with enough force to ram a piece of wood that size all the way through his body?"

I winced at the description and shivered as I relived the scene momentarily.

"Jim," Molly said in admonishment, touching the chief's uniform sleeve.

"Sorry—it's hard to believe you had the strength to do that."

There was no way I was going to explain that the spirit of my dead brother helped me, unless I wanted to end up in a completely different kind of hospital. "I don't know how I did it. I just did. I was so angry. I knew by then he was my father's murderer, and he or the cop were probably going to kill me and my mother, too." My voice was venomous and had more force to it than I knew I possessed given how tired I felt.

I noticed the shocked looks that Molly and Chief Barnett exchanged with each other and was sick all over again about being underestimated.

"I'm glad I did it."

The chief nodded. "Then what happened."

I recounted our escape up the steps into the main chapel and then abruptly quit talking as the vision of my mother diving in front of me as the gun went off vividly replayed in my mind.

"My mom saved me," I whispered.

"What?"

"She dove in front of me so I didn't get shot."

"Oh, wow," Molly said.

"Did she make it?"

"She's in surgery," the chief said. "We don't know anything else. Did she talk to you about the night your dad was murdered?"

"Yeah, she said she wasn't part of it. That she was trying to stop Lance. She said she'd been watching over me, to keep me safe. I sort of believe her, but I'm not sure. I guess he thought she was the beneficiary on my dad's life insurance policy and if he killed my dad, she'd be able to pay him back the money she owed. But that wasn't true—the policy was old. My mom knew that, but I guess he didn't. After that, I was the only leverage he had, and he threatened to hurt me if she didn't get him the money, so she stuck around to protect me. When they realized my aunt was such a big deal on TV, Lance and Mank hatched a plan to kidnap me and make my aunt pay a ransom."

I laid my head back against the pillow and closed my eyes.

"That's about right. I had Officer Mank's communications being monitored. We suspected him since we'd noticed his discrepancies in your dad's murder investigation. We actually have a recording of him calling your aunt and telling her that you'd be killed if she didn't pay a ransom."

"Oh, no. Aunt Maggie must be frantic."

"She's fine. Not long after I saw you when you *said* you were walking to your friend's house, your aunt finally got in touch with me. The minute she received the ransom demand, she ignored the warning not to involve the police and called me back."

"We already knew what was up from our surveillance of Mank, but we helped her play along."

"Play along?"

"We didn't know where they were holding you, Chloe," Chief Barnett said. "They disabled the security camera and the last videos had been erased, so we didn't have that to go on. We had to follow them until we knew for sure. So until we saw them entering the chapel, we weren't sure where you were being kept."

My eyes were starting to drift closed.

"Jim, let's leave her be for now," Molly said as she stood up.

"Okay. Chloe, if any other details come to you, let me know."

I was barely awake when they left, but I remember being glad that Jarvis had scooted his chair closer to my bedside, and reached out to hold my hand, careful not to jostle my raw wrist.

64

Chloe

WHEN I WOKE UP much later in the night, it was Molly who sat next to me. I scooched up in the bed and took a big drink of water before I asked where Jarvis was.

"He had to go home. He was worried about his dad getting mad again."

"Again? He told you about his dad?"

Molly nodded. "I kind of pried it out of him. It was obvious how much he was hurting on Saturday when we packed up your stuff, and it seemed like he might have some new injuries today. He really didn't want to talk about it."

"Did you tell the chief?"

"I will if I have to, but right now, I'm leaving that up to Jarvis. He was pretty adamant that I not do that."

"He has his reasons," I said, even though I wasn't sure his reasoning was sound. I was truly afraid that his dad was capable of killing him.

"What time is it?"

"It's late or early, depending, 4 a.m.-ish," Molly said. "Your aunt is getting into the Madison airport around eleven. The chief will pick her up and bring her here."

"That's nice of him. He's got to be busy with everything that's happening."

"He is, but he wanted the chance to talk things through with her."

"Uh-oh, that means they'll be talking about me."

"Probably." Molly smiled at me. "You doing okay with – with everything?"

"You mean with the fact that I killed someone?"

"Yeah, that, but everything else, too. It's been a bad couple of weeks for you."

"The worst weeks of my life, or at least the worst weeks I remember."

"True."

"I'm not upset."

"Truly? Or are you trying to convince yourself? No one would blame you if you were a complete basket case."

"No, I mean about killing Lance."

Molly only nodded.

"I know you all think I should regret ending his life, but he deserved to die. I'm glad I was the one able to dispense that justice – for – for my dad."

"Don't put words in my mouth. I never said that you should regret what you did. In fact, I totally understand. If I had the chance to dish out my own brand of punishment to the man who attacked me, I wouldn't have regretted it either."

"Okay." I'd almost forgotten about the violent assault Molly had endured.

"You're strong, Chloe. You're tougher than most guys out there, and law enforcement, even the good guys, hold some stereotypical views. At least now you don't have to worry about him ever getting out of jail."

That made me think of my mother. "Did my mom make it?"

"She came through surgery. They say she'll be fine—eventually. She did violate her parole and the restraining order, so she's going to have to answer for that back in Florida. But they won't move her until she's better."

"I want to see her."

"I'm going to leave that up to your aunt when she gets here." Molly checked her watch and stood up. "I have to open the diner in like two hours, so I'm going to go home and get ready for the day."

When my aunt arrived a few hours later, I heard her voice in the corridor before she pushed open the door of my room. Chief Barnett pulled the door closed behind her, staying in the hallway.

She crossed quickly to my bed, leaning down and pulling me in for a long hug.

"Mags," I whispered. My emotions let loose and through my sobs, I mumbled, "I can't believe he's gone."

"I know, I know, honey." She slid her butt onto the side of my bed but didn't let go for a long, long time.

Finally, I stopped crying and pulled back, trying to wipe my face with my hands.

Maggie grabbed tissues from the box on the table, handing some to me and keeping a few for herself.

I dabbed at my face and blew my nose, now really looking at Maggie's injuries. A stark white bandage on her forehead stood out against the awful bruising on the skin around it. Her hands and arms were flecked with scabs of different sizes.

She caught me looking. "Flying glass," she explained.

"God, we're a mess," I said, laughing a little through my crying. "What are we going to do?"

"I don't know, but we'll figure it out. I'm here now, and I'm not going anywhere."

"Do you know the whole story?"

"Yes, the chief filled me in on the way from the airport."

"Good. I don't really want to tell it again."

"I don't blame you."

"I met my mom."

"I heard."

"She saved me from getting shot."

"I heard about that, too."

"I want to see her."

"Is that really a good idea?"

"I should thank her."

My aunt sighed then and shut her eyes momentarily. I realized then how pale she was. She'd been through a horrible trauma as much as I'd been in the past few days.

"I can understand that, Chloe," she said slowly, seeming to pick her words very carefully. "But you do realize that none of this would have happened if it hadn't been for her. Bad things are always happening when she's around. From the day your dad met her, there's never been anything but trouble. Sure, there were other people involved, but I'm sick of her bringing tragedy to my doorstep. Look at all we've lost because of her."

My aunt wasn't wrong. I was equally careful when I spoke. "You're right—for sure. But if she hadn't jumped in front of the bullet meant for me, you might have lost me, too."

Maggie nodded.

"I wished you and Dad had told me she was still alive, and that I had a brother."

"I know, kiddo. That was Dean's call, and I wasn't in complete agreement. I understood why he wanted to change your name to protect you from the people your mom had been involved with, but I was less sure about wiping your brother from your life. I mean you were twins, I thought you deserved to know, but as your dad, he got the final say. We argued about it. I didn't care what he told you about your mother. The minute she was so reckless as to let your brother die and you get burned so bad, she was dead to me."

"What's your last name, Maggie?

"I use Gill professionally, but legally it's still Johnson."

"I can't believe I didn't know that."

"Well, I never use it, so how would you know?" Maggie chuckled.

Jarvis leaned in from the doorway then and asked, "Can I come in?"

"Sure," I said. "Maggie this is my – my friend, Jarvis." I stuttered over what to call him. I considered him my boyfriend, but we hadn't defined things yet.

"Hi, Jarvis. Nice to meet you." Maggie reached out and shook his hand. "I'll leave you two to talk. I could use a coffee."

Jarvis gave me a kiss, but I wanted more and hugged him as tightly as I could. He flinched and sucked in his breath.

"Sorry – sorry. You're still sore from your dad on Friday morning?"

"Yeah, and he decided that wasn't enough, I guess. He shoved me into the doorframe as I was sneaking back in on Saturday. I'm pretty sure I was knocked out. Still have a headache."

"You really need to get out of that house."

"We talked about this. I know him. He'll be fine now for a few weeks. He always feels bad for a while and acts like a normal dad.

"I was more worried about you. You scared the shit out of me when we didn't know where you were. We searched everywhere, but we couldn't find you. We were all looking. Emma even had the entire cross country team out searching."

"Really?"

"Yeah, really. You should have told me what you were up to. I knew you weren't going to stay at Emma's."

"I didn't know that anyone would actually show up at the cemetery. It was a long shot. I didn't ask you to stay with me because I was afraid you'd get another beating from your dad."

"Look how that turned out." Jarvis started to laugh but ended up holding his ribs and groaning. "Laughing—not a good idea," he said, grimacing. "Chloe, none of this is because of you. My dad's the only one to blame."

I held his hand and tried not to cry. "I don't know how I would have gotten through the last couple of weeks without you. Thank you, Jarvis."

Jarvis leaned over again to kiss me. This time I knew better than to hug him.

"You're welcome. I was glad to help. To keep you safe—at least until my dad made it impossible for me to get back to you."

"Would you be willing to help me with one more thing? Something I can't ask my aunt to do."

"What is it?" Jarvis eyed me warily, looking a little afraid at what I might say.

"It's nothing illegal or dangerous, I swear."

Jarvis snorted. "Well, what fun is that?"

"Can you go with me to my mom's hospital room? I want to talk with her."

"Is that a good idea?"

"Maggie blames her for everything, and in a way, it's fair, but I owe her a thank you at least for protecting me. She saved my life."

"I'm guessing Maggie thinks she should have done a better job of that when you were a toddler."

"True, but I need to see her. I've spent years not even knowing she exists. I've got to do this."

"Fine." Jarvis shrugged. "Let's go." He held his hand out to me and it was my turn to groan. Oh, man, was I sore. I swayed from the headrush. I'd clearly been lying down too long.

"Whoa," Jarvis said as he steadied me against him. "You good? Can I let go?"

"I'm good, but you don't have to let go." I smiled.

The chief was in the hallway talking with Maggie as she sipped from a white styrofoam cup.

"I'm going to visit my mom for a couple of minutes," I said.

The chief looked to Maggie as if for approval. She gave a quick nod but her expression was grim.

"I'll need to take you. She's in police custody, so there's an officer guarding her room, and he won't let you in without my say-so." He led the way and cleared it with the deputy on duty.

Jarvis and I slipped inside to find my mother hooked up to a bunch of monitors. One of her wrists was handcuffed to the side of the bed. I could see the marks the zip ties had made on her skin and worried that the cuff was only making her more sore. She looked like she was sleeping.

I stood near her bed. "Diana," I said quietly.

She didn't wake up.

Her free arm was relaxed at her side. I noticed the same lacerations on this wrist, too. Right over the tattoo of the handless watch.

"The tattoo," Jarvis said. "I wished I'd seen that before."

"Why?"

"That's a prison tattoo for people serving long sentences."

"How do you know that?"

"You know how I don't forget things once I've read them."

I slipped my hand into hers. I didn't remember holding hands with my mother when I was little—before the fire. I was sure I did. All toddlers did. But for me, this was my first time holding her hand.

I leaned close to her ear. "I don't know if you can hear me. It's Chloe. I just wanted to say thanks. Thanks for saving me," adding in the quietest of whispers, "Mom."

Her hand gripped mine for a second and then relaxed.

65

Chloe

WITH NO HOME TO go back to, Maggie booked us into the only bed and breakfast in town. She thought we both deserved a little pampering. I didn't argue with her when she explained that her month in Turkey meant that if she slept at all she did so on the ground or in bombed out shells of buildings. We ate and slept our way through the rest of Monday and Tuesday. Maggie also spent a lot of time on the phone.

On Wednesday, Maggie had a rental car delivered and told me she had something to show me. We drove to a house in a neighborhood near Emma's.

"Who's house is this?" I asked.

"Hopefully ours," Maggie said. "Thought we could take a look together and see if it will work."

"We're staying? What about your job?"

"Oh, I'm taking a leave. I need a break, and you need to finish up your junior year with your friends."

"Not sure I have many anymore."

"Quit being so dramatic. Of course, you have friends. What's Jarvis if he's not a friend or a boyfriend?" she added that last part coyly. "And Emma and Jordan."

"Okay, Jarvis and Emma are friends. Not sure about Jordan. The cross country team is mad at me for quitting so I could work at Molly's."

"They'd welcome you back to the team."

"How do you know?"

"The coach called me and reminded me that if you want to come back, you can. But you have to be at practice tomorrow, so you can compete at sectionals."

"He called you?"

"Yeah, and I'm glad he did. Why didn't you tell me about cross country?"

"It just wasn't the most important thing."

"Do you like it? Running?"

I thought for a minute. "No," I said, "I love it."

"Well, then you'd better get your butt to practice tomorrow. Now, let's see if this house will work for us."

It was perfect, and Maggie signed a year's lease. A year. I'd be well into my senior year by then. My worry that I'd end up in boarding school or back in New York with Maggie, was unfounded. I should have known Maggie would make things work for me.

I went back to school the next day. And it was as weird as I expected it to be.

Emma came up and hugged me, so did Jordan. Mrs. Hartman hugged me too—in front of everyone, saying, "You could have trusted us to help you, Chloe. We were all so worried."

I nodded. It didn't pay to argue, but I knew that if I hadn't tried to figure out my dad's murder, it was likely that it would never have been solved.

I finally got into my first class, thirty seconds after the final bell.

"Nice of you to finally join us again, Miss Cowyn. Is it okay if I start class now?"

Good ol' Mr. Hughes. I appreciated he was being himself. It would have been weird if he had been nice to me, too.

I laughed and took my seat by Jarvis. His bruises were fading. Hopefully, those were the last injuries his dad could ever inflict on him. In true Molly fashion—he'd been taken under her wing and now had a safe place to stay away from his dad's violent temper—at least for now.

Jarvis grabbed my hand and held it out of sight under the lab table.

This was good. It was different, but I was okay.

———◆———

My muscles ached like crazy as I tried to hit an end-of-season stride that I should have worked up to over the course of a few weeks. It was like cramming for a test. I soaked in the giant tub in the beautiful bathroom of our new house every night—sometimes warm water, sometimes ice cold. But my race time got close to where it'd been before my dad's murder.

The morning of sectionals, I stared out the bus window as we passed the glowing lights of Molly Bell's, remembering how I watched the bus pull out for the invitational right after I'd quit the team. I'd explained to Molly that I could come back to work once the season was over, and she said she'd be glad to have me back. I kind of missed it.

Emma and I were sharing a seat. She bumped my shoulder. "Whatcha thinking about, Cowyn?"

"I saw you wave that morning when I was going into work—the morning of the invitational."

Emma nodded. "I didn't know what you were going through. I would have helped you, y'know. With your dad's murder investigation. I would have." Emma's voice was thick as she struggled to hold back tears.

"I knew how your parents felt. I wasn't going to put you in the position to have to lie to them."

"You could have been killed, Chloe. I was so scared for you. When we were all looking for you, I was sure we were going to find you'd been murdered."

"I almost was." I shuddered thinking about how close I'd come.

"So, you had a twin brother."

Have a twin brother, I corrected in my head. "Yes. His name was Caleb."

"Ha," Emma said. "That makes sense now. You used to talk about your imaginary friend Leb. That's your brother."

"Yeah, but I didn't really know it at the time."

"Is he really around you, like, can you see him?"

"He's around when I need him, and it's more like a feeling when he's there. Is that weird?" I already knew it was weird, but I hoped Emma didn't think so.

"No, I think it's nice. It's special. But what about your mom? That's crazy that she's not dead like you thought. Your dad kept a lot of secrets."

That description was a little too tame. My dad lied to me about a lot of really, really important things. And I was still processing that. I simply nodded to Emma.

"Where is she now?"

"She's still here in the hospital, but she'll be going back to prison in Florida. She violated her parole. Now she's gotta serve out the rest of her sentence and the added time for violating the restraining order and stuff. It's like two more years."

"What was she like?"

"She was okay, I guess. I mean not like a real mom to me or anything. I don't really know her. But she apologized for not saving us from the fire."

"That's good, right?"

"Yeah, and she kind of made up for it by taking a bullet for me. Not many people would do that."

Emma looked at me for a moment. "A mother would."

I tried to hold back my tears. "You're right, a mother would." I sniffled.

Emma put her arm around my shoulders and hugged me. "You good?"

"I'm good." I wiped my tears away with the cuff of my warmup jacket.

"We gonna kick some ass today, Cowyn?"

"We're gonna leave them in the dust today, Phillips."

And we did, easily qualifying as a team for the state cross country meet.

Less than two weeks later, we were at state. I couldn't believe it. I thought I'd given up any chance of being here. Since sectionals, we'd worked at practice to maintain or possibly nudge our times down a little. Hailey and Alyssa had, individually, apologized again to me. I knew Hailey had always felt bad, but this time Alyssa's apology *seemed* real. It was really hard to forgive her for making jokes about how my dad died. I did my best to appear gracious for team harmony, but I knew I would never feel close to her again.

We appeared to be a cohesive team as we ran back and forth near the starting line to warm up—and for the race we would be—but socially?—not so much. We'd all competed at big meets before, but this was the most important one. We were all a little nervous. We gathered in a circle together like we did before each meet.

"Everyone ready?" I asked.

"Yes!" Everyone shouted

"Are we going to kick some butt?" Emma asked.

"Yes!" Everyone shouted again.

We put our hands together in the center of the circle, shouting, "Gooooooo Tigers!" as we whipped our hands skyward before jogging to our spot at the starting line.

Race strategy ran through my head, but the second the gun went off and we were jostling for position, I was in the zone. I loved running! Emma and I found our stride and ran side by side until the last half kilometer, when I always made my move.

We'd been in the middle of the leading group of runners, and I made my way to the edge to find the space I needed. My energy surged, and I gained on at least five runners. With four of us trying to maneuver into the lead, I gave it everything I had in a sprint to the finish line, passing one of them and coming in third.

Emma and Jordan weren't far behind. And Alyssa and Hailey placed in the top twenty. We watched the score board as the times were tallied. When our school's name flashed into first place, we couldn't stop screaming. We'd done it! Coach Brooks ran up and high fived us all.

I searched for Aunt Maggie and Jarvis in the crowd. Surrounded by other teammates' families, mine looked a little different than the others. A wave of sadness washed over me as I thought about how much my dad would have loved this moment. And how much I would have loved sharing it with him.

Aunt Maggie hugged me first. "So proud of you, kiddo."

When she let me go, I turned to Jarvis and hugged him. "I'm proud of you, too," he whispered into my ear. Then he pulled back and held my face with both hands, wiping away the one tear that had escaped, before leaning in and kissing me.

My teammates whooped at the public display of affection, and I didn't mind—at all.

66

Chloe

WE'D DELAYED SAYING AN official goodbye to my dad. There'd been an ongoing investigation with how my dad's corpse, *it still made me nauseous to think of my dad that way,* had been released from the morgue without the police chief's approval. It all led back to Officer Mank, who was trying to destroy evidence. I'd unknowingly helped by pretending to be my aunt and pressuring the local funeral home to cremate him. In the end it didn't matter. There'd be no trials as the culprits were dead.

It was time—past time really—to plan my dad's funeral. I knew a lot about what Dad liked and didn't like about funerals—at least graveside services, due to his job. Maggie and I decided to pick out a plot where we could have a headstone and bury his ashes rather than spread them somewhere.

It was strange to be back in the cemetery to meet the new caretaker. When he strode across the frosty ground toward us, I gasped, clutching Maggie's arm.

"Hi, I'm John. I'm so sorry for your loss. I'm guessing you know your way around here better than me." He nodded my way, taking in my shocked expression. "What is it?"

"You – you – I saw you. Looking in the windows of my house one night."

"What?" Maggie and the new caretaker said at the same time.

"Do you care to explain yourself?" Maggie stepped in front of me protectively with her arms crossed, giving off a don't bullshit me vibe.

"I'm so sorry. I never meant to scare anyone. The day I got hired, when I was still in town, I wanted to see what the house was like. I should have asked first, but I didn't think anyone was living there anymore. When I saw that wasn't the case, I hightailed it outta here. I felt bad—like a peeping Tom."

I shook my head. "We thought you were the murderer."

"Oh, geez. I didn't know about any of that until *after* I took the job. I'm really sorry."

"Well, you're not squeamish, that's for sure," Maggie added. "A lot of people would have decided not to take the job after learning that."

The man shrugged. "Working in a cemetery is not for the squeamish, is it?"

In the end, I was glad to have that last mystery solved.

John showed us the available plots. These were mostly in the newer part of the cemetery, but I knew how much dad loved the old headstones, and thought he might appreciate being closer to them.

We didn't need a full-sized plot to bury the urn with my dad's ashes, and there was space available near the avenging angel statue, which I continued to love even though my dad died at its very base.

———————•◦•———————

On a gray November Saturday, the fog of our breath mixing with snow flurries in the chill air, we stood in the cemetery as mourners. There were more people than I expected, many I didn't know, or didn't know well. But many I did—Chief Barnett stood with his arm around Molly, the cross country team huddled together, Emma stood nearby with her parents, and the guys from the coffee shop nodded as I glanced their way. With Jarvis on one side of me and Maggie on the other, we stood together.

A short graveside service was all my dad wanted. In a few minutes, the minister's prayers were complete. We stood silently for a moment, my heart hurting. I would have given anything to have him back.

As a military veteran, my dad was entitled to that honor for his burial. And, even though I knew it was coming, the first crack of the rifles made me jump. I was ready for the second and third volleys. Molly and Jarvis hugged me from either side.

With taps echoing in the distance, through my tears I looked up at the angel statue with his mighty sword and shield and found some comfort in knowing there'd been justice of a kind for my dad.

Caleb enveloped me with his familiar warmth. My Leb. My best protector. And suddenly another presence joined us, and I swore I heard my dad whisper, *I love you, baby girl.*

67

The Watcher

THE STATE OF FLORIDA graciously let me stay in Wisconsin while I recovered from the gunshot wound, even allowing me to complete my physical rehab here—under lock and key—of course. I knew that had more to do with who was picking up the medical tab than it did out of concern for moving me too soon.

I noticed Dean's funeral announcement in the local paper one of my therapists had left behind—conveniently scheduled for the day that I'd be leaving.

I ask the officer accompanying me on my travels south if we might drive by the cemetery on the way to the airport.

"Lucky for you it's on the way out of town anyway. We don't do detours," he says sternly.

As we pass, I ask, "Please, pull over for just a sec. Please." Begging is not my strong suit, but he grants this wish.

The service is nearly over. The rifle shots are loud even inside the car, and the haunting melody of taps hits me hard. I try not to cry.

I see Chloe. My beautiful, brave daughter.

It's almost like I'm standing watch anonymously like I did for so many days and nights. Almost.

Just like then, I don't want her to see me now either.

"Thank you," I say to the officer.

As we pull away, I watch her as long as I can.

She still needs me. I know she does.

Dear Reader,

I'm so glad that you are here! Thanks for reading! If you enjoyed this story, please take a minute to write a review on your favorite social media platform or book retailer website. I'd be very grateful as it helps so much for other readers to know why you loved this book!

This story started out like so many do with just a snapshot of an idea and then the burning question — *then what?* I had so much fun answering that question over and over again as I wrote this novel. So much so, that partway through, as I began to love my characters more and more, I decided I wasn't ready to say goodbye to them after just one book, and that's how the Chloe & Maggie Mystery Series was born.

If you want to come along on my writing adventures head to my website at ValerieBiel.com where you can connect with my social media and read more about my other books.

Happy reading, Valerie

ACKNOWLEDGMENTS

The biggest of thank yous to my critique group who saw the earliest drafts and provided essential feedback and encouragement; Silvia Acevedo, Keith Pitsch, Christine Keleny, and the late David Emanuel Nelson. Thanks also to beta readers who helped me immeasurably with valuable reactions and insight; Mary Behan, Tillie Roth, G.P. Gottlieb, Barbara Smith, Mary Biel, Angie Stanton, Denise Erickson, Victoria Rydberg-Nania, Tracey Phillips, and Brenda Schaefer. Thanks to The Blackbird Writers, a fabulous group of mystery, thriller, and suspense authors, for their support and camaraderie. I'm so grateful to be part of the flock!

I'd be remiss if I didn't give a shout out to Write On! Door County. My residency with them gave me a precious uninterrupted week that allowed me to write the first one third of the book.

And finally, unending thanks to my ever-patient husband and children who understand my need to inhabit fictional worlds much of the time.

 Valerie Biel writes books for middle grade to adult audiences—stories inspired by her travels and her insatiable curiosity. Her award-winning, young adult fantasy series, *Circle of Nine*, includes stories of the myth and magic of Ireland's ancient stone circles. She's also the author of *Haven*, a tough-topic contemporary middle grade novel as well as this novel—the first book in the Chloe and Maggie Mystery series. She helps other authors with their book promotion and marketing and frequently teaches writing workshops to students (of all ages). When Valerie's away from the computer, you might find her wrangling her overgrown garden, traveling the world, and reading everything she can get her hands on. Once upon a time, she graduated from the University of Wisconsin with degrees in journalism and political science. She lives with her husband on a (tiny) portion of her family's century-old farm in rural Wisconsin, but regularly dreams of finding a beautiful cottage on the Irish coast where she can write and write.

Other titles by Valerie Biel ...

ADULT
Taking Flight – Blackbird Writers' Anthology

ADULT / YOUNG ADULT CROSS OVER
Maggie & Chloe Mysteries
Beyond the Cemetery Gate: The Secret Keeper's Daughter

YOUNG ADULT
Circle of Nine Series
Circle of Nine: Beltany
Circle of Nine: Novella Collection
Circle of Nine: Sacred Treasures

MIDDLE GRADE
Haven